## Praise for Some *Kind of Happiness*

★ A quiet magic is at work in Legrand's novel, in which she adeptly interweaves Fin's imaginative writing with the real-life narrative, underpinning all with an appeal to honesty and self-acceptance."
—*Booklist*, starred review

★ "Legrand handles the tough subject of childhood mental health gently and honestly. . . . Finley's quest to uncover family secrets reveals not just what kept her father away from his relatives but how a family sticks together through good times and bad."
—*Publishers Weekly*, starred review

"Finley's marvelous adventure will resonate with anyone who has battled a broken heart through the power of story. The courage she finds along the way will leave you cheering—and believing in magic—even in the darkest part of the woods."
—Natalie Lloyd, author of *A Snicker of Magic*

## Also by Claire Legrand

*Foxheart*

*The Year of Shadows*

*The Cavendish Home for Boys and Girls*

*Winterspell*

# SOME KIND
# OF
# HAPPINESS

Claire Legrand

## Simon & Schuster Books for Young Readers

NEW YORK  LONDON  TORONTO  SYDNEY  NEW DELHI

If you purchased this book without a cover, you should be aware that this book is stolen property. It was reported as "unsold and destroyed" to the publisher, and neither the author nor the publisher has received any payment for this "stripped book

SIMON & SCHUSTER BOOKS FOR YOUNG READERS
An imprint of Simon & Schuster Children's Publishing Division
1230 Avenue of the Americas, New York, New York 10020
This book is a work of fiction. Any references to historical events, real people, or real places are used fictitiously. Other names, characters, places, and events are products of the author's imagination, and any resemblance to actual events or places or persons, living or dead, is entirely coincidental.
Text copyright © 2016 by Claire Legrand
Cover illustration copyright © 2016 by Júlia Sardà
All rights reserved, including the right of reproduction in whole or in part in any form.
SIMON & SCHUSTER BOOKS FOR YOUNG READERS
is a trademark of Simon & Schuster, Inc.
For information about special discounts for bulk purchases, please contact
Simon & Schuster Special Sales at 1-866-506-1949 or business@simonandschuster.com.
The Simon & Schuster Speakers Bureau can bring authors to your live event.
For more information or to book an event, contact the Simon & Schuster Speakers Bureau at 1-866-248-3049 or visit our website at www.simonspeakers.com.
Jacket design by Krista Vossen
Also available in a Simon & Schuster Books for Young Readers hardcover edition
Cover design by Krista Vossen
Interior design by Hilary Zarycky
The text for this book was set in New Caledonia.
Manufactured in the United States of America
0417 OFF
First Simon & Schuster Books for Young Readers paperback edition May 2017
2 4 6 8 10 9 7 5 3 1
The Library of Congress has cataloged the hardcover edition as follows:
Names: Legrand, Claire, 1986– author.
Title: Some kind of happiness / Claire Legrand.
Description: First Edition. | New York : Simon & Schuster Books for Young Readers, [2016] | Summary: Finley Hart is sent to her grandparents' house for the summer, but her anxiety and overwhelmingly sad days continue until she escapes into her writings which soon turn mysteriously real and she realizes she must save this magical world in order to save herself.
Identifiers: LCCN 2015033782| ISBN 9781442466012 (hardback) | ISBN 9781442466036 (eBook)
Subjects: | CYAC: Depression, Mental—Fiction. | Family problems—Fiction. | Secrets—Fiction. | Fantasy. | BISAC: JUVENILE FICTION / Family / General (see also headings under Social Issues). | JUVENILE FICTION / Social Issues / New Experience. | JUVENILE FICTION / Social Issues / Depression & Mental Illness.
Classification: LCC PZ7.L521297 So 2016 | DDC [Fic]—dc23
LC record available at http://lccn.loc.gov/2015033782
ISBN 978-1-4424-6602-9 (pbk)

*If you are afraid, sad, tired, or lonely*
*if you feel lost or strange*
*if you crave stories and adventure,*
*and the magic possibility of a forest path—*
*this book is for you*

# Acknowledgments

- Zareen Jaffery knew exactly how to make Finley's story shine and trusted that I could make it happen.
- Diana Fox wisely pointed to this idea out of all my others and said, "Write this one. This one feels right."
- Krista Vossen, Hilary Zarycky, and Júlia Sardà
  - wildly talented artists with flawless taste (see: the look and feel of the book in your hands)
- The Simon & Schuster team, especially
  - Mekisha Telfer, lady knight
  - Katrina Groover, Karen Sherman, Bara McNeill— scholars three, patient and sharp-eyed
  - Justin Chanda, Anne Zafian, Katy Hershberger— mighty champions and heralds
- Tim Federle and Natalie Lloyd, whose endorsements mean the world to me. (*endorsement*: eleven-letter word for "thumbs-up, buttercup!")
- Alison Cherry, Heidi Schulz, Corey Ann Haydu, Ally Watkins—faithful friends and early readers.
- Kama Lawrence and Dennis Pitman lent me their lawyerly wisdom.
- Matt (my love) gave me the idea.

- Mom (my forever anchor) gave me the courage.
- And mighty, unsinkable Battleship Legrand—how could I have done this without you? (I couldn't have.)
  - Drew and Kelsey and Kyle—let's never forget those tree-topped days.
  - Grandma and Grandpa—your house was our kingdom, your love our sword and shield.
  - Dad and Anna, fearless captain and first mate of our motley crew! Steer us steady and true. You always have, and you always will.

NCE THERE WAS A GREAT, *sprawling forest called the Everwood.*

*Magic lived there, and it lit up every tree and flower with impossible beauty.*

*But even so, most people stayed far away from the Everwood, for it was said to hold many secrets, and not all of them kind.*

*According to rumor, the Everwood was home to astonishing creatures and peculiar, solitary people. Some were born in the Everwood, and some had wandered inside, whether they meant to or not.*

*No one in the Everwood got along, for they had no ruler to unite them, no neighborhoods or cities. They lived like wild things and kept to themselves, but they all loved the Everwood, and its strangeness, with their whole hearts. For it was their home, and it was all they knew.*

*Or so the rumors said.*

*Most people were afraid to enter the Everwood, but some brave souls made the journey anyway: adventurers, witches, explorers.*

*They never returned.*

*Perhaps the wild creatures who lived in the forest had trapped them there. Or maybe the Everwood's secrets were so enchanting that those who made it inside did not care to leave.*

*Everyone who lived near the Everwood knew that it was home to two guardians. They were as ancient as the Everwood trees, and they protected the forest's secrets from outsiders.*

*Throughout their long lives, the guardians had learned how to read certain signs: the wind in the trees, the chatter of the Everwood creatures.*

*One summer, not so long ago, something happened that would change the Everwood forever. The ancient guardians determined that soon a terrible Everwood secret—one they had kept hidden for years—would come to light. And if this happened, the guardians feared, the Everwood would fall. They would no longer be able to protect their forest. Its secrets and treasures would be laid bare. The people of the Everwood would lose the home they so loved and be forced out into the cold, wide world.*

*So the guardians studied their signs, desperate for hope— and they found it. A small, cautious hope, as clear to them as though it were a page in a book:*

*The Everwood might fall—but it could still be saved, even then. The trees whispered it; the birds sang it: A fall does not have to be forever.*

*All they would need to save the Everwood, said the guardians' signs, was a queen.*

# 1

## WHY THIS SUMMER WILL BE THE MOST TERRIBLE OF MY LIFE

- I will be spending the entire summer at Hart House with my estranged grandparents. (*estranged*: nine-letter word for "kept at a distance")
  - My cousins will be there too, off and on. That's what Mom and Dad tell me. "Oh, they pop in and out, Grandma says."
    - ◆ I hate when people "pop in and out." Popping in and out is not very list-friendly behavior.
- Mom and Dad are taking me to Hart House because they are "having problems" and "need some space to work it out."
  - This, I assume, is a euphemism for divorce. Or at least something leading up to divorce. (*euphemism*: nine-letter word for "term or phrase, seemingly innocuous")
- I will be far away from my bedroom at home, which is the only place where I can be entirely myself.
- There is a heaviness pressing down on me that makes it difficult to breathe.

IT'S TRUE: I AM FINDING it difficult to breathe. A heavy feeling inside my chest squeezes and pulls.

I rest my head against the car window and watch the world outside race by. Pale green prairie grass and the wide blue sky. Old barns with peeling paint and lonely houses surrounded by cows instead of neighborhoods.

I imagine I am running through the tall grass alongside the car—no, I am on a horse: a white horse with a tail like a banner.

A horse from the Everwood.

Nothing is fast enough to touch us.

Mom is obsessively switching radio stations. I think she probably has ADHD, which is a term I have learned from listening to kids at school. Mom has a hard time sitting still and is never satisfied with a radio station for longer than the duration of one song. Her work as an interior designer is perfect for her; it keeps her hands busy.

Dad is talking about things that don't matter:

"I wonder if this summer will be hotter than last summer."

"What's a seven-letter word for *sidesplitting*?"

"I'm not sure I can get behind the new tone of this station."

They like to pretend I don't sense the stiffness between them, that I don't notice how much more they've been working lately, even more than usual.

They like to pretend I don't notice things. I think it makes them feel better, to lie to themselves and to me.

Which is kind of insulting. I may be a lot of things, but I am not stupid.

For example, I recognize how strange it is that I have never met my grandparents. I do know Mom's parents, and her brother, though they live so far away that I hardly ever see them and they might as well be strangers.

But when I ask about Dad's parents—Grandma and Grandpa Hart—Mom and Dad fumble with their words, offering explanations that don't explain anything much:

"Well, Grandma and Grandpa are always so busy. It's a matter of scheduling."

"*We're* always so busy, your dad and I. You know that, Finley."

"I don't know, Fin," Dad often tells me. "Your grandparents and I . . . we've never been close."

Through my observation of the world, I have concluded it is not normal for a girl to be kept away from her grandparents, her aunts and uncles, her cousins, as if they could hurt her.

Testing myself, I inhale slowly. The heaviness inside me has faded.

I can breathe again.

I glance at the back of Dad's head, at Mom's eyes in the rearview mirror. She must be nervous; she has never met Dad's family either. She is staring hard at the road, sitting perfectly straight, not paying attention to me.

So she and Dad didn't notice a thing. Good.

I am safe. For now.

(I will not think about Hart House, or about how my

cousins will stare at me, or about pretending it isn't weird to spend a summer with my grandparents after years of not knowing them.)

(No, it isn't weird at all.)

I cannot keep thinking about these things. That is a recipe for disaster.

I check the reflection of Mom's eyes. Still glaring at the road, Mom?

Yes. Good.

I am safe.

I flip past my pages of lists and to the portion of my notebook reserved for stories about the Everwood.

I don't know what I will write about today.

Perhaps about the Everwood's evil cousin forest, the Neverwood, and their terrible, thousand-year war. Or maybe about the various Everwood witch clans, and how people say you can tell them apart by the smell of their magic.

Rhonda, my next-door neighbor, and probably the closest thing I will ever have to a best friend, says I am a huge nerd.

She is probably right.

Given my father's love of crossword puzzles, his job as a literature professor at the university, and my preference for books over people, I've acquired an impressive vocabulary for an eleven-year-old.

But when my parents sat me down to explain where I'd be going this summer, and why, all the words seemed to fly right out of my head.

I hope I can find them again soon.

My notebook—the latest in a series of twelve—has loads of blank pages in it, waiting to be filled.

And if I'm going to keep my grandparents from discovering my secret, I will need to write.

A lot.

HE IS COMING.

She is coming.

*It was the beginning of summer. There were soft breezes in the air, and the Everwood was using them to speak.*

*The ancient guardians used spells and charms to weave a golden cage around the secret at the heart of the Everwood.*

*But still the secret grew and darkened, deep underground. It reached for the roots of the great Everwood trees like poison. Someday it would rise. Someday, soon, it would escape.*

*But those who lived in the Everwood—the witches and the goblins, the barrows and the fairies and the wood spirits— knew nothing of this. They turned their faces to the trees and listened, as they did every day.*

*Today the message was different.*

She is coming, *whistled the Everwood winds.*

She is coming, *rustled the Everwood leaves.*

*"Who?" the creatures of the forest asked. "Who is coming?"*

The little orphan girl, *groaned the trees.* She carries a great sadness inside her. We must put our hope in her nevertheless.

*And the guardians stood at the edge of the wood and gazed into the sun, waiting.*

# 2

WHEN WE MAKE OUR WAY down Brightfall Lane and Hart House comes into view, I see a curtain fall over Dad's face, closing him away from me.

He is driving now; Mom switched with him at a gas station at the edge of Billington, where Grandma and Grandpa Hart live.

Dad told her outside while he filled up the car, "I want to be the one to drive up to their door. I don't know, it feels like it ought to be me."

I don't understand why that's such a big deal.

Hart House is enormous and white, the largest house I have ever seen in real life. Hidden by a sea of green leaves, it sits back from the road, the only house at the end of a long driveway lined with trees.

Our car and this house and these trees feel like the only things left in the world.

For the next two and a half months, this will *be* my world.

*I want to leave,* I try to say, but my voice doesn't seem to be working.

As we drive up to the house, we see Grandma standing on the wraparound front porch beside a column, waving.

Dad squares his shoulders and plasters on a smile. Mom does the same thing—straightens her blouse, puts her chin up and her shoulders back.

I hope I am not so obvious when I try to hide myself.

I want to tell them about the stones piling up in my stomach. That my thoughts are tangled and wordless.

My brain does not like being brought here against my will. It is shouting at me to make Mom and Dad turn the car around.

Grandma Hart steps out the front door onto the porch.

Dad shifts the car into park. His hands grip on the steering wheel hard.

"It'll be okay, Lewis," Mom says quietly. "You're doing the right thing."

Does she think I can't hear her? *What* will be okay? *What* right thing?

My chest is knotted up. I feel like a person standing in the middle of a crowded street. The person is screaming, but nothing is coming out, and no one's paying attention anyway.

Grandma stands there, on that porch the size of our apartment, holding up a pitcher.

Everything looks like a painting: blue sky, white house, bright flowers.

How can the world look so perfect when I feel so broken?

There are so many of them.

A swarm of Harts: They all have their own faces, but each

face has a piece of me inside it. Almost everyone's hair is thin and blond, like mine, but none of them have Mom's freckles, like I do.

I catalog as much information as I can while Grandma gives me and my parents a tour of the house:

Seven bedrooms, five bathrooms, two living rooms, a dining room, a parlor, a kitchen, a sunroom, a rec room. A dark study with glass doors. This is Grandpa's private space. Children aren't allowed inside unless Grandpa says so.

I am used to an apartment in the city. This house is a planet.

I hear whispers, bare feet slapping on wood floors, bodies moving throughout the house. Some of my cousins are following us. Some of them scamper away and others take their place. I see adult women. My three aunts.

There are smiles, and hugs that are honestly painful to me because I'm not accustomed to strangers invading my personal space.

The Harts are a storm, and I am its bewildered eye.

I wonder what they are saying about me.

I feel like I'm being dragged through a fun-house mirror maze that reflects distorted versions of myself.

I see two little kids, much younger than me. A girl my age, another one a little older, and a teenage girl.

The teenager is inside a bedroom, lying on her bed, playing on her phone. She glances up as we pass her open door. Her hair is a waterfall of gold rushing over the side of her bed. She looks irritated that we have disturbed her peace and quiet. She does not get up.

"And this is where you'll be staying, Finley," says Grandma, opening a heavy white door. "This is your father's old room. We don't use it much."

"It's lovely, Candace," says my mother. I can see her work self take over.

(Gwen Hart of Gwen Hart Designs! Your one-stop renovation destination!)

Mom silently critiques the paint colors, the fabric choices, the arrangement of the furniture. Over the bed hangs a miniature chandelier made of crystal and dark brass. Against one wall stand shelves full of books organized in alphabetical order by author. The curtains are lace, and the rug is white.

The wrinkle between Mom's eyebrows vanishes. She approves.

I wish the wrinkles inside me could disappear so easily.

"It looks so different," Dad says quietly.

Grandma fluffs a pillow, not looking at him. "I redecorated some time ago. I didn't think you'd mind. We weren't sure you'd ever come back, so I thought, what did it matter?"

Dad rubs the back of his head and says nothing. The room is full of secrets—on Dad's face, hanging in the air like clouds of dust—but I don't know how to read them. Dad looks smaller than he ever has before.

"Don't you think this is a beautiful room, Finley?" Mom's eyes are wide. *Say something nice. Quick.*

"Yes. It's exquisite." (Nine-letter word for "mighty fine.") I try to smile, but it feels all wrong, like someone else's smile is being sewn onto my face. "Thank you."

Grandma's smile has been plucked from the pages of a magazine. She could be an actress. A ballerina in silk and pearls with piles of soft white hair.

Four of my cousins hover at the door—the girls around my age, the two little ones.

I feel like a creature at the zoo being gawked at. I roll my notebook into a spyglass.

"Kennedy," says Grandma to the oldest girl, "why don't you come say hello to your cousin? Where are your manners?"

"Hi, Finley." Kennedy wraps me in a hug. She is tan and blond and perfect. She looks like she has leaped right out of the ocean; she smells like vanilla. "I'm so excited to finally meet you." She turns to the other kids. "We all are."

I am probably supposed to say something, but all I can think about are these five pairs of strange eyes staring at me. This house that smells different from mine and is far, far too big.

Mom and Dad will be gone soon. They are going to leave me.

My brain has yet to stop screaming. It bashes against the walls of my head in protest.

I can't help it: I start to cry. Not loudly or anything; I am not one for fits. One minute I am not crying, and the next minute tears are sliding down my face, and I wish they weren't, but I can't stop them, and that makes me cry even harder.

I don't want to be here. This place is all wrong.

Grandma's mouth goes thin. She turns away from me. "I'll go put on some tea."

Dad says, "She's just overwhelmed. This is all new for her."

"Yes," says Grandma, "I suppose it would be. Tea is the thing. We'll have tea and get her washed up."

I hear my cousins: "Is she all right?" "What's wrong?" "Why is she crying?"

Grandma: "She's only tired. Come, now. Don't stare."

I am sitting on my bed, and Mom is holding me, telling me things:

"Please stop crying, sweetie. Please."

"The summer will be over before you know it, and then we'll be back to get you."

"You have to be brave. This will be fun. I promise."

She pries my rolled-up notebook from my fingers.

After a while I appear to have cried myself out. My head is so heavy, I can't lift it from the pillows on this bed that is not mine. The room is empty except for me and Mom.

She kisses my forehead and tells me I should come down soon. She and Dad can't stay long.

The longer they stay, she tells me, the harder it will be for her to leave me. And this is the right thing to do, she says. She and Dad have decided it will be good for me, to spend time with my family.

I think she sounds like she has been crying too, but I don't want to know if that's true.

Once she leaves the room, I lie flat and stare at the chandelier above my bed. This is a room for a princess, and I am anything but that.

What am I?

A lump of heaviness. A stranger. A thing that does not fit.

I can't seem to stop the poison inside me from spreading.

(I mean, I've never been poisoned, so I am only speculating.)

(But I do feel something spreading inside me. Something heavy and dark.)

I can't let them see it.

They can't know my secret. Not these people in this clean, white palace. Not even Mom and Dad know. And they never will.

Later Dad comes in and hugs me. "We'll talk every day," he tells me. "I love you."

He and Mom are leaving now. No, they cannot stay for dinner. Yes, they love me, forever.

A few minutes later I hear voices drifting up from beneath my window and get up to look outside. My parents and grandparents are standing by the sidewalk that leads to the driveway.

Dad tells Grandma, "Finley likes her space." He speaks quietly, but I am good at listening. "She's a dreamer. She loves to write. Just don't . . . push her."

Grandma's chin is square. "I think I'm used to taking care of grandchildren by now, Lewis."

Dad hugs Grandpa, who claps him on the back. Grandpa

says, "It was good to see you. You look good. You look . . . tall."

Dad clears his throat. "Yeah. You too."

Dad and Grandma do not hug. She tells him to drive safely.

Then Mom and Dad get into the car and drive away. I watch them until the trees swallow them up.

I am alone.

I wipe my face with tissues I find on my nightstand, unroll my notebook, and begin to write.

The Everwood won't leave me.

The Everwood is always right here, in my notebook, on these straight lines.

The Everwood is one thing I can always understand.

# 3

AT HOME, DINNER IS TYPICALLY a haphazard affair.

Mom camps out at the kitchen table, scarfs down her food in five minutes, and spends the rest of the night poring over some client's renovation blueprints.

Dad sits at his desk in the corner of the living room to work on lesson plans or write the novel he'll never finish because he gets distracted too easily.

Every now and then he'll take a bite of food. Mom inhales; Dad pecks.

I sit on the couch with my TV tray and my homework, usually with some kind of nature documentary on in the background. Dad says the narration soothes him and helps clear his mind.

Some people might think it's odd that we hardly ever eat dinner together at the table. I like our way, though. It makes me feel grown-up, like Mom and Dad don't have to pretend to care about typical dinnertime rituals.

We're all adults here. We eat how we want to eat.

But dinner at Hart House is like a dance. Not only do I not know the steps, but I seem to have forgotten how to move my legs entirely.

All twelve of us sit around the polished dining room table.

The room is full of glass. There is a sparkling chandelier. Old-fashioned music plays from a long, skinny stereo on a side table. Even though the stereo looks new, the music crackles and pops.

My aunts bring in dishes, serve drinks.

I have a list of the Harts in my notebook. For a couple of days I have studied their names and the photographs Dad gave to me. Grandpa sent them, in an e-mail.

(Obviously it is beyond strange to not have photographs of one's own family.)

(When I asked Dad about this, he rubbed his head and said, "Fin, it's complicated.")

(Whatever that means.)

My aunts whisper to one another as they set out silverware.

"I can't believe they didn't stay for dinner," says one of them. Her face is soft, and she keeps looking at me like she is terrified I might start crying again.

Aunt Deirdre. Dee for short, Dad said.

"I'm not surprised," hisses another of my aunts, thin and sharp all over. Her shiny blond hair is pulled back into a tight bun. "I *am* surprised they actually showed up."

Aunt Bridget. I must never call her anything but Aunt Bridget. Certainly not Bridge. In real life she looks even scarier than her photograph. Dad said Aunt Bridget kept her last name instead of taking Uncle Reed's, which I think is pretty wonderful. I wouldn't want to give up *my* last name.

But I'm not going to tell Aunt Bridget that. I'm not sure I'll say anything at all to her, in fact; she reminds me of a beautiful bird you would want to pet if you weren't afraid it might peck out your eyes.

"Stop it," says my third aunt. Aunt Amelia. Long, tan legs and arms. Lots of teeth. She is a runner, always has been. Everyone calls her Stick. "Not in front of Finley."

I inspect my napkin like it is the most interesting thing in the world.

"Girls," Grandpa says to my aunts, folding his napkin into his lap, "don't cause trouble. Bridget Lynn, that means you."

Aunt Bridget frowns, sits, takes a gulp of her drink. The ice cubes clink against the glass.

Grandpa's chair is at the head of the table. He has a lot of hair, combed into stiff silver waves. When he catches me staring at him, he winks. He is not very good at it.

Everyone is looking at me now, which makes me want to slither under the table and eat on the floor, but I think that is probably not allowed here.

(Focus, Finley.)

I must think of my list.

Aunt Bridget is married to Uncle Reed, who isn't here. He's hardly ever around, Dad said, because Uncle Reed took over Grandpa's business, which is basically about buying and selling companies and sounds to me like the most boring thing imaginable.

One of Aunt Bridget's eight-year-old twins shrieks. Dex, the boy.

"Ruth!" Aunt Bridget snaps. "Stop shaking pepper on your brother."

"But, Mom, he's been poisoned! This is the cure! He has to sneeze it out!"

Ruth's shouting makes me nervous. I wish my notebook weren't all the way up in my room.

I wish I were home.

I wish—

(Focus.)

Aunt Dee is married to Uncle Nelson, who drawls his words and looks like a cowboy without a horse. They have two kids: Kennedy, twelve years old. (The girl who looks like she belongs on a beach somewhere.) Avery, seventeen years old. (The girl I saw playing on her phone, the girl so pretty she doesn't look real.)

Then there's Aunt Amelia—Stick—and her daughter, Gretchen. Stick is 90 percent smile, 10 percent human. Gretchen has frizzy brown hair.

Mom told me Gretchen is the same age as me. She said it in this cheerful way, like the fact that there is another eleven-year-old in the house is supposed to make me feel better about my situation.

(Doubtful, Mom.)

And then there's me.

Grandma, Grandpa. Aunt Bridget, Uncle Reed (away on

business), Dex, and Ruth. Aunt Dee, Uncle Nelson, Avery, and Kennedy. Stick and Gretchen.

And me. Finley.

Aunt Dee sets a plate in front of me and smooths back my hair in a way that reminds me of Mom. I decide it probably isn't a great idea to start crying again, so I grab a fork and dive in before my body has the chance to betray me.

Maybe if I stuff my mouth with enough food, it will prevent me from saying what I want to say:

*There has been an awful mistake.*

*I'm not supposed to be here.*

*I'm not one of you.*

Someone kicks me under the table.

When I look up, everyone is staring at me—except for Grandma, who stands at the head of the table with her hands clasped at her waist.

My lips are smeared with salad dressing.

What did I do wrong? Who kicked me?

I glance across the table. Gretchen shakes her head, her eyes wide.

Grandpa clears his throat. "Finley, here at Hart House nobody eats until Grandma sits down."

"She's the key," Dex explains cheerfully. "You can't eat until she unlocks the meal."

Ruth claps her hands over her mouth and giggles hysterically.

"Ruth, for God's sake, calm yourself," says Aunt Bridget. "Right this minute. Stop laughing."

"Also, you're using the wrong fork." This is Avery, who looks like she's trying not to smile. "You're supposed to use the salad fork. You know, to eat your salad."

I look down at my table setting and see six utensils—three forks of different sizes, two spoons, and a knife.

"Uh. Okay."

Stick replaces my fork with a clean one and nudges my shoulder with her elbow. "Not to worry. How could you possibly be expected to know that?"

She smiles, but I'm not sure I believe her.

"It's not like Lewis would teach her," says Aunt Bridget. "He doesn't care about such things. He thinks everything we do is . . . What did he call us? Obsessed with the superficial."

Aunt Dee touches Aunt Bridget's arm. "Bridget, let's not do this right now."

"I'm just saying what everyone else is thinking," Aunt Bridget snaps.

Beside her Avery smirks and looks down at her lap. I see a soft glow on her shirt and realize she's playing with her phone under the table.

"That's enough, Bridget," says Grandma, and then she sits down at the only empty chair. "We do not talk about upsetting topics at the dinner table."

(*Upsetting topics.* Does she mean my dad?)

(If he is an upsetting topic, what does that make me?)

Grandpa leads a prayer—another thing I'm not used to,

another thing that makes me feel small and bulky at the same time.

Everyone begins to eat, and I pretend to, but I have lost my appetite.

People are talking to me—Gretchen and Stick, whose default setting appears to be talking. Kennedy, whose smile looks like it is straight out of a teeth-whitening commercial.

But I am too afraid to say anything much.

I am afraid that if I open my mouth, the wrongness inside me will come gushing out.

The wrongness of using the incorrect fork.

The wrongness of not knowing that Grandma is the key.

The wrongness of the tight, jumbled knot that is my insides. And how heavy it feels. And how it is pulling and pushing and molding me like clay.

I grab the crystal glass to the right of my plate and gulp down some water.

When I set the glass back down, I see the prints my sweaty fingers have left behind. I feel a sense of deep, sudden friendship with that smudge.

That is me. My aunts and uncles, my grandparents, my beautiful, beautiful cousins—I am a smudge on their glass.

# 4

I WAKE UP SWEATING AND pinned to my bed with terror.

Once, at home, I woke up like this and ran crying to my parents.

I told them I felt like I was going to throw up, that I heard terrible thoughts screaming in my head and couldn't make them stop.

They brought me a glass of water and sat with me until I fell asleep.

Nothing was wrong with me, they said. I had had a nightmare. Sometimes bad dreams linger.

I didn't believe them; I'd had nightmares before. This wasn't the same thing.

I knew something must be wrong, for me to feel like that. Something deep down where no one could see.

Since then I have never told my parents when I wake up sweating, feeling hot and sick and small. Instead I write about the Everwood until nothing else matters.

I never want to scare my parents again.

I don't want them to look at me like I am broken in a way they don't know how to fix.

(We are already broken enough; it's the reason I'm here.)

Gray light seeps in through the long white curtains of my bedroom, and I finally remember that I am not at home.

Everyone has spent the night at Hart House. The twins made a tent on the porch. My aunts and uncles and cousins all live nearby, but apparently they do this a lot: sleep over like a bunch of kids at a party.

Before I can talk myself out of it, I throw on some clothes and slip downstairs, out through the glassed-in sunroom attached to the kitchen.

At first the backyard looks pretty typical: Thick green lawn. Swing set with two swings. Bushes overflowing with pink flowers. Wind chimes tinkling on the patio.

There is no fence around the yard; Hart House is virtually in the middle of nowhere.

A path of pebbles leads to a slope in the ground. I creep closer and see stone steps set into the dirt, leading down into a pit of leaves and grass. It is almost as if someone carved a pond into the earth, sucked it dry of water, and filled it with trees.

There are so many of them that the air feels heavy and alive, like it's full of people. But I am the only one here.

Beyond the pit there is a small river. And beyond the river there are woods.

There is no fence to block my view, nothing to separate my grandparents' property from the woods beyond.

Wind blows past me, pricking me with goose bumps. The branches overhead knock against one another. The leaves whisper and shiver and sigh.

Something inside me unclenches.

I have read stories where the main character encounters a door—a window, a gate—and on the other side lies a magical land where anything is possible. If, that is, you dare to step through.

That is what I feel like right now: ready to leave the world I know and enter another.

The trees tower over me; I am small, but I am brave, and my heart is everywhere inside me. My fingers tingle. *Now.*

I take a deep breath and begin down the stone steps, into this pit that is another world.

A rope swing hangs from an impossibly tall tree. I have never been so close to so many humongous trees; they must be decades old. Maybe even centuries old.

Like the Everwood.

I sit on the high riverbank and let my feet swing out over the water.

In my stories about the Everwood, I have imagined a vast and tangled forest, a dense web of dark trees. I have imagined it to be dangerous inside, a forbidding place where only the wild-hearted live.

In my stories I have never visited it. Others have, and I have collected their tales.

But clearly they were wrong. I was wrong.

*This* is the Everwood—this towering green place full of sunlight.

And I belong here.

I forget about wrong forks and Hart House etiquette and my bedroom as white as clouds. I smell dirt, decomposing logs, river water.

Beneath these trees I feel the same way I have always felt when opening my notebook to a clean page:

As long as I am here, I am safe.

ONCE THERE WAS AN ORPHAN *girl*.

*She had been wandering for months, lost in an unfamiliar country.*

*Sometimes her loneliness felt so overwhelming she found it difficult to continue her search—for family, for a home—but she always did.*

*She wanted to see the world and discover its secrets. Curiosity burned inside her and kept her strong.*

*One day a great forest came into view. The orphan girl's heart stirred to see it.*

*"I wouldn't go in there," warned an old traveling musician, playing his violin beside the path.*

*"Why not?" asked the orphan girl.*

*"Too many questions," he grumbled, "and not enough answers."*

*The orphan girl thanked him and continued south, down the forest road. The next day she bought an apple from a farmer.*

*"You're not going to the Everwood, are you?" asked the farmer.*

*"Of course I am," the orphan girl replied.*

*The farmer shook her head. "Then you're a fool. People who go in there don't come out."*

*This did not particularly trouble the orphan girl, for she had no one to leave behind.*

"I thank you for the warning," she said, and continued down the road.

On the third day the orphan girl came to the forest's edge. A witch sat high in the trees, knitting dreams.

"Looking for something?" the witch asked, peering down from her perch.

"Adventure," the orphan girl answered promptly.

The witch's smile was full of holes. "Then you've come to the right place."

The orphan girl felt a tiny fear. A thread of darkness hissed in the witch's voice.

But a tiny fear was easy enough to push aside. The orphan girl was used to ignoring feelings that pained her.

So she thanked the chuckling witch, clenched her fists, and pushed through the brambles into darkness.

# 5

"WHAT ARE YOU DOING DOWN here?"

I jump to my feet and whirl around. Gretchen stands a few steps behind me, staring.

At least she isn't Grandma. Or Avery, who watched me at dinner last night like I was a puzzle for her to decipher.

Avery's hair makes me nervous. Unless it's in a shampoo advertisement, hair should not be that shiny.

"Hello?" Gretchen waves her hand in front of my face. "Earth to Finley?"

"Oh. Hi."

"Hi. What are you doing out here?"

"Um. Nothing?"

"Is that a question?"

My face grows hot. "No. I was just looking around. I woke up early. I was afraid of using the wrong fork at breakfast."

Gretchen stands beside me on the riverbank. "Don't worry about the forks thing. Avery says that's one of the Hart family pretensions. It's not something that matters in the real world."

"The real world?"

"The world outside Hart House." She squints at me. "Do you know what *pretension* means?"

A black-and-white grid flashes before my eyes, and I hear Dad's voice mumbling over the Sunday *New York Times* crossword. Thinking of his voice feels like someone has reached inside me and twisted.

*Pretension.* Ten-letter-word for "snobbery, a claim to importance."

It can also mean "false."

"It's like when you're snobby about something," I explain.

"Oh. Okay. Yeah, I get that." Gretchen puts her hands on her hips and faces the woods. "So you're just out here looking at everything?"

"Yeah, I guess." My mouth feels like a machine that isn't quite working. "It's pretty out here."

"Huh. I never really thought about it."

Gretchen plops down onto the riverbank. I sit beside her, prepared to run if need be. She did kick me under the table last night, after all.

"I can't believe you came out here by yourself," Gretchen says.

"You never go out to the woods?"

"Grandma's never forbidden it, exactly, but she doesn't like us being out here where she can't really see us. Mostly when we come over, we help her clean the house."

"That doesn't sound very fun."

"It's not. But Grandma likes things to look nice. So it's like we all come over, and the aunts sit in the kitchen and drink, and Grandma puts us kids to work. She's all 'you must learn to respect what you have' and 'people expect us to look a certain way.'"

I giggle. She does a pretty good Grandma voice.

"So what do you like about it?" she asks. Our feet swing over the water. Gretchen wears red galoshes over her pajamas.

"The woods?"

"Yeah."

"Well . . . it's complicated."

"Finley, we're Harts. We share blood, you know. You can tell me."

What does that even mean, being a Hart? It has to be about something more than blood; otherwise Hart House wouldn't feel like it is the wrong size for me. Maybe I should start a new list: What It Means to Be a Hart. If I can figure that out, maybe I'll be able to survive the summer.

*We share blood.* Kind of creepy, really.

I take a deep breath. "I like it because . . . it's the Everwood."

Gretchen frowns. "What's that? Like Narnia?"

"It's a real place," I clarify, "not imaginary, and not in another world. It's in our world, but you can only find it if it wants you to find it. I've been writing about it forever. Since I was seven."

"And you think this place is it?"

"Maybe," I say. "It looks like it always has in my head, but even better. I had some of it right, but I also got a lot of things wrong. Now I see how it all really looks."

"Like what?"

"Well . . . that's the Green." I point up the hill of the pit, toward the bright green lawn. "You know, for festivals and things. And that's the Great Castle." Now I point to Hart House. "It sits right at the edge of the Everwood, guarding against trespassers."

"Is there a king and queen?"

I think for a second. "No. The Everwood has never had a king or queen. It's really old, and it's been hidden away for a long time. Only one who is truly worthy can be ruler of the Everwood, and no one has ever been worthy enough."

"What makes a person worthy?"

"Only the Everwood knows that."

Gretchen nods, leans back on her elbows. "So does anyone live at the castle?"

"Of course. Someone has to, until the king or queen arrives. The two ancient guardians live there, all alone."

"That's sad."

"Not really. It's their solemn duty."

"So how old are they?"

"Think of the oldest thing you can imagine, and that's them. Their duty is to watch over the Everwood and guard its secrets until the rightful ruler is found."

These words spill out of my mouth as if they have always been there, waiting to become themselves. I have written dozens of Everwood stories, but now everything is different.

Now I am actually *here*.

"Are they the only people who live in the Everwood?" asks Gretchen.

"Oh, no, lots of other people live there. There are witches, and barrows—these digging creatures with huge mouths like shovels. They live underground, and you have to be careful where you step, because they can reach up and grab you. And there are fire-breathing salamanders with poisonous drool, and fairies that will play tricks on you if they decide they don't like you, and sometimes there are knights, if one gets lost during a quest—"

"Oh!" Gretchen shoots upright, her hand in the air. "Me! I want to be a knight. Can I?"

"What?"

"A knight! I'd be a great knight. Would I get a horse? Would I fight dragons?"

My thoughts spin out of control.

What does Gretchen mean, can she *be* a knight? The Everwood is not a game. It is not a thing you play at; it is a thing that already exists. You can't simply become a part of something that doesn't belong to you, something you've only just learned about.

I find myself wishing Gretchen had never come out here. Then she would never have found out about the Everwood, and it would still be safely mine.

Now that *she* knows, who else might soon know? And what will they think of me? The Everwood has only ever belonged to me. We understand each other.

If I swear Gretchen to secrecy, will she agree?

I wonder if Harts are good at keeping secrets. I am good at that, but then, I don't feel like a real Hart.

Maybe blood doesn't matter at all.

"Please? *Pleeeease?*" Gretchen clasps her hands under her chin and pouts.

She looks so ridiculous that I burst out laughing. It feels strange, and wonderful, like jumping out of deep water to breathe. I have not laughed for days.

"Okay," I say. "You can be a knight."

Gretchen pumps her fist into the air.

"But be warned: As a knight, it will be your duty to help the ancient guardians protect the Everwood from evil."

"What kind of evil?"

"Invaders. Highwaymen." I look around, and then whisper, "Pirates."

Gretchen scoffs. "Please. I could take on a whole ship of pirates with one hand tied behind my back. Without armor, even. *Blindfolded.*"

"Not even the most valiant heart, good lady, can know every wonder the Everwood holds. Both gentle . . . and dangerous."

What has come over me? I don't normally talk to people like this. The only time I use my Everwood voice is around Mom or Dad, and they're only halfway listening anyway.

Gretchen jumps to her feet. "Okay, so if I'm a knight, what does that make you?"

"I'm . . ." I pause, flushing. "I'm an orphan."

That is who I have always been, in all my stories. Dad used to read to me before bed every night, and we read about a lot of orphans. They were often strange in some way—they had unusual powers or ugly scars, or carried terrible secrets inside them. But they always turned out to be heroes in the end.

I like that idea, of the strange, lonely character being the most powerful.

Gretchen makes a face. "Being an orphan doesn't sound fun at all."

"It isn't about *fun*. It's how the story goes."

"Okay, if you say so. It's your game."

"It's not a game!" The words explode before I can stop them.

Gretchen blinks at me, and I wonder if she will laugh at me and leave, or get mad, or think I'm a freak, or . . . what? Do I care?

Maybe it would be for the best.

But Gretchen simply kneels. "Forgive me, oh fair orphan child! As a knight I have awful manners and do not always think before I speak."

Warmth rushes through me; maybe I will start laughing again. Gretchen is not making fun of me or running away. She's . . . staying. She's smiling. She has a decent English accent.

What now?

"You are forgiven," I declare. "After all, I am but a humble orphan child, and you are a great knight."

"Well, not yet," she says, in her normal voice. "I have to prove myself first. So should we go?"

"Go where?"

She throws out her arm toward the woods on the other side of the river. "Exploring! Questing! Not sure how we'll cross over, though."

I search for a moment and then point down the river at a tree trunk–sized pipe that stretches across the water, its ends buried in the riverbanks. "We'll cross over the First Bridge."

"Well . . . technically, we're not allowed to go near that pipe. Grandma doesn't think it's safe. . . ." Gretchen trails off, watching me closely.

I hesitate. Breaking Grandma Hart's rules on my second day here doesn't seem like a good idea. But the call of the Everwood is not something I can ignore, and now that Gretchen is beside me, waiting, I don't want her to leave.

I think I want her to understand.

I certainly don't want her to think I'm afraid of crossing a pipe.

Maybe it is important for me to impress Gretchen. If I do, I will have passed some sort of test, and my cousins will accept me.

"If we explore fast and get back before breakfast," I say slowly, "maybe no one will ever know?"

Gretchen grins. "And a knight wouldn't care about breaking rules, would she?"

"Not if it was for a noble cause."

"I'm in. Let's do it." Gretchen runs toward the pipe, her galoshes kicking up clumps of mud.

For a moment I imagine Grandma Hart peeking out a window, and I freeze with fear. But it's too late; I have a responsibility to accompany Gretchen. No one should enter the Everwood alone, especially not a knight who thinks she can fight pirates blindfolded.

"Orphan girl!" Gretchen whisper-shouts, ready to cross the bridge. "Hurry up! I need a guide!"

A guide. Because no one knows the Everwood like I do.

Because the Everwood *wanted* me to find it.

I grin, and run to catch up.

*NE DAY THE ORPHAN GIRL was walking through the Everwood alone, when she came upon a lady knight polishing her armor.*

*The orphan girl was careful around any stranger, for in strangers lay the possibility of pain. But the knight greeted her warmly and proposed that they travel together.*

*And so they did, exploring an area of the Everwood that was new to them both. The trees stretched into a high world of green; neither the orphan girl nor the knight could see the sky above.*

*The farther they walked, the quieter the woods became. The world took on an eerie feeling, as if the air had been disturbed by something malicious and slow-moving.*

*"Something terrible has happened here," whispered the orphan girl.*

*"How can you be sure?" asked her friend.*

*"Can't you feel it? The air is heavy with secrets."*

*Then the orphan girl saw a shape in the shadows beneath a thin white tree. The shape gave off a quivering power—weak, but once strong.*

*"Be careful," said the knight. "I don't know this part of the forest. Perhaps we should turn around."*

*But the orphan girl was too curious. She reached into the briars and pulled out a fine bridle laced with gold. It hummed with power, rattling her teeth and leaving her breathless.*

"Put it away," urged the knight. "There is something evil about this place."

"I cannot," said the orphan girl. "I must find to whom it belongs." She tucked the bridle into her pack.

Not long after this, they found another object, half buried in the dirt.

"A boot?" mused the orphan girl.

"A fine one," added the knight. "The leather is like velvet."

"'Tis a shame to misplace something so valuable," the orphan girl observed.

"Misplaced, perhaps. Or stolen. Or worse."

The orphan girl shivered at her friend's dark words. The boot's power was even stronger than the bridle's, making her bones ache as if with fever.

"Do you think it has been enspelled by a witch?" whispered the knight. "Enchanted by a fairy?"

"It has certainly known pain," said the orphan girl soberly, "for when I touch it, I feel it too." She tucked the boot into a pouch on her pack.

Deeper in the Everwood, where the light was as dim as evening, a wave of power washed over the orphan girl and her knight. They staggered, gasping.

The orphan girl caught a glint of metal.

"A dagger," she said, lifting the weapon from the tangled forest floor.

"It is a fine blade," said the knight. "But what has happened to it? I feel ill to look at it."

"Something cruel," concluded the orphan girl. "Something that left much pain behind."

"Wait a moment. Look!"

The orphan girl raised her head and saw a strange light shifting through the Everwood leaves. Following it, she emerged into a gray field. Few trees stood here, and no birds sang.

In the middle of the field stood a small castle of crumbling stone. Wind whistled through the dry grass, and a torn flag hung from a crooked tower.

"It is a wasteland," whispered the orphan girl, for she could think of no other way to describe it. Determined to explore, the orphan girl wrapped the dagger in cloth and tucked it into her pack with the boot and the bridle.

No sooner had she done this than three figures tumbled out of the castle door. Their laughter was high and sharp, their voices vicious. They wore filthy rags tied around their heads, and their coats were black with mud.

The lady knight unsheathed her sword.

"Who are they?" asked the orphan girl.

"Rotters!" shouted the lady knight. "Come, my brave friend! We cannot let them catch us!"

"You would run from a fight?" asked the orphan girl.

For answer the knight raced back into the trees, away from the castle and its gray field, and the orphan girl had no choice but to follow.

# 6

I sprint after Gretchen, dodging trees and jumping logs. I do not want to leave the house we found without seeing what is inside it, but these boys are definitely chasing us, and they are fast.

"Wait, the who?" I shout.

"Come *on*, Finley!"

"But who are the Baileys?"

Even in galoshes Gretchen is lightning fast. "They're these kids from next door," she yells back at me. "Well, across the river, I mean!"

As we run, my mind races.

The Baileys. In the Everwood they would not be neighbors across the river; they would be pirates. The Rotters, to be specific: an infamous trio of rogue pirates hailing from the Bitter Sea, who befoul and besmirch everything they touch, and who have come to the Everwood to plunder it of its riches.

Thinking about the Everwood turns my chest light and my legs powerful. I dodge trees and jump over logs, passing Gretchen. A creeper vine whips past my face, and I almost drop the tiny shoe I found.

Behind us the Bailey boys holler at us:

"Trespassers!"

"You'd better run faster!"

"No Harts allowed!"

I look back and see one of the boys grinning at me. He darts through the trees and disappears, but I still hear him laughing.

Back at the river Gretchen and I scoot across the pipe bridge as fast as we can. Once we get to the other side, there is no sign of the Bailey boys.

"Where'd they go?" I ask, panting.

Gretchen points across the river, and I see it now: a house, hidden in a mess of trees. It is as grand as Hart House, with a massive porch and too many windows to count, but this house is brown with dirt. The roof sags, and the paint is peeling.

"Are you friends with them?"

Gretchen clutches her side. "Are you kidding? No way."

I stick my hand into my pocket. I wonder what Mom would think if she knew I was running away from boys, through a forest, with a wrapped knife in my jeans.

The Bailey boys climb up the hill to their house. It's so steep on that side that they have to pull themselves up tree roots, like climbing the rungs of a ladder.

One of them, the one who smiled at me, turns around at the top of the hill. He makes a gesture that would no doubt make my issue with the dinner forks seem like nothing to Grandma.

Gretchen flings sticks across the river. They plop into the water. "Stay out of our woods!"

"I don't think they're our woods," I point out, once I have gotten my breath back. "Right? I don't think where we were is Grandma and Grandpa's land."

"Whatever. God." Gretchen's face is red and splotchy, but on her it is somehow appealing. How does she do that?

## WHAT IT MEANS TO BE A HART

• You look pretty even after sprinting across a forest.

I am not sure how to talk to Gretchen right now. "Are you . . . mad?"

"Yes, I'm mad! The Bailey boys are such trash. I can't believe they chased us. They know they're not supposed to come near any of us. Grandma says so. She told them so."

"Well, we were the ones messing around by their . . . whatever that was. That house."

"Nah, that's not the Baileys'. It's just some house that's been abandoned forever. We're *definitely* not allowed to go there. I tried to stop you, but you wouldn't listen." Gretchen grins a little. "I didn't think you'd be such a rebel."

I have to write a story about this house, and the pirates, and everything. The words racing through my head aren't big enough to describe what has happened.

Before today I didn't know there was an abandoned old castle in a gray field, deep in the Everwood, but now it seems obvious it has always been there, hidden and waiting. For me.

I have to sit down with my notebook and think. I have to write it just the right way, pick my words carefully. The Everwood deserves to be written about like it is important.

My fingers itch for a pencil.

"But why aren't you allowed to go there?"

"To that house? I don't know, because it's condemned or whatever. Ugh!" Gretchen kicks dirt toward the Bailey house. "Just look at that place. It's a disaster. Grandma calls them a blight on the town. Sometimes when I sleep over, I can hear them up in the middle of the night, yelling and blasting music. Like, what, they can't sleep like normal, civilized people?"

I wonder if Grandma has told Gretchen bad things about me and Mom and Dad, like she has about the Baileys.

She has had a lot of time to do so.

The Bailey boys disappear inside their house. A screen door slams.

"Have you ever talked to them?"

Gretchen stares at me. "No. Why would I?"

I am not sure how to answer her. I don't want her to think I don't belong here, that I don't understand how things work at Hart House.

"You don't get it, Finley. These aren't normal boys. It's like they're . . . I don't know."

"They're pirates," I say. "Ferocious scoundrels come to pillage the Everwood. They're known as Rotters, wicked and completely without honor."

"Ha! If those are the pirates I have to fight, I can totally handle it." Gretchen finds yet another stick to throw. "You hear me? I can take you!"

She runs after the stick, kicking up chunks of mud.

As I watch her, I consider asking Gretchen what Grandma has said about me.

Does Grandma think I am a blight on the family?

Does she think I am a disaster?

These questions make me feel like I am shrinking inside myself, but I will not disappear. Not now that I've found the Everwood.

Gretchen is marching around, whacking branches with a stick, still grumbling about the Bailey boys.

To distract myself, I take out our finds to examine them:

A shoe. Child's size 11. For the left foot. Black with mud and mildew. The fabric is a faded pink.

A pocketknife that flips open when you press the side. Rusty blade. The hilt is marked with initials, but they are so faded I cannot read them.

Then there is the bicycle, buried back in the woods, where Gretchen and I were exploring—blackened and twisted, its spokes warped.

Something about these three objects, quite frankly, creeps me out. They do not seem to fit with the gleaming white world of Hart House. They belong to the dry field where we found them. To the crumbling old house.

Especially this child's shoe. When I hold it, the Everwood

seems to shift around me, as if to say, *Here. This. This is important.*

I wonder if these objects are connected somehow, and if what I have always guessed about the Everwood is true:

Such a large forest must be full of secrets.

Now that I am here, I will find them.

HE TREES IN THE EVERWOOD were turning gray. Their leaves began to fall, dry and shrunken, although autumn was still months away.

These trees smelled sour and sharp—burned, though there were no flames.

The orphan girl noticed the change one day not long after her first encounter with the Rotters. She sensed a great pain lying hidden at the heart of the Everwood, a secret connected to the boot, the bridle, the blade.

Whatever this secret was, it had begun seeping into the Everwood trees like disease. The lady knight plucked a withered leaf from a low-hanging branch; it crumbled into ash at her touch.

"What does this mean?" the knight whispered. "What has happened here?"

The orphan girl did not answer. She was staring at the bridle. The ash from the crumbled leaf had fallen onto the bridle, and now the cords of leather were beginning to twist and grow.

The knight withdrew her sword.

"Do not interfere," warned the orphan girl. "There is dark magic here. If we try to stop it, we might make it worse."

Soon the bridle was no longer leather and gold but scales and skin—an enormous brown snake with bright turquoise eyes.

"What do you want?" demanded the orphan girl.

The snake hissed. "I know a secret."

"Tell us," yelled the knight, "or I'll cut off your head!"

The snake let out a wheezing laugh. Smoke curled up from its mouth. "I'd like to see you try."

The orphan girl knelt to look the snake in its gleaming eyes. "What is the secret of the Everwood?"

"Oh, it isn't my place to tell you that," said the snake coyly.

"Then why do you taunt us?" cried the knight.

"I said I know a secret. I didn't say I could share it."

"Please, tell us what you know," said the orphan girl. "We must save the Everwood."

"You can't," said the snake, with a cold smile. "Not with what you carry."

The orphan girl stepped back. "What do you mean?"

"You know very well what I mean." The snake raised itself up until it was as tall as a man. "Here. I'll show you."

Then, too quickly for the knight to even raise her sword, the snake lunged at the orphan girl. Holding her upright in its coils, it opened its jaws wide over her mouth.

The orphan girl felt something deep inside her unraveling, sliding up her throat and out her mouth. She gagged.

The snake set her down in the dirt and spat a coil of darkness into her palm.

"There," the snake said. "I cannot remove all of it. It is lodged too deeply. I am not powerful enough. And besides, it is not my darkness to fight."

The knight crept closer. "What is it?"

The orphan girl stared at the slick, wriggling lump in her palm. When the orphan girl flung the thing away, it rolled through the mud, spitting smoke, until it, too, crumbled into ash and drifted away on the wind.

Raising her sword high, the knight shouted a battle cry and ran after it.

Once they were alone, the snake turned to the orphan girl. It was no longer smiling. "Whatever we carry within our hearts, the Everwood's power makes it real. And soon what you carry will destroy not only you but everything you touch. The Everwood is not as strong as it once was; your darkness will bring out its own. To save the forest you must face this thing inside you."

The orphan girl held back tears of shame. Her great secret, the one she had worked so hard to conceal, lodged in her heart. "But how?"

"First you must give it a name," said the snake. "Naming a thing takes away some of its power and gives it to you instead."

The orphan girl backed away and shook her head. "But I cannot!"

The snake narrowed its eyes. "And why not?"

"Because I am afraid."

"If you want to save the Everwood—and save yourself—you will have to find a way."

The snake slithered off into the shadows.

"I cannot just stop being afraid!" the orphan girl shouted after it. Then she said quietly, "I have been afraid for so long."

"Only fools try to run away from fear," called the snake. "What you must do is learn to walk alongside it."

Then the snake was gone. In the silence the orphan girl heard three distant keening howls. The darkness she carried inside her moved, restless, as though her secret were a beast and those howls were waking it up.

The knight returned. "My friend, I fear we cannot do this on our own. The evil here is too monstrous for only two warriors to conquer."

"You are right," said the orphan girl, watching the path the snake had taken, until her eyes burned. "We must find more brave souls for our quest.

"We need to bring others to the Everwood."

# 7

I AM EXPECTING A CALL from home. Mom doesn't call that much—she has a secret phone phobia, so unless it's for work, she hardly ever uses it—but I talk to Dad almost every night at eight. It is now 8:05.

I pace up and down the hallway and then walk circles through the rec room. I peer out the tall windows, trying to see through the trees to the Bailey property.

One window of the Bailey house is lit up. The others are dark. A boy-sized shape walks along the river, then disappears up the hill.

I walk back to my bedroom, staring at my phone. 8:10. 8:12. I wipe my palms on my pajama pants.

The phone rings, and the screen lights up, displaying Dad's picture. He is dressed up for Halloween, even though Mom says he is too old for that. His costumes are always literary characters. Last year he was Miss Havisham from *Great Expectations* and carried around an actual spoiled cake.

"Lewis, why are you dressing up as a *woman*?" Mom asked.

Dad looked at her as though she had asked him to wear his shoes on his hands. "Because she's the best character in the book? Plus, my eight o'clock class dared me."

Dad Havisham is calling me.

I answer. "Hello?"

"Fin! How's my girl? A whole week away from you, I'm going nuts."

"I'm fine, I guess. Grandma's listening to the blues. Here, wait a sec."

I creep to the landing and peek downstairs, holding out my phone. The air is full of music. It makes me think about one of my favorite words, a nine-letter word for "slow, heavy, rhythmic": *ponderous.*

In the living room Grandma and Grandpa dance in a slow circle. Grandpa presses his cheek against Grandma's hair. He says something soft, and Grandma laughs.

Something inside my chest gives way.

I cannot remember the last time Mom and Dad danced, or touched, or laughed, unless it had something to do with me.

The hand holding my phone is sweating. I go back to my room.

At the end of the hallway the door to Avery's room stands open. Everyone else went home days ago, but she is still here, and I can't figure out why. I assume it's because she loves our grandparents, but I haven't heard her say so.

There she is, sitting back in her pillows, playing with her phone.

She glances up, and I freeze. Her eyes cut into my skin, like my secret is this thing inside me, knotted up and quivering, and Avery knows right where it is.

I duck back inside my bedroom.

"Got to love Ray Charles," Dad is saying in my ear. "Your grandma has good taste."

"You never listen to Ray Charles."

"I used to. You go through phases, you know?"

"Yeah. So how are you?"

"Excellent, excellent! The first section of summer school. Every day is packed full. Lots of grading. But the kids this time around are great."

As Dad talks, I turn to the Favorite Words list near the front of my notebook and find *ponderous*. I enjoy how its letters look all together. This list has become so long that, to keep it to one page, I have begun writing words wherever I can find space, even in the margins.

*Rivulet. Wanderlust. Flagrant. Gewgaw.* Three hundred and forty-six words so far.

I run my finger down the list, feeling the pen marks. "How's Mom?"

"Oh, she's engrossed in the Robertson renovation. You remember, that house on the lake? She's got swatches spread out all over the kitchen table. She's in heaven."

There is that tiny pinch in his voice, the one that means Mom has been working too much. Again.

"Dad?"

"Yeah, sweetie."

"Mom's really busy, huh?"

Dad sighs. "We both are. Sometimes I think . . ."

My heart pounds into the silence. "What?"

"Ah, nothing. You know me. I ramble."

"How's . . ." I can't say it. It catches on my tongue like a swear word. "How's everything going? You know, with the stuff you and Mom are . . . figuring out?"

Dad is quiet for too many seconds. "Well, Fin. We've been talking about a lot of things."

"Like what kind of things?"

"About me, and about your mom, and about our life together. School, her design firm. Whether . . . we're as happy as we should be." He pauses. "It's pretty boring, actually. You're not missing a lot! But we miss you. We miss you like crazy."

He's so cheerful, not saying much that is real, not really answering my question. I try to imagine him and Mom sitting around at home by themselves, talking and laughing without me, and I can't do it.

All I can picture is Mom working at the table and Dad working at his desk, and my empty spot on the couch, and silence.

All I can think is that, without me there, they don't have to pretend everything is okay.

They don't have to pretend smile, and say pretend *have a good day* and pretend *I love you*.

Pretend words sound so different from real ones. Like you've got something stuck in your throat that won't come out, and you're trying to act like it isn't there.

I feel sick to my stomach all of a sudden. "Grandma made pot roast tonight. And asparagus."

"Asparagus? Hmm. Spindly green things, right?"

Dad hates vegetables. Mom says he had better be careful about that. He's not eighteen anymore.

"Ha, ha. Very funny."

"When you get home, I'm going to make you such a welcome home dinner, it'll put your grandma's cooking to shame."

"Dad. Be serious."

"I am, Fin. I am." Dad gets quiet again, and I sit there waiting for him to speak, and wanting to ask to talk to Mom, and wanting to hang up on him, and twisting my shoelace around my finger until it is so tight my skin turns red.

I miss him. I'm angry they have left me here.

But I would stay here for ten summers if it meant, at the end of them, I could come home and everything would be the same as it used to be.

Then I remember something that has been on my mind. "Dad? I have a question."

"Yeah? Shoot."

"You know the Bailey family? They live across the river from Grandma and Grandpa?"

I wait. Have I lost the call? "Dad?"

"Yeah? Yeah! I'm here. Sure, the Baileys. They're still there, huh? What about them?"

"Yeah. Gretchen and I were outside, and they just started chasing us. The Baileys, I mean. We chased them but we couldn't catch them. Gretchen said Grandma told them they're supposed to stay away from us, and we're supposed to stay away from them. She said Grandma said they're a blight on the town. But I don't get why. Gretchen acted like she really hated them, and I thought it was weird to hate someone for their house being messy. Don't you think it's weird? Unless they did something bad or wrong or something." I pause.

I didn't mean to say so much, but it feels better now that I have. I miss having Mom and Dad around to talk to. "Dad?"

He draws in a long, slow breath and then says, "Finley?"

"Yeah?"

"I don't want you talking with the Baileys either. And I mean it."

The seriousness of his voice frightens me. "But why?"

"Because . . ." Dad sighs sharply. "Look, Finley, when we were teenagers, the Baileys—their dad, I mean—he wasn't a good kid. He did . . . bad things. He's not safe to be around, and if he has kids now, I bet they're not much different. I wouldn't trust them for anything. And your grandparents don't like talking about this, so I wouldn't bring it up. Okay?"

"But I don't get it—"

"Finley. I'm serious. Do this for me, okay? Please?"

None of this makes sense. My head buzzes with questions. "Yeah. Okay. I won't say anything."

"You promise me, Fin?"

"I promise."

"Okay. Good." Dad's voice relaxes. "I'm going to let you go now, all right? You should go downstairs, spend time with your grandparents. Or with Avery."

"Avery's scary, Dad."

"I know you think so, but I'm sure she's not once you get to know her."

"You don't know her. You don't know any of them, and neither do I. They're like strangers, and you left me here with them like it was no big deal."

There is an awful silence. I wish I could take it all back.

Dad says, "Finley, it was a big deal. Don't think it wasn't. It was hard for us to leave you, okay?"

"Then why did you?" I get up, start pacing. Maybe I'm glad I said something. Maybe I don't want to take it back after all.

"We've talked about this. Because your mom and I—"

"Need space to work things out. I know."

"Finley . . ."

I wait for him to say something that will make this better. "What?"

He sighs. "You know, I talk to your grandpa a lot, actually. On the phone."

I don't say anything.

"He's been asking me to come by for years, to bring you to visit. When I told him about—when I mentioned that your mom and I needed some time together, he was the one who suggested I bring you down for the summer. He's been saying that for a while now, and he was right. As much as I hate to admit it when he's right . . ."

"How come you never let me talk to him?" My eyes are hot.

Avery walks by on her way to the bathroom. She's typing

on her phone, but she glances over anyway. I run over and shut the door.

"I don't have a good answer for you, Finley," Dad says. "I should have let you talk to him. I should have done a lot of things. I've been selfish and stubborn. But I'm trying now, okay? We're all trying. You're getting older, and I don't want you growing up and leaving for college and heading out into the world without knowing your cousins."

"*Dad.* College is a million years away."

"Time's a slippery little jerk, Fin." Dad sounds tired. "Things happen more quickly than you think. One minute you're a kid, and the next minute you're grown up and wondering what the heck happened when you weren't looking."

"You're being so dramatic."

"Seriously, Fin."

I stare at the closed door, breathing in and out. "Okay."

"Are you going to be all right?"

"I'm fine."

Silence. He doesn't believe me. I don't care.

"Your mom's going to try to call you tomorrow, all right? She's busy prepping for a big meeting with the Robertsons."

"That's okay. She can call me whenever. Tell her it's okay."

It's not okay.

I don't care about the Bailey boys and whatever it is their stupid dad did.

I don't care about the Everwood, or the shoe and the knife tucked under my bed.

I throw my notebook against my pillows. I consider asking Dad not to hang up, but that would mean I'd have to keep talking to him.

"Okay, sweetie." Dad blows me a kiss through the phone. I can almost feel it hit my cheek. "I love you. I love you so much. I'll talk to you tomorrow. Okay?"

"Okay."

"Go talk to your grandma. Ask her about her favorite Ray Charles song. She'll talk your ear off. We used to listen to him all the time when we were kids."

When they were kids.

And *then* what happened?

"Okay." I feel like my voice is not my own. I have too many questions and I can't figure out how to ask any of them.

After Dad hangs up, I climb into bed and try to read one of my old Everwood stories, one I wrote before coming to Hart House. But it seems all wrong, now that I've seen the real Everwood. It seems like I didn't know what I was doing, like I was just a silly kid playing make-believe.

Before long these thoughts are so loud they start to feel true:

I am just a silly kid playing make-believe.

I don't know what I am doing.

I am all wrong.


When Grandma comes up to say it's time for bed, I pretend I am already asleep.

I am too close to blurting out my secret to her:

How I didn't get up to brush my teeth or wash my face, not because I am lazy but because I couldn't. It was physically impossible. My body was too heavy to move.

How I am sinking into cold, blue water, a blue nothing like the warm music filling the house downstairs.

How I am finding it difficult to breathe. How my skin is crawling with something like fear.

I cannot say these things to anyone, especially not to Grandma.

So I lie there with my eyes closed while Grandma turns off the light.

It is easier this way.

# 8

ON THE MORNING OF MY second Friday at Hart House, everyone returns for the weekend. Grandma immediately puts us to work cleaning.

"How else will you learn to respect what you have?" Grandma points out when Dex and Ruth start whining.

Gretchen shoots me a look around Grandma's back. *See?*

"Or we can let everything sit and rot and turn into some overgrown pigsty," Grandma adds.

She doesn't say anything about the Bailey house directly, but I'm sure that's what she means. I glance out the kitchen window, through the woods, and find the Baileys' vine-swamped porch.

Grandma catches me looking. Our eyes lock.

"What do we have to do *this* time?" Ruth moans, draping herself theatrically over the back of a chair.

"Ruth, you and Kennedy have the downstairs bathrooms. Gretchen and Dex will take the upstairs bathrooms. Avery's dusting. And Finley?"

I swallow hard. "Yes?"

"You'll help me in the kitchen."

As I reluctantly follow Grandma down the hall, Gretchen

grabs my arm and whispers, "I told everyone we'd meet tonight. Outside, in the pit, after the adults have gone to sleep."

"Even Avery?" Please not Avery.

"Are you kidding? She'd tell on us, and she wouldn't want to come anyway. *Be there*, okay? No chickening out."

"Chicken out? I was the one who got you to cross the river in the first place, you know."

"I'm just saying, the Everwood is a whole other world after dark." Gretchen grins and waggles her fingers at me.

"Finley?" Grandma calls out. Her heels click on the kitchen floor. "Quickly, we have a lot to do."

"Be. There." Gretchen pokes my shoulder twice and hurries off to find Dex.

In the kitchen Grandma is taking plates, pots, and pans out of the cabinets. Stick just got back from one of her runs and is making a protein shake.

When she sees me, she attacks me with a hug. She does not look much like her daughter; Stick is long and golden, like Avery. Gretchen must have gotten her frizzy dark hair from her father. Dad told me Gretchen's father died when Gretchen was very young. Stick kept his name and never remarried.

(If anyone around here should feel sad, and heavy, and unable to get up and brush her teeth before bed, it should be Gretchen, or Stick.)

(Not me.)

(So get it together, Finley.)

"Here, Finley." Grandma hands me an old cloth. "Start wiping down those bottom cabinets, please. I'd like to get this done quickly so I can be at the clinic by one o'clock."

"Clinic?"

Grandma waves a hand. "Just something I do when I have the time."

"Your grandma's being modest." Stick loops her arm through Grandma's. "She volunteers at the clinic, works the front desk. Whenever they need her, she drops everything and goes. *And* she organizes this back-to-school program at the Y, where they stuff backpacks full of school supplies for kids who need them. You know, so their parents don't have to worry about spending money on notebooks and pens and such. Your grandma, Fin." Stick beams at me. "She's the best, in case you didn't know."

Stick plants a sweaty kiss on Grandma's cheek, and Grandma's nose wrinkles. I try not to laugh.

"It keeps me from getting bored around here in this old house, is all," Grandma says crisply. "Now get to cleaning, you two."

Stick flips on the radio. "Gretchen has been talking about you nonstop all week, Finley," she tells me while she sweeps. She stops to gulp down some of her shake. "She couldn't wait to come back—and for once it had nothing to do with Grandma's cooking."

I wait 'for Grandma to laugh, but she's elbow deep in a

soapy sink, scrubbing hard at a pan that looks perfectly clean to me.

"I'm just so excited you two have hit it off," Stick continues. "It's been a long time since I've seen Gretchen so excited about playing outside. Trees? And mud? Come on. Usually it's nothing but video games and texting her friends. I should never have gotten her a phone so young. But all her friends had them, so if I didn't get her one, she'd be constantly whining about it. Here." Stick holds out her shake. "Wanna try?"

Stick looks so hopeful that I take a sip. It tastes like a combination of gritty cake and liquid metal. I fight not to make a face.

Stick bursts out laughing. "Not for you, huh, babycakes?" She kisses my forehead and ruffles my hair. "Don't worry, I still like you."

I smile up at Stick. Her short hair pokes up behind her headband. "You do?"

"Of course! You're my coolest niece by far."

"Even cooler than Avery?"

Stick winks at me. "Don't tell her I said that."

"You were playing outside?" Grandma has stopped scrubbing to look at me.

It takes me a minute to remember what we were talking about—the Everwood. Playing outside with Gretchen.

I wait for Stick to say something, but suddenly she seems to be very interested in sweeping.

"Um. Yeah?"

"*Yes,*" Grandma says. .

"I mean . . . yes. It's no big deal. We were just messing around."

"Doing what, exactly? And where?"

Stick stops sweeping. "Mom, come on. They're just having fun."

"Amelia, I asked Finley, not you."

"We talked. Hung out in the pit." My mind ping-pongs around, searching for a reason why Grandma would be acting this way. Playing outside seems like a normal thing to do, but I get the sense that isn't true at Hart House.

Then it hits me:

Maybe Grandma knows about what Gretchen and I found: the child's shoe, the twisted bicycle. The knife.

Maybe she knows about something that happened in the Everwood.

"I don't want you girls playing around back there," Grandma says.

"Not even in the pit?"

Her lips purse. "If you must. But not beyond that, Finley. It isn't safe."

My shoulders tense. She dares to forbid me to enter my Everwood? "What do you mean? It's fine out there. It's just woods."

"I know you aren't used to how things work around here, Finley, but in this house, when I give you instructions, I expect them to be obeyed. Is that clear?"

Her words are quiet, clear, polished. They slice right through me. I could cry; I could scream. It isn't fair, being here. It isn't fair, having to pretend to fit in and understand these rules that make no sense.

Avery comes down the back stairs into the kitchen, one earbud in, her arms full of sketch pads. She wears what I have come to know as her painter's uniform—a ratty oversized T-shirt and orange shorts splattered with color.

"Grandpa told me to tell you he's leaving," she says to Grandma.

"Thank you, Avery. Finley, I asked you a question: Is that clear?"

Stick is staring out a window, holding her shake tightly in one hand, her back to us.

Avery watches, paused by the door to the garage.

Grandma's smile is polite, but her eyes are sharp.

*I know you aren't used to how things work around here, Finley.*

Grandma knows the truth: I am not one of them.

"Yes, Grandma," I say quietly. "I understand."

Grandma's face relaxes. "Good. I'm glad we're clear. I'll be back shortly. I need to ask your grandfather something before he leaves." Then she tugs off her soapy gloves, brushes a paper-dry kiss on my cheek, and leaves us. Her earrings glitter in the sunlight.

Without another word Avery slips into the garage.

Stick resumes sweeping. "Your grandfather and his drives,"

she says cheerfully, rolling her eyes. "Ever since he retired and Uncle Reed took over the company, it's become his quiet time. He's always liked long drives. It's his way of meditating, but don't ever tell him I said that. He'd disown me if he knew. He thinks meditation is a bunch of new age hokum."

I stare at the refrigerator, at the pictures of my cousins stuck on with magnets. All my cousins, all the aunts.

Not me. And not Dad.

*He'd disown me if he knew.*

I swallow hard. "You mean like how they disowned my dad?"

The kitchen goes still. Stick crouches in front of me, taking my hands. Her smile is gone; she looks older without it. I can see the tiny lines around her eyes.

"Finley . . . Finley, listen to me, sweetie. I'm sorry I said that. It was thoughtless of me. I never wanted Lewis to stay away. None of us wanted that."

I look Stick in the eye, and I try to imagine myself as beautiful and untouchable as my grandmother.

"Grandma did," I say, and return to my work. Stick doesn't correct me.

I polish the cabinets until every inch of them shines.

# 9

THAT NIGHT, AFTER THE ADULTS have gone to sleep, we all sneak out of the house and down into the pit.

The trees shiver around us, silver with moonlight; the air is soft and warm on my skin. We sit in a circle, and I dig my fingers into the dirt. Four pairs of eyes lock on to me: Kennedy, her hair in a messy bun on top of her head. Dex and Ruth, wide-eyed, sitting on either side of her. Gretchen.

*Hello,* I think to the Everwood. *I am here.*

I think, *Protect us, hide us,* because if Grandma wakes up and finds us, I'm not sure what she will do.

And then I think to the trees, *I hope you will like my cousins*—because I'm not sure if they will. Or if *I* will like having my cousins here, in my trees, by my river.

It's silly to think of this place as mine, after only a week. I haven't had the time to properly explore yet, since that first day with Gretchen. But they say people can fall in love in a day, or even in a moment.

I wonder if Mom and Dad fell in love in a day, or if it took much longer, and if it makes a difference. If the way you fall in love determines how long you will stay in love, or if you will stay in love at all.

I clear my throat. "What we're here to discuss tonight is the Everwood, and the artifacts Gretchen and I found, and the pirates."

"And their secret house," Gretchen adds.

Kennedy looks skeptical. "What pirates?"

"The Bailey boys. It's part of the game."

I bite my tongue at Gretchen's continued use of the word *game*, too nervous to reprimand her. Kennedy is *twelve*. She must be hiding how ridiculous she finds this situation. She can't honestly care.

Gretchen nudges me. "A-*hem*."

"A long time ago," I say, not looking at Kennedy, "I started writing about the Everwood. It's not another world. It's in our world, but you can only find it if it wants you to find it."

With Gretchen's help I tell them about the Bailey boys, and how they chased us away from the old house back in the woods. Then I take out the shoe and knife from my backpack.

Everyone stares at the knife.

Kennedy frowns at me. "You didn't, like, touch the blade or anything, did you? You were careful? If you cut yourself, you'll need a tetanus shot. Grandma told me that once."

"Of course we didn't *touch* it," says Gretchen. "What kind of knight do you think I am?"

"I'm sorry, a what?"

Gretchen throws her arm around me. "I'm a knight, and Finley is the poor orphan child. Everyone needs a part to play."

"But it's not a game," I say, avoiding Kennedy's eyes, "or a play."

I wish we were back inside.

Kennedy is quiet. Then she says, "Okay, cool. What are our choices?"

I look up. *Really?* Kennedy smiles at me. If she thinks this is childish, if she is playing along for the sake of the twins, I can't tell.

I smile back at her.

"I want to be a witch!" Ruth cackles, her fingers curled.

Kennedy covers Ruth's mouth. "You weirdo. Stop screaming. Grandma'll flip if she finds us out here."

"You can't be a witch," I explain, "because witches in the Everwood are villainous. Do you *want* to be a villain?"

Ruth appears to be thinking hard about that.

"Well, you can't be," I say quickly. "We already have the pirates to deal with. Don't you want to be a hero, like Gretchen?"

Gretchen jumps to her feet and flexes her skinny biceps.

Ruth and Dex start laughing—but then the sounds of a slamming door and a crash come from the direction of the Bailey house.

Everyone falls silent.

"We should go inside," Kennedy says, standing up. "We're so not supposed to be out here. I shouldn't have let this happen."

"Oh, don't go all *Grandma* on us," Gretchen hisses. "It's no big deal."

"Come on," I whisper. "We have to see what's going on."

Kennedy frowns but says nothing. We crawl up the far side of the pit and peek out over the top. From here we can see the Bailey house clearly—and the boy sitting on the opposite ledge of the high riverbank.

He is swinging his legs through the air. Picking at the ground. Throwing rocks into the water.

I think it is the medium-sized boy. The one who laughed at me while he chased us. He doesn't look so wild and dangerous now.

"Something's going on over there," Gretchen whispers. "I just know it. What was that crash?"

Kennedy says, "It sounded like glass breaking. Maybe we should wake up Grandma."

"And get grounded until the end of time? No thanks."

"Why is he outside by himself?" Dex asks, squishing lumps of dirt with his thumb.

"I don't know," I say, "but something *is* going on over there. My dad said something happened when he was a kid. Or he kind of hinted at it, anyway. He said the Baileys aren't good people. That their dad did bad things. But we can't talk about it with Grandma and Grandpa. Okay?"

"What kind of bad things?" Kennedy asks.

"I don't know. But I want to find out what."

"Why do you care about whatever the Baileys did?" Kennedy crosses her arms. "You don't even know them. None of us do. I mean, we've seen them at school, but we don't actually *talk* to them. So . . . what is it? What's the big deal?"

I don't know how to explain it to her in a way that would make sense—that there is a story in these woods, waiting for me to write it.

That when I write about the Everwood, I don't have to think about anything else. Not Mom. Not Dad.

Not me, spending the summer away from them.

Gretchen pipes up. "Look, the important thing is that there's this really old, beat-up house back in the woods, and we found all this creepy stuff around it. And you can't find an old, beat-up house in the woods surrounded by creepy stuff and *not* go investigate. I mean, come on, *Kennedy*." Gretchen drops to her knees and tugs on Kennedy's tank top. "You're killin' me, Smalls! You're *killin'* me with your goody-goody ways! I'm *beggin'* ya, don't ruin my fun!"

Kennedy is trying not to smile. "Get off me—you're stretching out my shirt."

I clear my throat. "As a poor orphan child, with nothing to my name, I beseech you to join me and the Lady Gretchen, knight of the Everwood, in our quest: to explore the Everwood and discover its secrets."

"Especially the beat-up old house," Gretchen adds.

"Right. Especially the house."

Kennedy sighs. "Which is probably *condemned*."

"Kennedy," Gretchen whines, "don't be a butt."

"Kennedy's a butt," Ruth sings. "Kennedy's a butt."

"Great," Kennedy mutters.

"We won't do anything too dangerous," I say. "I promise, Kennedy."

Kennedy sighs. "Otherwise everyone'll hate me, I guess?"

"Yep," Gretchen says. "Forever and ever. Amen."

"*Ugh.*" Kennedy crosses her arms over her chest and stares up at the trees.

Gretchen pats her shoulder. "It sucks being the goody-goody, doesn't it?"

"I'm *not* a goody-goody."

"Are too," Gretchen whispers. Dex bursts out laughing.

Kennedy shrugs off Gretchen. Even in the dark I can tell that she's blushing. "Fine. I'll do it. But the second things get dangerous—"

"Sure, sure. Whatever. Let's do this."

Gretchen picks up a long, skinny stick and looks at me, waiting. I hesitate, but there's no going back now.

"Kennedy Howard," I say, "you will be our champion. You will serve as general if we should enter into battle, and act as speaker of the Everwood when we forge alliances with foreign parties. Do you accept this title and the duties and responsibilities it entails?"

For a minute it looks like Kennedy is going to change her mind. My heart freezes in my chest.

Then she takes a deep breath and says, "I do." She kneels, and Gretchen taps her shoulders with the stick. The twins watch, their mouths hanging open.

My opinion of Kennedy skyrockets.

"And you, Dexter and Ruth Prescott," I say, turning to the twins. "You will be squires to the Lady Gretchen until such time as either age or experience proves you worthy of knighthood."

Ruth makes a face. "What's a squire?"

"Basically it means you have to do whatever I tell you to do," Gretchen explains.

"That sounds dumb."

"Not as dumb as not getting to play at all."

"You'll still get swords," I say. "And horses."

Dex's hand shoots up. "Can I have a unicorn instead of a horse?"

"There are no unicorns in the Everwood. But you can have a *white* horse."

Ruth tugs on Kennedy's arm. "Do we really have to do everything Gretchen says?"

"Absolutely," Gretchen says.

Kennedy gives Gretchen a look. "Within reason."

"So," I say, "do you accept?"

Dex and Ruth exchange a glance, then kneel in the dirt to be initiated.

"Now what?" asks Kennedy. "What's next?"

"We must take a solemn oath." I dig in Gretchen's bag for the oversized shoe box she brought from home. "Did you bring your dues?"

Everyone hands me their personal items: a black, ferocious-looking model unicorn from Dex, and from Ruth a collar she is saving for the kitten she wants for her birthday. Gretchen brought a scruffy plush dolphin named Echo. Before handing him over, she kisses him on the nose.

Kennedy holds on to her MVP soccer medal. "We're keeping these somewhere safe, right?"

"Absolutely," says Gretchen. "On my honor as a knight, I won't let anything happen to these, our most powerful treasures."

Ruth giggles. "Why are you talking so funny?"

"Because that's how knights talk, stupid."

Kennedy says, "Gretchen, come on, don't call her stupid."

"Kennedy, you have to," whispers Dex, bouncing on his toes. "Otherwise you can't come to the Everwood!"

Kennedy regally adds her medal to the pile. "Such an important gesture must be given due consideration."

"Duh!" Ruth hisses. Dex sticks his tongue out at her.

As for me, I tear out my Favorite Words list from my notebook and fold it into a tiny square.

"That's it?" says Gretchen. "You're giving up a piece of paper?"

"You don't understand. There are three hundred and forty-six words on this list. If I lose it, I'll lose years of work."

Gretchen doesn't look convinced, but I nevertheless put our items into the shoe box and tape it shut. Everyone places their hands on the lid.

"Repeat after me," I say. "Upon the valuables in this box, I swear to never reveal the secrets of the Everwood quest to anyone not present tonight. And if I break this promise, I give up all rights to my property contained herein."

Everyone repeats the oath and crosses their hearts. Now three more people know about the Everwood. It is no longer only mine.

I am not sure how I feel about that. It seemed like a good idea, and yet now I am not so sure.

I follow my cousins up the stone steps. We are going slowly, because Dex keeps slipping in the dark.

Too slowly.

I would like to get back inside now, please, so I can have some time alone to think.

I need some time.

I need to be alone.

Now.

Before Grandma finds us. Before anyone sees me. Before the others change their minds and start laughing at me for playing my stupid Everwood game.

Now.

Now.

*Now.*

But it is too late; it is already happening.

It slides over me like I have walked through an icy veil:

*Fear.*

# 10

IT STARTS DEEP IN MY STOMACH and crashing out to my fingers and toes. I know this feeling well by now. It means I am close to losing myself.

When my body becomes hot and cold at the same time, and itchy all over.

When my stomach goes queasy, and I find it hard to breathe, and all I know is that I am afraid for no particular reason.

When I wake up wanting to call out for Mom and Dad, but I don't.

My breath starts to come faster, thinner.

I do not understand. I should be happy right now, shouldn't I? With a champion, a knight, and two squires at my side?

A normal person would be happy right now, I think. Why is this happening to me?

(I never know the answer to that question.)

Is it because my Favorite Words list is all taped up in a box?

That flash of white at one of Hart House's upstairs windows—is it Grandma, spying on us? What will she do to us? What will she do to *me*?

I cross my arms over my chest and stare at the ground.

Maybe if I think hard enough, this feeling will go away. I cannot lose myself, not right now, not in front of everyone.

From what I can tell, no one else I have encountered has ever lost himself or herself. If they have, they certainly have not talked about it.

My cousins do not seem like the kind of people who lose themselves.

Go away.

*Go away.*

*GO AWAY.*

As we climb up the pit, all I can concentrate on is my sweaty hands, my prickly skin, the rhythm of my breathing. Kennedy might be watching. If she thinks something is wrong with me, she'll wake up Grandma, and everything will be ruined.

So I will walk, and keep my fear locked up inside me.

(Breathe in and out, Finley. In and out.)

(Just hold on.)

(Don't let them see.)


By the time we get back inside and upstairs, I am feeling a little better—but only a little.

I sit against the wall, Dex and Ruth on either side of me. It is my responsibility to make sure they stay quiet while Gretchen hides our stash in Avery's room, underneath her bed.

It seems like the safest place. Who would want to sneak into Avery's room to steal back their dues, and risk awakening what is sure to be a mighty teenage wrath?

Kennedy, standing watch at the end of the hallway, whispers, "Hurry up, you guys!" She bounces on her toes.

Gretchen crouches at Avery's bedroom door, our stash under one arm. "Shut up, Kennedy! Do you want me to do this or not?"

As soon as Gretchen slips inside Avery's bedroom, Dex and Ruth start giggling.

The edges of my body still feel sharp, unsteady. The fear is not far from me; even breathing the wrong way could send it flying back.

Then I have an idea.

"Do you hear that?" I whisper. It is difficult to speak.

"Hear what?" asks Ruth. "I don't hear anything."

"The Everwood. It's speaking to us."

Ruth frowns. "Really?"

Dex scoots closer to me. "What's it saying?"

"It's saying . . ." I close my eyes.

(In and out. Just breathe.)

(Think of the Everwood. Think of the oak trees, the ash trees, the gold-and-green light.)

"It's saying it was impressed by the bravery of the two young squires who dared enter the forest so late at night. It senses you have courageous hearts, that you will one day be glorious knights." I open my eyes and look at each of them. "But if this quest fails tonight, you can never be knighted. The Everwood has strict rules, you see."

Ruth immediately clamps her hand over Dex's mouth. I

pry it loose and pull them close. "Hush, squires. The Everwood is listening."

They sit as still as statues beside me. From down the hallway Kennedy gives me a thumbs-up.

Then a light switches on in Avery's bedroom. "Gretchen? What are you *doing*?"

Gretchen bolts out of Avery's room, and we tear down the hallway, sliding across the hardwood floor in our socks, trying not to laugh. Kennedy grabs the twins and pulls them inside their room.

From behind us I hear movement. Avery stands at her door. Her hair is a mess, like mine in the mornings. It makes her less scary somehow.

*"Freaks,"* she whispers, and shuts the door behind her.

The next morning at breakfast, Avery ignores us all, like usual. If she knows Gretchen put the stash under her bed, she doesn't say anything.

We pass giggles around the table like a secret code.

Aunt Dee puts down her toast, smiling at us. "Okay, what's the story? What happened? What did we miss?"

But no one says anything. We are bound to secrecy now, the five of us.

Gretchen starts laughing through a mouthful of scrambled eggs. Aunt Bridget has to clap her on the back. A chunk of yellow goes flying and hits Uncle Nelson's forehead, and the twins start shrieking.

Grandpa glances up from his newspaper, his mouth

twitching. "If you let me in on the secret, I'll take you to the swimming pool this afternoon."

Dex's eyes light up. "Really?"

Ruth grabs his arm. "We'll think about it," she says primly, then glances at me and winks.

She is better at it than Grandpa.

Grandpa returns to his reading, but his eyes twinkle at me over the top of the newspaper.

The kitchen is bright and smells like coffee, and at this moment I cannot remember what it is to feel afraid.

T HE ORPHAN GIRL AWOKE IN *the middle of the night to the feeling that she was being watched.*

*She looked about the camp she shared with her sleeping companions.*

*A circle of trees surrounded them, their trunks twisted together in mighty knots. Ash fell from their withered leaves like snow.*

*"Hello?" the orphan girl whispered into the darkness.*

*"Hello," said a small, clear voice.*

*The orphan girl reached for her pack and saw that it had been opened. Nothing was missing—except for the soft leather boot.*

*The orphan girl followed the voice. "Who are you? Show yourself."*

*Two amber eyes appeared in the gloom. "You know who I am."*

*As the voice spoke, cold waves of power glided across the orphan girl's skin.*

*"The boot," she whispered.*

*The voice laughed, and a red fox padded into the moonlight.*

*"I didn't think you'd recognize me," said the fox.*

*"I met your friend," said the orphan girl, "the snake."*

*The fox's yellow eyes narrowed. "The snake and I are not friends. Not everyone in these woods is friendly, child. Do not make the mistake of assuming so."*

"I thought—"

"Yes, you thought and you thought. What good did thinking ever do anyone?"

The orphan girl considered this a silly question. "Well, a whole lot of good to a great many people, in fact."

The fox grinned. "You speak your mind. I like that."

"My friends and I are looking for the secret of the Everwood," the orphan girl explained. The fox's grin unnerved her. "Why the trees are dying, what those howls are at night."

"You know the answers to these questions," the fox said, curling its tail about its paws.

"I don't."

"You do, and don't lie to me. The snake told you, I know. Snakes talk too much."

"The Everwood makes whatever is inside us come to life," admitted the orphan girl. "That's what the snake said."

"And?" prompted the fox.

"And my darkness will bring out the Everwood's darkness."

"The forest is not as strong as it once was," said the fox.

The orphan girl wanted to look away, but did not. "Yes."

"And what is inside you, child?" The fox's expression turned serious. "What have you brought into these woods? Fear, perhaps?"

The orphan girl stiffened. "I am not afraid of forests."

"No. You are afraid of yourself."

A chorus of howls cut through the night, closer than they had ever been.

"Like is drawn to like," the fox murmured. "Darkness finds darkness."

"You speak in riddles," accused the orphan girl.

"I speak in truths." The fox slunk about the orphan girl's ankles. "Have you heard of the Dark Ones?"

The orphan girl shivered. "They only come out at night."

"But they don't truly love the night. What feeds them is a different kind of darkness."

The orphan girl did not want to say it, but the black woods trembled around her, and she ached for them. Were the trees in pain? Was it because of her?

"The darkness I carry inside me," whispered the orphan girl.

"We all carry secrets," said the fox. "The more we ignore them, the heavier they become." The fox fixed his hard, golden gaze upon the orphan girl. "Are you ready to name it yet, this thing you carry?"

The orphan girl squeezed her eyes shut. "No. I am not."

"Then they will keep coming for you," said the fox, "and for all of us."

When the orphan girl looked up, the fox had gone, and the trees moaned in the wind, as if they knew she had failed them.

# 11

ON SUNDAY MORNING I GO with Grandma and Aunt Bridget to Barclay Park. There is a 10K race there today.

The group Grandma organizes—A Pack for Every Back—will set up a table in the parking lot so people can learn about the program and give donations.

In the car, on the way to the park, Aunt Bridget is on the phone with Uncle Reed. He is in London on a business trip. I watch Aunt Bridget's face while she talks to him about Dex and Ruth, and how they are having such fun playing with me.

"Ruth said something about being a squire, whatever that means," Aunt Bridget says. She sighs and rolls her eyes. "Come on, Reed. You know, like a junior knight? I don't know if they fight dragons. Probably. Wouldn't you?" She catches my eye and smiles, like we are sharing a joke.

Music plays softly on the car stereo. It sounds kind of like the Ray Charles music playing downstairs at Hart House the other night, except it's faster and makes me want to dance.

Grandma's fingers tap on the steering wheel in time with the music. I can only see her eyes in the rearview mirror. Even though they are a different color, something about them reminds me of Dad.

At the park Grandma and I set out bright green information flyers and a basket of flat, round pins and green pencils
with the Pack for Every Back logo on them. Aunt Bridget
takes a clipboard and launches into the crowd.

"Good morning," Aunt Bridget says to a group of three
runners stretching under a tree. "My name's Bridget Hart.
Hi, how are you?" She shakes their hands; her eye contact is
spectacular. Her hair shines in a tight ponytail. "I'm with A
Pack for Every Back. We're an organization that helps families in need get school supplies for their children . . ."

Grandma and I sit alone at the table. An oak tree sways
overhead. It reminds me of the Everwood trees, only this one
is out here all by itself. A scout.

"Hello, Candace!" A man in running shorts waves as he
passes us. Grandma waves back, straightens the pile of flyers
on the table.

It is always strange to me to realize that parents and grandparents have actual names. I find myself wanting to correct
the man: Her name is *Grandma*, sir.

A woman with a T-shirt that says RUN JANE RUN comes up
and grabs a flyer. "Candace, you look wonderful!" she gushes.
"And is this Lewis's daughter?"

Grandma places a soft hand on my arm. Her wedding
ring is warm with sunlight. "Yes, this is Finley. Finley, this is
Roxann Bates. We help at the library together."

"Your grandma's the *best*," says Roxann Bates, beaming.
"You look like her, you know. Oh! Here. It's not much, but I

hope it helps!" She drops a ten-dollar bill into our donation bucket.

Grandma smiles. "Thank you, Roxann, that's very generous."

"Anything for you, Candace!" She kisses Grandma's cheek. "See you on Thursday?"

"Of course."

Roxann Bates hurries away, calling out someone else's name and waving frantically. When the sun hits her, the glitter on her T-shirt shines a silvery pink.

Every now and then someone passing by the table takes a flyer, donates money, or says hello to Grandma, but mostly it is just me and her. I keep checking to make sure I am sitting as straight as she is.

*You look like her, you know.*

What an odd thing to say. Grandma is old and has white hair. I am young and have blond hair. Grandma wears just the right shade of lipstick. I do not know what forks to use. How could I possibly look like her?

She starts humming the song we were listening to in the car. I want to say something, but I don't know what. Then I blurt, "Ray Charles?"

Grandma stops humming to look at me. "Pardon me?"

"Um. Ray Charles." My cheeks feel sunburned even though we are safely in the shade. "Isn't that what you were singing?"

"No, actually, that was Jimmy Reed. Are you a fan of the blues?"

"I don't think so. I'm not sure. I mean, I don't know a lot of the songs."

"Ah."

We sit there, staring at each other. I know I should say something, but I don't know what. I am distracted by Grandma's sharp blue eyes.

What does she see when she looks at me?

I tuck some hair behind my ear. I should have combed it better this morning. Grandma's is in a soft, neat bun.

"Dad says all of you listened to Ray Charles. When he was growing up."

Out of everything to say, I have to bring up Dad.

Grandma's mouth twists into a funny shape, like she has heard something strange and does not know what to make of it.

"He said that, did he?" Grandma straightens the stack of flyers for the seventh time today. "Well, yes, we did do that."

I wipe my palms on my pants. It occurs to me that most people are probably not this terrified of their grandmothers.

But do most grandmothers avoid talking about their sons at dinner?

Do most grandmothers keep secrets, like why their grand-daughter has never visited?

Then Grandma says, "We had so many parties, in the summer especially." She pauses; a group of children laugh, chasing one another through the parking lot. She folds her hands on the table, puts them in her lap, returns them to the table.

"Not big parties," she says, "not with anyone else. Just family. We would open the windows and string up lights on the patio. Your grandfather grilled burgers, and we'd turn up Ray Charles and Jimmy Reed and Bessie Smith and B. B. King. The girls would put their hair in rollers, wear face masks and old dresses from the attic. They'd do it to feel fancy. Old-fashioned Hollywood glamour."

Grandma smiles, her voice quiet. "There'd be fireflies in the azaleas, and we would dance and eat for hours, and the music would fill up the woods. We only went inside late, when the mosquitoes got bad. Sometimes not even then."

My heart is in a race with itself. I can see it so clearly that it is like I was there, years ago: Aunt Bridget, Aunt Dee, Stick. Kids like me, all of them short and small. Dad, with his floppy hair. Our photo albums at home have some pictures of him looking like that—but they are always pictures of him alone. No sisters. No parents.

Grandma stares at her hands. "I miss him, Finley."

I feel like I am standing on the edge of a cliff. "You mean . . . Dad?"

"We did what we had to do. I thought your father could understand, but . . . I never wanted him to stay away. *He* chose that. Not me. *He* decided we weren't good enough for him. Do you understand?"

Have her hands been shaking this whole time? Or have they just started?

"Yes," I whisper, although I understand nothing. What did

she *have* to do? Why did Dad stay away? Why did he keep *me* away?

Grandma turns to look at me, and I feel like I am actually seeing her now. Like what she has shown me before is a Grandma mask, and this is what lies beneath.

I open my mouth to say one of several possible things:

*Grandma, what has happened to your face? Your makeup suddenly looks all wrong on it.*

*Grandma, what did Dad do? Was it something he did?*

*Grandma, tell me more about your blues parties. Tell me more about my dad when he was little.*

*Tell me why we never visited. If you miss him, why don't you ever talk to him?*

My hair falls into my eyes again, and Grandma brushes it away. What does she see when she looks at me?

"Sorry," I mumble. "My hair's kind of messy."

"Lewis's always was too."

"Excuse me." A tired-looking man comes up to the table. Two small boys hang off his leg, and he's giving another one a piggyback ride. "Are you Candace Hart? The backpack lady?"

Grandma's face fills with a silver-bright smile. "That's me."

"My kids' teacher told me about your program. Where do I sign up?"

I watch Grandma talk to this man. She holds one of the kids on her lap while the man fills out three forms. She lets them pick out pencils and helps put the pins on their T-shirts. She shakes the man's hand and straightens the kids' collars.

When one of them hugs her legs, she bends over and hugs him right back. While they walk away, she watches them go, and she waves when they get to the swing set.

"Candace Hart!" A woman waves from the snack table. "I knew you'd be here! Come here, tell me what's new!"

"Watch the table, Finley," Grandma instructs without looking at me. "And tie your shoe, won't you, please?"

As I watch Grandma head for the snack table, I wonder which is more true:

The Grandma who knows everyone, who scrubs pans that are already clean, who runs organizations and holds messy kids with crooked collars in her lap.

Or the Grandma with shaking hands and a tired face. The Grandma who hates the Baileys because their house is an embarrassment.

The Grandma who misses her son.

That night I dream of fireflies, and of Dad dancing with Grandma in the Everwood beside the old castle in the gray field. When I wake up the next morning, the dream feels thick around me, like a scratchy blanket too heavy for the summer.

I find my notebook and start to write a new list.


WHY MY DAD LEFT THE FAMILY

- Because he was called away on an adventure that required him to sacrifice all personal ties.
  - But then he got married, so that can't be it.

- ◆ Unless . . . am I part of some secret international plot? (Unlikely.)
- Because they wanted him to take over Grandpa's business with Uncle Reed, but he didn't want to. (But why would that be a secret?)
- Because he was different. (Like me.)

# 12

BUILDING A TREE HOUSE IS more difficult than I had anticipated, but it had to be done. No quest is complete without a base of operations.

However, even with Grandpa's supervision, what we end up with on Tuesday is something more like a tree . . . patio.

Once we nail the final board into place, we all step back for inspection.

Grandpa is the first to speak.

"Well," he says, scratching his chin, "now that is something."

Specifically, it is a platform three feet off the ground, built around a cluster of three thick trees. There is a slanted roof, and it has walls on two sides. Steps lead up to the front, with a rope ladder hanging off the back.

It is one of the most beautiful things I have ever seen.

"It's ugly," Ruth announces. "I thought it would be, you know, up *high*. In the *trees*. It's supposed to be a *watchtower*."

"Oh, come on, Ruthie." Kennedy adjusts the bandana tied around Ruth's head. "This way you can go inside without asking someone for permission."

"You can also fall off it without breaking your neck," Gretchen points out.

Ruth frowns. "But it's not high enough to *see* anything!"

"I'll tear it down, then." Grandpa approaches the steps with his crowbar. "If you're not going to appreciate it, that is."

I am happy to hear a collective gasp of horror.

"That's what I thought." Grandpa turns to me. "Now, remember the ground rules: Not one inch outside the pit, like Grandma said."

"Yes, sir," we all say.

"And you won't let the twins climb around here by themselves?"

"No, sir."

Grandpa looks at each of us like he is searching for evidence of a lie. Gretchen stares back so intensely that I almost crack up. Dex picks his nose and inspects the findings.

Satisfied, Grandpa nods. "Well, then. Go nuts. But not *too* nuts. And take your shoes off before you come in for dinner."

Gretchen asks, "What if we *didn't*? What then?"

"Apocalypse, probably."

Once Grandpa has packed up his tools and gone back into the house, I climb inside what we have named the Tower and hang the shoe Gretchen and I found from the ceiling by its laces. It dangles over the center of the floor like a bizarre chandelier.

Doing this gives me a moment to think.

Everyone else is going home after dinner, but Gretchen has talked Stick into letting her stay at Hart House for the rest of the week.

On the one hand, out of everyone, Gretchen is the person I know best.

On the other hand, I have spent the past two days building a tree patio with five other people, one of whom is Grandpa, who wears button-down shirts even while building tree patios in the dirt—and I feel a bit like I am crawling inside my own skin.

I keep thinking about what Grandma said at the park: about missing Dad, that *he* was the one who chose to stay away.

What does Grandpa think about Dad? Does he miss Dad too? Dad said they talk on the phone—but about what? And how often? And what do they say when they hang up? Do they say *I love you*? What would those words sound like, coming out of Grandpa's mouth?

I want to ask him about these things, but whenever I imagine doing so, I freeze up.

I have always been better at writing things than saying them.

"I'm going for a walk," I say, casually, hoping no one will follow. Just a walk, to clear my head. That is all I need.

"Oh, me too!" Gretchen loops her arm through mine.

I try to pull away. "Gretchen, really, it's no big deal—"

Then Gretchen tenses up beside me. I see him too.

It's that Bailey boy, the medium-sized one. He is crouched behind a stump a few yards away.

And he is holding our stash of valuables. Gretchen's dolphin. Kennedy's medal.

My list of words.

I am seized by righteous anger.

It was Gretchen's idea to bring the stash out here, to christen our headquarters, even though I protested.

How did the Bailey boy slip past all of us without anyone seeing him?

Gretchen's hands are in fists. "Give that back. *Now.*"

The boy grins, winks, and takes off in the other direction. Into the Everwood. With *our stuff*.

Gretchen growls an extremely forbidden word under her breath.

I have to agree. "We can't let him get away with this."

Gretchen snorts. "Oh, don't worry. He won't." She yells, "Back in a sec!" over her shoulder.

Kennedy whirls. "Wait, *what*—?"

But we ignore her. We don't stop to think about Grandma or Grandpa seeing us. We run.

We scoot across the First Bridge, jump over ridges and weave through trees, skid down slopes of mud and leaves like surfers.

The Bailey boy's laughter floats back to us. Trying to catch him is like trying to catch a shadow.

"We're losing him!" Gretchen shouts. "Come on, Fin!"

I have never run like this in my life. We're practically flying, dodging tree roots and fallen logs like they're nothing. My breathing starts to burn, and my side aches.

Then Gretchen skids to a halt. "Oh *man*."

I catch my breath and blink hard against the sun. We have reached the Wasteland—the field with the old gray house.

The Bailey boy jumps onto its porch and yells back at us, "Come inside . . . *if you dare!*"

He laughs, slams the door, and disappears.

"What'll we do?" Gretchen whispers. "We can't go in there, not with the Baileys inside!"

A dry summer wind sweeps across the field toward the house. I have to follow it. When the Everwood speaks, only fools choose not to listen.

"Yes, we can," I say. "And we will. Right now."

# 13

I START WALKING TOWARD THE house before I can change my mind.

The Everwood may be calling me, but I am not an idiot. Going after an enemy on his home turf is a huge risk.

"Are you crazy?" Gretchen runs after me.

"No."

"Well, I'm not going in there. You'll have to go by yourself!"

"Fine."

Up close, the house looks even worse. A huge hole where the roof is missing opens up one half of the building to the sky. Dark stains cover the house like bruises. Black wooden beams stick out of collapsed walls, and the windows are either smashed or missing.

There must have been a fire here.

The summer wind blows past me again, and I imagine it is the heat of flames. It shouldn't make sense to shiver when you're hot.

"This place gives me the creeps." Gretchen pokes through the grass with her foot. "Look at all this trash. God, it's like the house threw up or something. Empty bottles, clothes, toys . . . *ugh!*" Gretchen kicks away a one-eyed doll wearing a faded red dress. "Get away, you freaky little monster."

"Oh, *wow*, would you look at this awesome medal?" a voice calls out from inside the house.

Gretchen and I both stare up at the second floor, where a tanned hand dangles Kennedy's MVP medal out a window.

"It sure is *shiny*," the voice continues. A boy's head pops out, grinning down at us. It's the boy who brought us here, his bangs dark and wild. He slips the medal around his neck. "I think I'll keep it! What do you think, Cole?"

Another, older boy looks out the window. "I think you should keep that, and I'll . . . keep *this*." Cole waves around Gretchen's stuffed dolphin, Echo, and kisses its nose. "Oh, what a cutie-wutie wittle dolphin!"

"Stop touching him, you gross . . . *toe fungus!*" Gretchen shrieks.

"Come and stop me," Cole suggests, which makes the other boy crack up. They disappear back inside.

"I am literally going to knock their heads off," Gretchen growls. She finds a stick and whacks the house with it. Faded green paint flakes off and blows away. "Either that or call the cops. They are so getting arrested. Do you have your phone? Hey! Where are you going?"

I follow the trail of garbage behind the house. The backyard is a mess: overgrown trees, grass that comes up to my waist, piles of broken bricks and rotting wood. An old, rusty pickup truck sits off to the side, weeds grown up around its tires.

In the corner, back where the woods start up again, is a giant oak tree with curved branches that hang so low you could walk right up and sit on them.

I crawl inside the tree's canopy. Above me the world is green and cool. The grass here is thin; it must not get enough sunlight. I place my hand on a nearby branch. The rough bark feels familiar, like this tree and I are old friends.

"Fin?" Gretchen barrels into the tree after me. "Do we have a plan here or what? Kennedy will flip if we don't get back soon."

"Hold on a second," I say.

"Why? What's going on?"

I do not know how to tell her about the hot wind whispering to me, or the fact that I think I have fallen in love with a tree.

"Nothing's going on—" My foot catches on a dip in the ground, and I fall.

"Fin? You okay?"

I do not answer her. I am staring at the small, gray shape sticking up out of the dirt in front of me. It is so covered with moss and leaves and mud that I can't see much of it.

Even so, I know it is a gravestone.

There are three of them.

"Holy . . . Are you kidding me?" Gretchen squats beside me. "Are those what I think they are?"

She reaches out to touch the nearest one. I slap her hand away.

"Hey! What was that for?"

"Don't touch them."

"Why not?"

The truth is, I want very much to touch them. I want to scrub off that moss and mud and find out who they belong to. But the quiet of this place beneath the tree suddenly seems like it might be a sign. "Maybe they don't want to be touched."

Gretchen inches away from the gravestones. "You mean, like . . . ghosts?"

"Maybe." I get up and march toward the house. "I'd like to know a little bit about them before I stick my nose into their business, is all I'm saying."

I creep up the back steps, making sure the wood is steady before I put my weight on it, and knock on the door. The wall beside it gapes open, but it feels wrong to step inside without asking.

A piece of paper slides out from beneath the door. It says, *If you want your stuff, you'll have to steal it back.*

I shove the paper back into the house. "We're not stealing anything. We want to talk to you. It's important."

After a minute the door swings open. Three boys stand there. The medium-sized one passes a Slinky back and forth between his hands, his eyes narrowed.

"State your business," he says.

"My name is Finley Hart, and this is my cousin Gretchen—"

Gretchen nudges me. "What are you doing?"

"I'm Jack," says the medium-sized boy. Then he points to the oldest boy. "That's Cole. And the little one's Bennett."

Bennett waves cheerfully at us. Cole grabs his hand and stops him.

"You're trespassing," Jack says.

"You stole our stuff," I reply.

He shrugs. "Doesn't give you the right to trespass."

"We want it back."

"What if we don't give it back?"

"Then we'll call the cops," Gretchen snaps.

Bennett's eyes go wide. "Cole!"

"No one's calling the cops," Cole says. "And even if you did, they don't care about stuff like that."

Jack is watching me. I stare right back at him. I am not afraid of pirates.

"You'll give us our stuff back," I say. "You don't look dishonorable."

In fact they do, but flattery might be our best bet in this situation.

"Ha!" Cole grins. "Sure we do. We're *Baileys*. Didn't your grandparents warn you about us?"

"Actually, they did," says Gretchen.

"Yeah? And what did they say?"

I don't want Gretchen to make things worse, so I interrupt. "Did you know there are gravestones under that tree in the back?"

"Yeah," says Jack. "Why do you care?"

"Whose are they?"

He shrugs. "Don't know."

"Well, didn't you ever try to look?"

"Nah. Don't care."

"Can I clean them off?"

Gretchen tugs on my sleeve. "Fin, let's just go."

"Why do you care about them?" Jack asks me.

"Because it's disrespectful to leave them dirty," I say. "People are supposed to take care of the dead."

No one says anything. Jack pulls a piece of paper out of his pocket—my list of favorite words—and carefully smooths out the wrinkles.

"Is this yours?" he asks me.

I could snatch it away from him and run, but I stay put. "Yes."

He reads over the list. "*Sinister. Footfall.* There are a lot of words here."

"I've worked hard on them. I love words."

Jack scratches the back of his head, messing up his hair. He disappears and comes back with our box.

"Jack!" hisses Cole. "What are you doing, man? Come on."

"You can have this back," says Jack, "but only if you clean up the gravestones."

I think about that. "We can't do it today. We have to get home."

"Then when you come back to clean, you can have your stuff."

Gretchen looks ready to bite him. "Why can't *you* clean them off?"

Jack grins. "Because Cole's scared of ghosts and doesn't want to 'curse our family.'"

"Shut up, Jack!" Cole pushes him, his face turning red. "I just hate cleaning. It's pointless."

I hold out my hand. "It's a deal."

Gretchen protests, *"Finley . . ."*

"Deal." Jack shakes my hand. His fingers are gritty with dirt.

Gretchen grumbles at me as we start across the field toward home. The Everwood wind blows against my sweaty skin, cooling me off. I have an idea and turn around. The part of the house with the roof missing looks like a jagged rib cage.

"Jack?" I call out.

Jack comes out onto the front porch. "Yeah?"

"Does the house have a name?"

"Not really. Why?"

"We should call it the Bone House." I pause. "You know, because of the graves."

He nods. "Yeah. I like that."

"We'll come back as soon as we can."

"Okay. Sorry about all this. I was bored. I wasn't trying to be mean. It's usually the same old stuff around here, you know?"

"I guess."

"And hey, Finley?"

"Yeah?"

He shoves his hands in his pockets. "Don't worry about your words. I'll keep them safe."

I don't say thank you. It seems strange to say thank you to someone who has stolen from you. But I think about Jack's voice all the way home, and how he held my list in his hands like he knew it was a piece of my own heart.

T HE ORPHAN GIRL'S SLEEP TURNED *restless and fitful.*
*Dreams plagued her night hours and fol-*
*lowed her into waking—dreams about the Bone*
*House, the Wasteland, the three small graves.*

*To clear her head, she took long walks through the for-*
*est, without her friends, and on these walks she saw strange*
*shapes on the edge of her vision: Birds and bats. Long, snake-*
*like vines. Tall, thin, faceless figures. Whenever the orphan*
*girl turned to face these shapes, they disappeared, and all*
*she could see were the Everwood trees, green and gray and*
*fading.*

*One day, however, the figure she saw did not fade.*

*She turned, and there it was: a shadow in the shape of a*
*man in flowing robes. The shape shimmered as if the orphan*
*girl were viewing it through water.*

*"Who are you?" the orphan girl demanded.*

*"I am the wizard," said the shadow.*

*"What wizard?"*

*"The only one."*

*The orphan girl took a careful step away. "Why do you*
*look so strange?"*

*"Because," answered the wizard, "I am no longer here."*

*A tendril of fear rolled down the orphan girl's spine.*
*"You're a ghost."*

*The wizard inclined his head.*

"Are you here to haunt me?" the orphan girl asked.

"I don't think so."

"Then why are you here?"

The wizard shrugged, his shoulders rippling. "You woke me up."

"The graves," the orphan girl whispered. "Are you in one of the graves?"

"I was. Now there is only dust and bits of bone."

"Was the Bone House yours?"

The wizard was quiet for a long time. Then he said quietly, "Once. Long ago."

"And the others? The other two graves?"

"Wizards," said the wizard mournfully, "always live in threes, for they are burdened with terrible secrets."

"What secrets?" The orphan girl tried to touch his arm, but it was like drawing her hand through icy water. "Do you know what's happening to the Everwood? Why are the trees dying? What are those howls at night?"

The wizard's shadowy eyes, darker than the rest of him, were large and soft. "Only you can stop them. That is what the trees tell me. Did you know trees are very fond of ghosts? I never would have guessed that, but it appears to be so." The wizard smiled faintly and touched the boughs of a tree. "Hello, my friend. Thank you. You look nice today too."

"Only I can stop who?" asked the orphan girl.

"Beware the ancient guardians," whispered the wizard. The clouds shifted, and in the sunlight the wizard began to fade. "They shine as white as snow, but they can be as cruel as winter."

Then the wizard was gone.

The orphan girl felt a rustling in her pocket, where she kept the wrapped dagger. When she placed her hand on it, she felt a warmth. A softness.

But when she withdrew the dagger and held it in the sunlight, it was only that—a blade, a hilt. Cold and unmoving.

A creeping sensation crawled up her back, nestling in her hair. Someone was watching her.

"Find me," whispered the wizard, from nowhere and everywhere. "Find us."

And the orphan girl promised, "I will."

# 14

IT IS FRIDAY, AND I am feeling calm. My cousins are staying over for the weekend, and we are making paper-bag monster masks in the dining room.

When I lose myself, my insides become a storming sea in which it is very easy to get lost. Even something as simple as breathing feels difficult.

But on days like today, the sea is tame, and I hardly feel heavy at all.

(Why can't every day be like this?)

Grandma brings us a plate of sugar cookies. She has been baking cookies all morning for the clinic volunteers, and we get the last batch. "I'm going to take a nap. The Friends of the Library meeting last night, baking all day today. I'm completely worn out." She touches Kennedy's golden hair. "Kennedy, are you all right with the twins?"

"Yes, ma'am," Kennedy chirps. When Grandma kisses her cheek, Kennedy beams.

I concentrate hard on cutting my construction paper into a spiky lion's mane for Dex. I want to ask Grandma to kiss my cheek too, but I haven't seen my cousins ask for kisses; perhaps they must be earned.

A few minutes later Grandpa comes in. He stands behind Ruth and examines her mask.

"What is that?" he asks. "A bear?"

Ruth puts her mask over her head and growls at Grandpa, "No, it's a . . . *monster*!"

"Needs more fangs," Grandpa suggests.

Ruth takes off the mask and examines it. "Good idea."

"I'm off for my drive," Grandpa tells Kennedy. "I'll be back in a little while."

I nearly jump out of my chair. This could be my chance to ask him about Dad. "Can I come?"

Grandpa raises an eyebrow. "With me? Your boring old grandpa?"

"I'm done with my mask."

"Monster? Bear?"

I pick it up to show him. "Fox."

Grandpa nods. "Good choice. Come on, then."

Grandpa's car smells like leather and air freshener. It's so clean you could eat off the floor mats. I feel fancy sitting beside him in the passenger's seat, the polished dashboard in front of me. When he turns on the car stereo, it plays a familiar song.

"Jimmy Reed!" I cry, pointing at the speakers.

"You like him?"

I look out the window. I need to calm down and act my age. "Yeah, I like him okay."

"He's one of your grandma's favorites. Your dad's, too.

That was a long time ago, though. I don't know what he listens to now."

Grandpa starts down the long driveway, lined with giant trees. The music plays into silence. I swallow hard.

"He likes classical music," I say quietly. "He listens to it while he writes. He says it helps him think."

"Oh? What kind of classical music?"

"Beethoven. Mozart. Schubert."

Grandpa smiles. "Do you know Beethoven's Sixth Symphony?"

"The *Pastoral* Symphony," I answer in a rush. "Eight-letter-word for 'about the country.'"

I bite my lip. Why did I say that out loud?

"I like crossword puzzles too," says Grandpa. "Your dad and I used to work on them together when he was little."

I can no longer stay calm. "We do that!"

"It's a good thing to do, especially when you get older. Keeps the brain sharp."

I feel small and huge at the same time, like I could either shrink into a tiny, happy ball or balloon up until I burst into pieces. I sit straight and still in my seat, but my insides are a wild party.

At the end of the driveway Grandpa changes the music to the *Pastoral* Symphony, and my heart jumps.

"Where do you think your dad first realized he liked Beethoven?" Grandpa pats my hand. "I'm glad you're here with me today, Finley."

I am in the car with Grandpa. We are talking about Beethoven and crossword puzzles. He is smiling at me, he is smiling at me, he is smiling at *me*.

"Why do you go on drives every day?" I ask.

Grandpa pulls onto the road. "It relaxes me. It's nice to get out of the house every now and then, don't you think?"

"Yeah. Where do you go?"

"Anywhere with trees."

I grip my seat to keep from flying away. "You like trees?"

"I love them. Why do you think I bought Hart House?"

"Because of the Everwood."

Grandpa laughs. "I forgot you kids call it that. How'd you decide on the name? It's really quite nice."

"I'm good at naming things," I say, and soon I am telling him all about my notebook—my lists, my stories, the different Everwood creatures.

(I do not tell him about the stories I have written since arriving here.)

(Those are still in progress, and I get the feeling he would not be happy if he knew I'd been out to the Bone House.)

Grandpa listens to every word. Then he says, "Oh, Finley. You're so like your dad."

My heart is a pounding drum. "I am?"

"Absolutely. He was always writing stories too, when he was little. Sometimes he'd write plays, and he and the girls would get all dressed up in the most ridiculous clothes: skirts and scarves and raincoats, whatever they could find. They'd put on these plays in the foyer—you know, where those doors open into the living room?"

I nod, imagining it. Beethoven's violins soar. "Did you and Grandma watch?"

"Every single one. Your grandma made me, even the ones we'd already watched a thousand times. Your aunt Bridget always liked to do things over and over, until they got it just right. And your grandma would sit and watch each performance like it was the first one, every time. She'd clap in all the right places. She was so good about that, Finley. She always has been."

"Good about what?"

"The family thing. Everyone eats dinner together. Everyone cleans house together. Everyone takes turns telling about their day, and everyone else has to listen. You know? Things like that. Not every family does that, but ours always did. And it was because of her." Grandpa's face is so soft that looking at it is kind of embarrassing, like I am spying on a secret. When I try to imagine Dad talking about Mom like this, I . . . can't.

I scratch the dry spot on my knee, over and over.

"I wasn't always good at being a dad," Grandpa says, "but your grandma was always good at being a mom."

I think about Grandma at the park, the little boy with the crooked collar in her lap. "Was Dad messy when he was little?"

Grandpa bursts out laughing. "Oh, goodness, yes. They all were, except for Bridget, of course. Your dad and Stick would always come in from outside with muddy shoes and scraped knees. Everything was an adventure."

We are quiet for a while. Grandpa turns onto a road with woods on one side and fields of crops on the other. I watch the rows of corn flash by. The stalks are still small, but by the end of summer they'll be taller than Dad.

"Grandpa?"

"Hmm?"

"When you and Dad talk on the phone, what do you say?"

Grandpa gently taps his thumbs against the steering wheel. "Well, we talk about you a lot. Your mom. Your grandma. He tells me about his classes, and about his writing. I tell him about my golf scores and about his sisters, your cousins."

I flex and point my bare feet. Kennedy painted my toenails pink. "Grandpa?"

"Yes?"

"Do you love him?"

"Your dad?"

"Yeah."

Grandpa sighs. It is a tired, heavy sound. "I do, very much."

"Then why . . . ?"

"Why are you just now meeting us? Why does your dad stay away?"

I nod. My voice catches in my throat.

"I'm going to tell you something, Finley," Grandpa says, "and I want you to listen carefully, because it's important."

"Okay."

"Your grandma had it hard, growing up. Nothing end-of-the-world terrible, but not much love, and not much money. Her parents were always fighting, always spending money on things they shouldn't. Once your grandma had her own family, she decided that this time things would be different. She was going to do whatever she could to make things good for her kids, make the kind of family she always wished she'd had, and she wasn't going to let anything get in her way."

I think about that while the symphony's third movement begins. "Did Dad get in the way?"

"She and your dad . . . they had a disagreement. And they could never settle it. They got madder and madder at each other until your dad got tired of being mad, and left. And that was that."

I try to imagine being so mad at Mom that I would leave her forever, but I cannot do it. "Were you mad at him too?"

"A little," Grandpa admits. "Mostly I wanted them to figure out a way to make peace, but . . ."

His voice trails off. The symphony dances on happily, which seems really rude of it.

"Grandpa?"

"Yes, Finley?"

"Does . . . does Grandma hate me like she hates Dad?"

Grandpa pulls the car over and looks right at me. "She doesn't hate your dad. She loves him, and she loves you, Finley. She loves you more than she knows how to say."

My eyes fill up with tears. "Then why won't they say sorry and get over it?"

"Sometimes things are too big for 'sorry.'" Grandpa wipes my cheeks with a handkerchief embroidered with his swirly initials: WH. "But I don't think they'll always be that way. You being with us this summer is big, Finley. It's tremendous. Maybe it's a step. A baby step. That's what life is, you know: a bunch of baby steps, one after another after another, and sometimes you fall, but you always get back up, and eventually you get where you're going. And, hopefully, you have people beside you to help you up when you need it. That's where family comes in."

I have many questions left, but they can wait. Right now I will nod and let Grandpa hug me, and I will think about how he loves Dad after all. Grandpa's shirt is white and wrinkle-free; he smells like laundry and this morning's pancakes. The sunlight makes his face look older than usual, but I like it. I imagine each wrinkle is a year, and each year was a good one.

"Shall we keep going?" Grandpa tucks his handkerchief away. "There's a farm stand down this way that sells the best strawberries you've ever tasted."

"Strawberries are my favorite," I tell him.

He squeezes my hand. "They're your grandma's, too."

As we get back onto the road, Grandpa skips the next movement in the symphony, the one where there's a storm, and goes right to the last movement, where the sun comes back out and everything sounds like flying.

I don't mind.

# 15

THAT NIGHT AFTER DINNER, WE are sitting in the Tower shelling pecans when the Bailey boys show up.

Dex sees them a split second before I do.

"Pirates!" he yells.

I clap my hand over his mouth. The adults absolutely cannot know the Baileys are out here.

Gretchen leaps to her feet and raises her stick high. "Come any closer and I'll poke your eyes out."

"No, you won't." I jump down from the Tower. "We said we'd come back when we could. What do you want?"

Jack kneels before me. His brothers, on either side of him, do the same. "Noble orphan girl, we are here to beg your forgiveness for our thievery the other day. Indeed, it is crazy boring around here and we think it would be less boring if you were our friends and not our enemies."

I stare at him, trying not to laugh. He looks so *serious*.

Ruth peeks out from under her monster mask, which she has not taken off all day. "*What?*"

"Why are you talking like that?" Gretchen snaps. "How do you know she's the orphan girl?"

"We listen," Jack says matter-of-factly. "You guys talk louder than you think."

"Plus, we're excellent spies," Cole adds.

"We brought cookies!" Bennett announces. Cole glares at him.

Gretchen perks up. "Cookies?"

I try to remain uncompromising.

(Fourteen-letter word for "I will not change my mind, no matter what!")

"You're not supposed to be over here," I say. "That wasn't part of our deal."

Kennedy grabs my hand and whispers, "What deal? Finley, this is not cool."

"It's okay," Cole says quickly. "We're not messing with you, promise." He pauses. "Kennedy, right?"

Kennedy puts her hands on her hips. "Yeah?"

"Yeah, I've seen you at school." He smiles a little. "Hi."

"Great. Hi. Somebody tell me what's going on before I get Grandpa."

We tell Kennedy about the Wasteland, the Bone House and its graves. How the Bailey boys stole our dues, and the deal we made to get them back.

"Uh-huh. I see. One sec." Kennedy pulls me aside. "Okay, this is so not allowed. We're not supposed to leave the *pit*, and we're definitely not supposed to go back into the woods that far. And you made a deal with the *Baileys*?"

"I'm sorry. It's just . . . we had to get our stuff back, and then the Everwood said—"

"The Everwood *said*?" Kennedy blows hair out of her face. "Finley, listen. I know you've got this great imagination, and that's awesome, and I know we're supposed to let you do your thing and be super nice to you, but—"

Suddenly I feel about five inches tall. "Who told you to be nice to me?"

"It's no big deal. Grandma just told me . . . Don't be mad, okay? She just said you're kind of sensitive, and to try not to upset you." Kennedy pauses, biting her lip. "You know, because of the stuff with your parents."

I cross my arms over my chest. Kennedy's eyes are so sweet and blue, looking at me like a worried mom, like Aunt Dee did that first night at dinner, when she seemed like she was afraid I would start crying any second.

I want to melt into the dirt.

"There's nothing wrong with my parents," I say quietly.

Kennedy puts a soft hand on my arm. "Sure. *I* know that. Grandma doesn't know what she's talking about, okay?"

"Okay."

"Hey." Kennedy's fingers pry mine loose. Her hand squeezes mine. "You're all right?"

I squeeze her hand back, and she smiles at me.

"If it makes you feel any better," Jack says loudly, interrupting us, "we've brought a few things to prove you can trust us."

Cole opens his backpack and nods at Bennett, who is bouncing on his toes. Bennett pulls out a handheld telescope, a bag of cookies, two flashlights, and a cloth banner decorated with painted vines and leaves and huge letters that say WELCOME TO THE EVERWOOD.

Everyone gasps. Kennedy lets go of me to run her fingers along the banner's edge. I almost grab her hand back, and then remind myself I am eleven years old and am *not* sensitive. I can stand here by myself like a normal person.

I clench my hands into fists at my sides.

"Who made this?" Kennedy asks. "It's beautiful."

Cole clears his throat and looks at the ground. "I did. It took me two whole nights."

Kennedy drops her hand. Her cheeks are red.

"And one more thing." Jack reaches into his own backpack and draws out a small, rusted mailbox painted with vines like the banner. A tiny flag sticks up from the top—yellow, with a green leaf painted in the center.

"That's the Everwood flag," Jack says proudly.

Gretchen looks ready to explode. "You can't just make the flag for everyone. This is *our* thing."

"Fine. We'll vote on it. And if you don't like it, I'll make another one. I figure we can put it by the river, between our houses, by that group of trees." Jack points down the river. "It'll be good for planning things, like when to meet at the Bone House to hang out. This way your grandparents don't have to see you talking to us."

Gretchen snatches up the cookies.

I try to ignore how wonderful this mailbox is. "Why do you want to be our friends? Our families don't like each other."

Jack shrugs and shoves his hands in his pockets. "I don't know. Nobody'll tell me why our families don't like each other, so I figure it's a dumb reason. And you seem fun. And it's summer. And like I said, we're bored."

Bennett wipes his nose on the back of his hand and grins up at me.

"So, orphan girl," Jack says, "what do you think? Do we have a deal?"

When I don't answer right away, Cole asks, "Do you always do what your grandparents tell you to do?"

I am not sure how to respond. "What about your parents? Do they care if you talk to us?"

Jack puts a hand to his heart. "Alas, we have no parents. We are in the custody of a gargantuan, poisonous troll!"

With each word he takes a step closer to the Tower and then lunges at Dex and Ruth with his finger crooked like a pirate's hook. Dex screams; Ruth growls.

Bennett stares at Ruth's mask and tugs on Jack's shirt. "Jack," he whispers, "I want a mask too."

Gretchen remains unimpressed. "You are *not* in the custody of a *troll*."

"What kind of troll?" I say.

Jack pauses. "What kinds of trolls live in the Everwood?"

I think fast; I haven't thought about there being trolls in

the Everwood before. "Well, there are the Fellfolk, who have scaly hides like alligators and can swallow a deer whole. Their breath smells like a thousand rotting corpses."

Kennedy shudders. "That's so gross, Fin."

"Oh, yeah," says Jack, "the troll guarding us is definitely one of those. But we can pretty much do whatever we want—as long as we don't wake him up. So." Jack puts out his hand. "Do we have a deal?"

I gather my cousins together for a conference. Gretchen is digging into the cookies and seems much happier about life in general.

"Finley, I don't know." Kennedy keeps looking over at the Baileys. I can't tell if she's worried or curious. "How can we trust them?"

"We just can."

"Why? Because the Everwood said so?"

I will not feel embarrassed. "Yes."

She shakes her head sadly.

"Kennedy, please. Don't you want to see the Bone House?"

"It's so cool," Gretchen says, her mouth full of cookie. "Like haunted-house-in-the-movies cool. Like if-a-tiger-and-a-dragon-had-a-baby cool."

I grab Kennedy's hands. "*Please*, Kennedy."

Kennedy sighs and rolls her eyes. "Fine. *Fine.*" She marches over to shake Jack Bailey's hand. "We have an accord," she says in an official tone of voice.

And just like that, an alliance is born.

# 16

IT IS SATURDAY AFTER DINNER, and Avery has retreated to her bedroom like usual. Her door swings open before I can knock.

"I thought I heard you fidgeting out here," Avery says, half smiling. "What do you want?"

I glance past her and see sheets of paper strewn across her bed. Her hands are covered with charcoal smudges.

"So." I can totally be casual. "Drawing?"

"Nah. Cooking."

I blush. "Yeah. I mean . . . sorry."

"Seriously, kid, you need to chill. What's up?"

I take a deep breath. "Well. Okay. So, we're all going outside to play for a while."

"What else is new?"

"And Grandpa and Grandma are downstairs, and the other adults are too."

"Okay . . ."

"So . . . if they ask you where we are, can you say we're just playing outside? Don't let them come looking for us."

Avery raises an eyebrow. "You want me to lie for you?"

"It's not lying," I say quickly.

(Not really, anyway. We will be playing outside. We will just be farther away than usual.)

(And with the Baileys.)

(And we will not be playing so much as we will be exploring a certainly condemned house.)

"We don't want them to worry. Not that there's any reason for them to worry. It's just we don't want them bothering us. Please, Avery. I promise we'll be safe. I promise."

Five seconds pass. Avery sighs and goes back into her bedroom. "Fine. Don't die, okay?"

I hurry downstairs before she can change her mind.

The five of us—me, Gretchen, Kennedy, Jack, and Cole—meet by the mailbox and trek through the Everwood. The fading sunlight is the color of Grandma's pale pink azaleas, and our pockets are full of flashlights. Kennedy carries a bucket of cleaning supplies, and Gretchen has a box of trash bags.

I hope we get them back before Grandma notices they're missing. This was my idea, and if we are caught, it will be my fault.

We made the little ones stay behind this time. First we must scout the area. Ruth would only agree to silence once we snuck her an extra scoop of ice cream after dinner.

Kennedy keeps taking out her phone and checking to make sure we still have a signal. "I don't know about this. . . ."

Cole moves closer to her. "It's okay. We've come out here for a while now. It's safe enough."

Ahead of me Gretchen slices through the undergrowth with her stick. When the grass turns dry and scratchy, I look up.

There it is—the Bone House.

Jack whoops and runs ahead. We follow him inside to the kitchen, where a folding card table is covered with boxes of cereal, three apples, decks of cards, empty root beer bottles, a ratty baseball cap, and a worn-out copy of *The Adventures of Tom Sawyer*.

"For school," Jack explains. "Summer reading. It's not half bad, though." He sits in one of the folding chairs and thunks his heels right on top of *Tom Sawyer*. "Welcome to the Bone House. First-time visitors must pay a fee."

Gretchen frowns. "What kind of fee?"

"You have to talk in English accents for the rest of the night," Cole suggests.

"Even after we go home?"

Jack's eyes light up. "Yes, definitely. For the rest of the weekend."

Kennedy giggles. "Everyone will think we're so weird."

"That's the point!"

I halfway listen to them while I walk around the kitchen. It is scattered with signs that someone once lived here— shattered coffee mugs, pots and pans piled in a corner. A framed piece of cloth embroidered with the words *Welcome Home* hangs in the corner by one nail. The refrigerator, oven, and sink are all full of charred trash, rotting cabinets, pieces of wall and ceiling.

Everything is black and warped, like the bicycle Gretchen and I found.

Gretchen and Cole gather a deck of cards and start a game of War while Kennedy puts on a pair of pink rubber gloves and starts bagging up trash like she was born to do it.

I cannot imagine what Grandma would think if she saw this place. She would probably not be able to sleep until it was as good as new.

"Weird, huh?" Jack comes up beside me. "Everything looks normal but completely messed up at the same time. Once I tried looking through some of their stuff, just to see, but it freaked me out too bad. Never did it again. We try to only touch whatever we bring from home."

"Why?"

"Cole's idea. Bad luck, he says. The curse thing."

I stare up at the ruined ceiling. "I wonder how long it's been abandoned. Is the whole house like this?"

"Yeah. Come on, I'll show you."

Jack leads me through the first floor. What used to be the living room has no roof, but the brick chimney is still mostly standing. There is a flower-patterned love seat stained gray and yellow, stuffing spilling out of the cushions. A tiny bookshelf still holds a few books, but most are on the floor, burned black and crisp, scattered in piles. There are heaps of trash, charred planks of wood, a ceiling fan with two blades missing and the lightbulbs shattered.

Except for the chimney, that far wall of the house is completely gone.

"Upstairs is worse," Jack says quietly. We walk back through the living room and up the stairs. Jack puts a hand on my arm when we get to the landing, and I jump.

"Careful." He points to a missing part of the floor. "Don't step there."

We scoot around the hole and into the only remaining bedroom. It's dark up here, and Jack turns on a flashlight. Piles of trash sit along the walls. They remind me of shadow monsters you might see in a junkyard, full of torn clothes, melted plastic toys, pieces of wall, pieces of doors, pieces and pieces and pieces of someone else's life.

The beam from Jack's flashlight hits a shard of glass, mostly hidden beneath a mound of clothes and a graveyard of stuffed animals stained with ash.

"Wait, over here." I crouch by the window, where Cole dangled Kennedy's MVP medal out for me and Gretchen to see. Jack follows me with his light, and I dig until I find what I'm looking for.

"It's a picture," Jack says, looking over my shoulder.

"A family picture?" The glass is cracked, and the photograph is stained from water or fire or maybe something else. I try to wipe some of it away, and through the smoky stains I see a man with blue eyes, a woman's smile, a kid's feet in two pale pink shoes.

(Child's size 11. For the left foot.)

I squint hard. "It's a man, a woman, and a kid. She's little."

"Three people," Jack says. "Three graves?"

We look at each other for two seconds before hurrying downstairs and out the back door. On our way out, I grab a towel, an ice scraper, and a bottle of water from our bucket.

"Where are y'all going?" Gretchen asks. "Come watch me kick Cole's butt at War!"

"Don't you dare wander off, Finley Hart," Kennedy calls out. "You swore you wouldn't!"

Jack and I ignore them, picking our way through the trash-filled backyard to the sound of cicadas pulsing in the trees. A train horn wails in the distance.

Once we're under the big oak tree, we find the gravestones and get to work, yanking off weeds and scraping away moss. Jack doesn't speak, and neither do I. He looks serious in the flashlight's glow. A grasshopper flits against my leg, but I don't even scream.

We scrub at the layers of caked-on mud until the towel is ruined and we run out of water. My fingers and leg muscles ache, and I am getting eaten alive by mosquitoes, but I don't much care.

"Finley?" Flashlights bob through the leaves, and the others join us. I hear the buzz of another grasshopper, and Kennedy shrieks.

Jack tells them all to hush. "Don't make so much noise. We don't want to disturb them."

"Who?" Gretchen peers around us to see the work we've done.

"The Travers family," I answer quietly, and point at the gravestones. Some of the engraved letters are hard to make out, and we could not clean everything completely, at least not tonight, but we can see enough to read their names:

CYNTHIA TRAVERS, *born* March 24, 1986 | *died* April 17, 1994
JOY TRAVERS, *born* September 3, 1958 | *died* April 17, 1994
FRANK TRAVERS, *born* March 1, 1954 | *died* April 20, 1994

"Holy God," Gretchen whispers, creeping closer. "One of them was a *kid*?"

"Seriously, guys, this is messed up," Cole says. "I told you not to touch these things."

"It's fine, Cole." Jack shows him the framed picture we found. "Look, it's them."

"Oh. Great. So you found a creepy picture of dead people. Is this supposed to make me feel better?"

"Come on, don't you get it? Now we know the names of the people who used to live here!"

Cole grabs Jack's shoulders. "I did *not* want to *know* this. It's *freaky*."

"The dad died a few days after the mom and daughter," Kennedy points out, trailing her fingers across Frank Travers's gravestone. "Why do you think that is?"

Gretchen stares at the graves. "Mom said my dad never wanted to be buried. They burned him and sprinkled his ashes across the farm where he grew up."

Everyone grows quiet.

"Your dad's dead?" Cole asks.

"Yeah, but I was really little. I don't remember him. Can you imagine? Being *buried*? I wouldn't want to be stuck underground for all eternity."

"You'd be dead," Jack points out.

"Yeah, but I'd still know."

"How?"

She glares at him. "I'd just *know*, okay?"

"I don't like this." Cole edges back toward the tree's outer branches. "Maybe we should go home."

"Wuss," Jack declares.

Cole cusses at him, but I am thinking about what Gretchen said and not really listening.

Being buried—the weight of all that dirt and rock on top of you, and you yourself sealed into a coffin. No air, no breeze, no sounds.

I am not sure I have ever imagined anything so terrible.

I want to leave.

I must leave. Now.

I cannot breathe.

No matter how hard I try to force down the feeling, my chest is shifting and sliding away from me.

It is a cascade of things:

Being spooked by my surroundings.

Imagining the body of Gretchen's dad being burned, and wondering if part of you, even if you are dead, can still feel things like that.

Wondering why Frank Travers died a few days after his family, and what kinds of horrible things he must have been thinking during that time, all alone, with no one around to ask him if he was okay.

Any sadness I may feel is nothing compared to what he must have been feeling, or what Stick must have felt when her husband died.

I have no right to my sadness when there are dead families and burned houses.

The memories of all the sadness I have ever experienced come rushing back to me in a stream. Days when I could not smile, when I felt heavy and pushed down. Nights when I could not sleep. Mornings when I could not wake up.

These moments of sadness seem so small, now. They seem pathetic.

"Finley?" Jack nudges me.

I jerk away. In these moments, when I am close to losing myself, one of the worst things that can happen is for someone to unexpectedly touch me.

When I am like this, my body feels stretched tight. Like it

is working extra hard to keep me together, and the slightest touch might send me cracking open.

"Are you okay?" Jack says. "You look funny."

I do not answer him. I crawl through the branches of the oak and escape into the open backyard, but not even fresh air can get rid of this fear living like bugs underneath my skin.

This fear that I have no reason to feel.

There is no reason for the heaviness I can feel pressing down on me. Like when you step outside before a storm and the air feels heavy and damp, like you're drinking it instead of breathing.

Like that, but worse.

It seems wrong to feel these things while standing in front of this poor, broken Bone House.

I ought to be able to get rid of these feelings—right?

Shouldn't I be able to live in my beautiful, clean house (which is not burned) with my family (who are still alive) and be happy about it?

I ought to be able to get rid of these feelings.

I *will* get rid of these feelings.

I walk circles around the house, close my eyes, and listen for the sounds of the Everwood trees, back in the thick part of the forest. I focus on pushing these feelings down to a place where they cannot touch me anymore.

I will push on them, and push on them, until they have nowhere else to go but out of my head entirely.

# 17

It is Wednesday morning. The house is quiet because Kennedy, Dex, and Ruth stayed over last night, but they are still asleep.

I did not fall asleep until four in the morning.

Since exploring the Bone House and cleaning off the Travers family gravestones, I have had trouble sleeping. Once my head hits the pillow, my thoughts start spinning and spinning. I think of being buried, and being buried alive, and being burned alive, and Hart House falling down around me, and what my parents are doing, and what the Travers family looked like, and what the Bone House will look like once we clean it, and what the upcoming school year will be like, and what story I will write next about the Everwood, and how quiet the house is around me, and how everyone else is sleeping, and why I can't seem to sleep, and

and

and

My brain just will not stop.

I creep out of my bedroom, my mouth dry and my head heavy. Soft, cheerful music and the smell of pancakes drift up the stairs. In the kitchen Grandma stands at the stove wearing her pearls; her white apron is spotless.

"Grandma? I have a question."

Grandma clucks her tongue. "How about, 'Good morning, Grandma'?"

"I mean, good morning. Sorry."

"Did you sleep well, Finley?" asks Aunt Dee, passing me a bowl of strawberries, ones I picked out with Grandpa.

Aunt Bridget swirls her glass of orange juice in one hand. "I hope Dex and Ruth didn't keep you up too late. You all seemed to be constantly whispering last night."

I am quite certain Aunt Bridget's orange juice has alcohol in it. Aunt Bridget hardly ever drinks something that does not have alcohol in it; her drinks smell bitter and sour, even drinks that are supposed to be sweet, like orange juice.

Even though Aunt Bridget smiles a lot, her eyes are thorny, like she is always picking apart everything she sees, to make sure nothing is hiding from her. Maybe she knows this, and matches her drinks to her eyes.

"I slept fine," I lie.

Uncle Nelson looks up from his newspaper. He is working on a crossword puzzle before leaving for work, so I scoot closer to see.

"Kennedy hasn't been able to stop talking about these games y'all have been playing," says Uncle Nelson. "I told her she was too old for that kind of thing, but she told me I was being ridiculous. She's probably right." He frowns at the puzzle, appearing to be stumped.

Eight-letter word for "family tree subject." I have to think about that one.

"They call it the Everwood." Aunt Bridget looks at me over the top of her glass. "Isn't that right?"

The word sounds so strange coming from Aunt Bridget that I consider denying it, pretending that Dex and Ruth are silly eight-year-olds.

Aunt Dee starts folding a pile of fluffy, cream-colored hand towels. "What's the Everwood, sweetie? Is it some kind of code word?"

"No," I say. The crossword puzzle is distracting me. "It's a forest full of witches and trolls and things. *Ancestry.*" I tap the newspaper. "The word is *ancestry.*"

Uncle Nelson smiles. "Hey, you're pretty good at this, kiddo."

"I collect words. Dad does crossword puzzles all the time. I help him."

"Does he? Tell me, Finley," says Aunt Bridget, "did your dad ever tell you he felt bad for keeping you away from your family all your life? Did he ever mention that?"

I freeze.

Aunt Dee stops folding.

"Bridget," says Grandma, her back to us. "That's enough."

The pancake batter sizzles in its pan.

"I'm sorry," says Aunt Bridget, although she doesn't sound

it. "I just think it's ridiculous that this is the first time I'm seeing my niece. You know, if he and Gwen weren't having problems, I don't think they'd have ever brought her—"

Grandma slams down her spatula. "Bridget, that is enough!"

The sound is an explosion. No one in this house yells, unless it is to call someone in from another room, and even then Grandma makes whoever it is stop at once.

She leans heavily against the countertop, her face pale.

"Mom?" Aunt Bridget sets down her drink and hurries over, Aunt Dee right behind her. They hover around her like birds.

"What is it?" Aunt Dee puts her hand on Grandma's forehead. "Your skin's clammy. Have you eaten yet?"

Grandma waves her away. In a flash she looks like herself again. "I'm fine. Just a little dizzy." She tugs her apron straight and smiles at my aunts. "Good thing it's almost breakfast time, I suppose. I had such a light dinner last night."

Aunt Dee smiles too, but Aunt Bridget looks pulled too tight, like she's waiting for something to crash. Aunt Dee grabs her hand, squeezes. Uncle Nelson returns to his newspaper.

In the span of ten seconds we are all back to where we started. I want to say something about how uncomfortable I feel, and about how something is obviously very wrong, even if they do not want to admit it, but I am not brave enough to do it.

"You had a question, Finley?" Grandma says.

Aunt Dee is back in her chair, peering at Uncle Nelson's crossword puzzle. Aunt Bridget sips her drink.

"Finley?" Grandma looks up, shoots me a bright smile. She holds a plate of pancakes. "You had a question?"

I could go ahead and ask Grandma to take me to the library. That's why I came in here, and everyone is acting normal now, so why not?

(Ask away, Finley.)

But I don't want to ask Grandma anything. She was just shaking, a few seconds ago. She needs to eat; she needs to sit down. She needs *something*. Why does no one else say that?

I want to hug her, but if I touch her, she might break.

"No, never mind," I tell her. "I figured it out."

# 18

THINGS I KNOW ABOUT THE EVERWOOD

- The Everwood
  - The Green (Grandma and Grandpa's backyard)
  - The Great Castle (Hart House)
  - The Tower (our tree patio)
  - The Pit (the pit)
  - The First Bridge (the sewer pipe)
  - The Wasteland (where the Bone House is)
  - The Bone House (the Travers house)
  - The Troll's Keep (the Bailey house)
  - The Post Office (our mailbox)
- The Baileys
  - Cole (thirteen), Jack (twelve), Bennett (eight)
  - Captives of the Fellfolk troll (obviously not true, but I must accept this explanation until I find more information)
  - Jack's dad (Fellfolk troll, I assume) did something bad when Dad was a teenager, can't be trusted. *Why???*
  - The "something bad"—don't ask Grandma and Grandpa about it. *Why???*

o Jack's mom—where is she?
- The Bone House
  o Severely burned. Lots of fire damage.
  o Once home to Frank, Joy, and Cynthia Travers (we think). All deceased.
  o What happened? What started the fire?

I STARE AT MY LIST for a long time. Aunt Dee is taking me to the library instead of Grandma, because when I finally felt brave enough to ask her, she said she was too tired.

Grandma says that a lot, and I understand. I am always tired too, and I don't do half the things she does—Friends of the Library meetings, A Pack for Every Back, the WIC clinic, baking for the neighbors.

(So get it together, Finley.)

(WAKE. UP.)

According to the note Jack left at the Post Office, he and his brothers want to meet us at the Tower after dinner.

I must show up with answers of some kind—why the fire happened, and how it happened, and how the Travers family died, and if that really is their house, or if we have somehow gotten it all wrong. Not because my cousins expect me to find answers, but because maybe if do find some, I will be able to sleep better.

Luckily, the library is about a thirty-minute drive because Hart House is so far out past the edge of town, so I have time to look over my list a few times.

Aunt Dee, however, is distracting. I watch her from the backseat. She offered me the front, but I wanted to sit back here, where she couldn't read my list. She chews on the inside of her lip, and her knuckles are white on the steering wheel.

"Aunt Dee, are you okay?"

"Oh, sweetheart, I'm fine." She reaches back to pat my knee. We ride in silence for a minute. "Aunt Bridget shouldn't have said those things about your parents. I'm sorry she did."

"It's all right."

"It was out of line." Aunt Dee keeps looking back at me in the rearview mirror, like she is afraid I might fly away. Her hair is soft and gold, curled right above her shoulders. Her face is soft; her voice is soft. I often find myself thinking I would like to snuggle up in her lap and read, because it looks like a cozy place to do such a thing.

"It's only that she loves you so much, Finley," she says. "We all do, and it's hard to accept that you've been away from us for so long."

"But how can you love me? You only met me, like, three weeks ago."

We stop at a red light, and Aunt Dee turns around in her seat to look at me.

"Finley, it isn't about when we met you, or how long it's been, or anything as complicated as that. It's about family. You're a Hart. You're ours, and we're yours. It's in the blood, okay? It's in the bones."

I cannot find any words to say after that, so instead I reach toward the front seat and take Aunt Dee's hand. "Gretchen told me that. About Hart blood."

Aunt Dee smiles. "Gretchen's a smart girl, like you. I knew you would be. Lewis was always the clever one."

Aunt Dee's eyes look like Kennedy's, but older. Crystal-clear blue. "Do you love Dad, too? Even though . . ."

(Even though what?)

(Why?)

(*Why?*)

"Even though," Aunt Dee says firmly, squeezing my hand. "He's my brother. You can't get rid of that kind of love."

"Then how come he stayed away?"

A car horn honks behind us; the light is green.

"Shoot." Aunt Dee starts driving again.

I think she has forgotten my question. Then she says, "That's his question to answer, Finley. Not mine." Aunt Dee taps her fingers on the steering wheel for a few seconds. "Well. How about some music? What do you say?"

Aunt Dee looks at me in the rearview mirror. I'm not sure what else to do, so I smile. Her eyes crinkle back at me, and she turns on the radio.

I do not press the issue. I am a smart girl.


Downtown Billington is four streets running from north to south, and four streets running perpendicular to them from east to west, and a courthouse in the center square, and tiny shops that look like they have existed there since the beginning of time.

The library is across the street from the courthouse, in a pale purple building that used to be a movie theater, according to Aunt Dee.

"I'll be next door at the Grind, okay?" Aunt Dee kisses my cheek. "Here's my library card. Come get me when you've finished."

Watching her disappear into the café, I get the sense she is relieved to not be in the car with me anymore.

The feeling is mutual. Aunt Dee is nice, but I need some space to think.

The library is exactly what it should be: lots of dark wood and winding bookshelves, and a smell of computers and old books in the air.

I stand in the middle of the room and consider where to begin.

"Can I help you?" A librarian peeks around her computer to smile at me.

"Perhaps." I set down my notebook on her desk. "I'm from out of town. My name is Finley Hart—"

"Oh! Are you the granddaughter who's visiting for the summer?"

Who is this woman, and how does she know about my life? "Excuse me?"

"Hi! I'm Pam." She holds out her hand.

Cautiously, I shake it. "Finley."

"Your grandma's been talking about your visit for weeks now. She's the president of the Friends of the Library and comes around all the time. I'm so happy you're here! Your grandparents are just the sweetest people. They've done so much for Billington."

But why would Grandma have been talking about me? I suppose she must have been excited. Or maybe she was pretending to be excited?

Or maybe, once I arrived, she realized what a disappointment I was, that I am too much like my dad, and felt her excitement drain away.

"They've done a lot for Billington?"

Pam beams at me. "You bet! Can I show you?"

Pam leads me to a glass display in the library lobby. She points to an old photograph, and sure enough, there are my grandparents, standing in front of the library. They look like themselves and not like themselves at the same time. Grandma's hair is golden instead of white; Grandpa's face has fewer wrinkles. Beside them stands a man in a suit holding a giant pair of scissors.

"That's Mayor Calvin," Pam explains. "He's ancient now, but isn't he handsome here?"

"I guess?"

"See, they're opening the new library. Your grandparents put a lot of money into renovating it. You should have seen this place before they donated. We had such a sparse collection. There was mold, the roof was leaking, mice had chewed through the wiring. Without your grandparents' help, we might not be having this conversation today." Pam sighs happily. "And it's not only the library. I guess—oh, what was it? A couple decades ago?—they started really pouring a lot of money into downtown. Restoring buildings, planting trees . . ."

I stare hard at the photograph. The three teenage girls standing beside my grandparents are unmistakably Aunt Bridget, Aunt Dee—who looks so much like Avery that I wonder if it *is* Avery, somehow having traveled back in time—and Stick.

A teenage boy stands a little apart from them, looking away from the camera, as if he is wishing he were somewhere else.

I know that look. It's how I look in photographs.

I touch the glass. "That's my dad. He looks . . . weird."

Pam laughs. "You mean young?"

No, not quite. What I mean is, I know my father met my mother in their first year of college. That could not have been very long after this picture was taken. And thinking about my father meeting my mother, both of them looking so young, makes my chest tight and uncomfortable, like I am seeing something I should not see.

I wonder if Mom and Dad knew, in those first moments when they met, that they would get married and have a daughter named Finley. That they would start working too much and ignoring each other and fighting with each other, the whole time pretending everything was okay.

I wonder if they knew that when they started to pretend, their daughter would be able to tell.

"Anyway, I'm probably boring you," says Pam, leading me back to her desk. "What can I do for you, Finley?"

"I'm trying to solve a mystery."

"Oh, that sounds fun! How can I help?"

I glance down the list in my notebook, playing with the curly strips of paper from where I ripped out my Favorite Words list.

"I'm looking for information about a man named Frank Travers, and his wife, Joy, and his daughter, Cynthia," I say at last. "And also about the Bailey family. I don't know the parents' names, but I know the kids' names. They live across the river from my grandparents. And . . ."

I pause. I do not want to say this part out loud, but I must. "And also, about any fires in the area. About twenty-five years ago, maybe?" (Stay cool, Finley. Stay casual. Pretend you know nothing about those gravestones.) "When my dad was a teenager."

When Mr. Bailey was a teenager too.

*He did . . . bad things.*

*He's not safe to be around, and if he has kids now, I bet they're not much different.*

But Dad's wrong about that last part, at least. Jack's safe, and Cole and Bennett are too. They wouldn't do anything dangerous.

Would they?

"The Travers fire," Pam says quietly, nodding. "I remember hearing about it from my dad."

I have read about out-of-body experiences, but I have never had one myself until now. My mind seems to drift out of my head and float there, observing, while my body stares at Pam.

*The Travers fire.* Hearing it said like that makes it feel real, like before now it was just this story in the Everwood, and now it is more. It has a history, a past.

Pam places her hand on mine. "I'm not sure you want to hear about it, Finley. It isn't a happy story." She tilts her head. "I'm surprised your grandparents haven't told you. If they haven't, then maybe I shouldn't—"

I slip my hand away from hers. "Please, I'd like to know. I like all kinds of stories. I'll tell Grandma about everything when I get home, and we'll discuss it together. I promise."

(Or not.)

After a pause Pam starts typing away on her keyboard. She shows me articles on her computer. She prints documents. She babbles on and on, telling me words too awful to stick. They jump and slip around in my skull like panicked fish, and it is hard to get a grip on them, but I try. I scribble in my notebook. I must get this information out of my head and onto paper.

Aunt Dee comes up behind me. "Finley? You about done?"

I jump and slam my notebook closed. "Yeah. I'm fine. Why?"

Aunt Dee takes a sip of her coffee and looks at me funny, but Pam hurries over before she can say anything.

"Dee! Hi." Pam gives her a hug. "Good to see you. I was just helping Finley with—"

"Some research," I interrupt. "For a story I'm writing. Thanks, Pam."

Now Pam's the one giving me a funny look.

"Well, thank you so much for helping her," says Aunt Dee. "I'll see you at choir practice this weekend?"

"Sure, sure. Oh! That reminds me: Is your mom okay?"

Grandma?

Aunt Dee frowns. "What do you mean? Of course she is."

"I was only asking because she missed our Friends of the Library meeting last week. Didn't leave a message or anything. It was so unlike her, and I wanted to make sure everything was all right."

Aunt Dee freezes for a tiny second and then relaxes into a smile. "Oh! That. Yes, I'm afraid we've all been a little behind on things since Finley arrived." Aunt Dee squeezes my shoulder. "Trying to make up for lost time, you know? The kids have been over almost every day, and Mom's been cooking up a storm."

Pam smiles at me. "I should've guessed. The famous Finley. Maybe if you have enough of your grandma's cooking, you won't ever want to leave! Her chicken spaghetti is my absolute favorite thing in the world, honest to God."

Aunt Dee says something, laughing, and Pam says something back, and somehow my feet are taking me out of the library, but I don't realize it until the sunlight hits me.

"I don't get it," I tell Aunt Dee. "Grandma said she went to that meeting."

Aunt Dee marches to the car beside me. "You must have heard her wrong."

"No, I remember it exactly. We were all in the dining room making masks, and she came in and said—"

"Finley, your grandmother's a busy woman. She probably got the schedule mixed up, is all. I wouldn't worry about it."

"But she *said*—"

"I really don't want to talk about it anymore, okay?" Aunt Dee holds the car door open for me. I can't see her eyes behind her sunglasses, but her smile is front and center. "What do you say we swing by Carter's on the way home, grab a batch of those frosted oatmeal cookies for dessert tonight, huh?"

"Okay." I climb into the car. The leather burns the backs of my legs. Aunt Dee turns on the car, and the air-conditioning roars to life. A song starts up, and Aunt Dee sings along. She doesn't look at me.

I concentrate on my notebook, trying to clear my head. I don't know what to think about Grandma lying to us, and I guess Aunt Dee doesn't want to think about it either.

So I stop thinking, and read over my notes:

NEW INFORMATION ABOUT THE EVERWOOD
- Geoffrey Bailey
  - Jack, Cole, and Bennett's dad
  - Frequently gets in trouble for drunk driving

- Maggie Bailey
  - Jack, Cole, and Bennett's mom
- Grandma and Grandpa Hart
  - Gave a lot of money to the city (library renovation, courthouse restoration, parks maintenance)
- The Travers family
  - Frank Travers: Worked at a small gas station on the outskirts of town (no longer exists). Deceased. Forty years old at time of death.
  - Joy Travers: Worked at Freddie's Diner on I-35 (went out of business in 1991). Deceased. Thirty-five years old at time of death.
  - Cynthia Travers: Attended Billington Elementary. Deceased. Eight years old at time of death.
- The Travers fire
  - April 17, 1994. Twenty-two years ago. (Dad was fourteen.)
  - Cause of fire: negligence; illegal garbage fire spread to house (from fire department records)
  - Joy and Cynthia Travers died in the fire.
  - Frank Travers died in the hospital three days later.
  - My aunts saw the fire, tried to save the Travers family, but couldn't.

As Aunt Dee brakes at an intersection, she finally looks back at me. "Are you all right, Finley? You look like you've seen a ghost."

How do I tell her what I am thinking?

Pam showed me an article about the Travers fire. I have two copies of it in my notebook. The article explains how my aunts saw the flames from the backyard of Hart House. They crossed the river and ran through the Everwood to help. But they couldn't.

They were heroes, the article says, the three beautiful Hart girls.

No one is surprised, the article says.

The Hart family is a pillar of strength in our community. Those Harts have always shined.

"Finley?" Aunt Dee looks worried. "Do you need me to pull over?"

Why has no one ever told me about this fire?

Why did I have to find out myself?

It seems odd that Grandma Hart would not have wanted to tell me about my aunts, after they did this great thing.

And why doesn't this article say anything about Dad?

I shut my notebook. I cannot ask these questions until I talk to someone about this. I need to talk to Gretchen, or Jack.

"I'm fine," I tell Aunt Dee. "Reading in the car gives me a headache."

# 19

I HAVE STARTED ACCOMPANYING GRANDPA on his drives—
not every one of them, otherwise I'd be out of the house
nearly every afternoon, but some of them.

I never ask him to let me go with him, not after that first
time. I do not want to bother him. I understand how a person
might want time to himself.

(Sometimes when I am sitting alone in a quiet room, with
only my Everwood stories for company, I feel like I am truly
*me*.)

(I do not have to talk when I don't want to.)

(I can get lost in my thoughts and not miss anything other
people think is important.)

(I do not have to pretend to be happy when I am not feeling happy.)

So usually I wait until Grandpa finds me.

Every afternoon before his drive, I hold my breath and listen while Grandpa moves through the house. I hear the jingle
of his car keys, the garage door open and shut. Then he is gone.

But today he finds me in the squashy armchair by the giant
living room window. The house is quiet because Grandma is
napping.

I am trying to work on an Everwood story, but I cannot stop thinking about the Bone House and the list of questions tucked inside my notebook.

"Feel like going for a drive?" he asks me.

"Can we listen to Beethoven?"

He smiles. "I'd like that."

Most of the time Grandpa takes the same route through Billington, and we end up at the farm stand and buy a basket of strawberries.

Today we go a different direction. Instead of turning left out of the Hart House driveway, we turn right. We take a country road out to these big rolling prairie fields full of grazing cows.

The sky is huge, a cloudless blue carpet that never ends. Nothing gets in its way—no trees, no buildings, no mountains.

The second movement of the *Pastoral* Symphony is playing. It is this really sleepy part of the symphony that sounds like a slow dance.

Grandpa isn't talking today, and I am not sure why. Usually he asks me about things back home, like my friend Rhonda next door or how in art class last year I painted a forest in tiny pieces of color, like a stained-glass window.

But not today.

He stares out the window ahead of us, not looking at the sky or the fields of cows. He turns the volume of the radio up and down.

He looks very tired. At a stop sign he rubs his face, sliding his glasses up his forehead.

My notebook, with the newspaper article inside, sits in my lap like a brick.

Words rush out of me:

"Aunt Dee took me to the library this morning. I found out about the Travers fire."

Grandpa finally snaps out of his tiredness and looks at me. "What?"

"It says Aunt Bridget, and Dee and Stick, they were heroes." I take out one copy of the article to show him.

Grandpa snatches it away from me. He looks at it for much longer than it would take to read the article. The paper trembles in his hands.

"How come no one ever talks about it?" Now that I have brought it up, I might as well ask my questions. "I think it's really nice. They must have been so brave."

Watching him, I breathe very carefully. My heartbeat gets louder and louder. Maybe this was a terrible idea, although I cannot imagine why. Does it have something to do with Dad? Why wasn't he in the article? Grandpa is scaring me with the terrible, lost-looking expression on his face, but all the same, I have to know.

My words rush out: "So how come Dad—?"

"Finley, this was a very painful time for everyone," he says abruptly, crumpling the article into a ball and throwing it out the window. "It was frightening for us, and for your aunts, and sad for a lot of people, and I'd prefer we not talk about it."

"But—"

"End of discussion. Can't we just enjoy the day?"

He drives away from the stop sign. Beethoven's music now sounds unbearably loud.

"Grandpa," I whisper, because it is really bothering me, "you littered."

He sighs sharply. "I know, and I shouldn't have."

"Can we go back and pick it up?"

"No!"

I try to scoot away without him noticing. My eyes are stinging, and I look out the window so he can't tell.

We drive for a long time, until we reach a dead end, a dirt road, a NO TRESPASSING sign. Grandpa sighs, turns the car around, stops.

"I'm sorry, Finley. I shouldn't have snapped at you. There was no excuse for that. Can you forgive me?"

I nod, because the last time I opened my mouth, things came out that apparently should not have. And my question about Dad, it still balances there on my tongue, itching to be said.

"Good. Thank you." Grandpa starts driving again. The music waltzes through our silence. "Why don't you read me something out of your notebook? Something that makes you happy."

That sounds like an awful idea; I do not read things out of my notebook to people. It is my own private space.

But Grandpa looks so hopeful, and if this will make his conscience feel better about littering, then perhaps I should help him with that.

"All right." I flip through my notebook, making sure to hide the second copy of the article so he won't crumple that one up too. "I like to make lists sometimes."

"Oh? What kinds of lists?"

"All kinds. Like . . . I have this one, for example."

He glances over. "What is it?"

I hesitate. "Why I Love My Dad."

(Don't ask the question, Finley.)

(Let's only talk about nice things, just now. Nothing about *then*. Nothing about *why*.)

Grandpa goes quiet for a while. Then he says softly, "Will you read it to me?"

I scan the page. "Some of these are from a long time ago. They're kind of cheesy."

"That's all right. Go ahead."

So I do:

WHY I LOVE MY DAD

- He is tall.
- He is strong.
- He sings songs.
- Brown eyes. Like me!

- He tells me funny stories before bed about Yellow Peach.

("My stuffed rabbit," I explain to Grandpa. He nods, and I keep reading.)

- He likes pizza.
- He dresses up for Halloween, and other dads don't.
- When he writes, he makes funny faces, but I pretend I don't see (but I think he knows I see).
- When I have nightmares, he doesn't think it's silly.
- He pronounces Beethoven "Beeth-oven" because it's funnier that way.
- He is a good teacher.
- He doesn't like scary movies either.

I read and read. The list is fifty-seven items long. When I get to item number fifty-seven, I say, "He—" and pause.

I added this last one a couple of weeks ago.

"What is it?" Grandpa asks.

"It's stupid," I tell him.

"I doubt that. You don't want to finish?"

"You won't laugh?"

"I won't."

I take a deep breath and say the last item on my list:

- He looks like Grandpa.

Like he promised, Grandpa doesn't laugh. He holds my hand instead, even though I am pretty sure one-handed driving is unsafe and illegal.

He does not say anything, but he does not need to. The symphony continues, and the cow fields roll us back toward home, and that is enough for me.

# 20

THAT EVENING BEFORE DINNER, I show Gretchen and Kennedy the newspaper article Grandpa did not throw away, and I tell them everything I have learned about the Travers fire.

We agree not to talk about it with the little ones, and we are certainly not mentioning anything to the adults. I learned my lesson after trying to discuss it with Grandpa.

Obviously something is being kept from us; otherwise I'm sure I would have heard about the fire by now, and how my aunts tried to save the Travers family. My cousins would have already known about it. They would have told me right away after finding the Bone House. They wouldn't want to hide that their mothers are town heroes.

I'm glad I'm not the only one who didn't know about this. We are in this mystery together, my cousins and I.

I tell Jack everything in a note and leave it in the Post Office with the article.

Jack's response, a couple of hours later, says this:

*Dear Orphan Girl,*
*I didn't know about your aunts and the fire either. Cole says same for him.*

*I noticed one thing. Why doesn't the article talk about your dad? It says your aunts saw the fire, and it talks about your grandparents. But it doesn't say anything about him. That's weird, right?*

*Your friend,*

*Captain Jack*

*P.S. Don't worry, we won't talk about this to the troll, either.*

Standing beside the Post Office, I stare at the article, which Jack has returned to me. A messy circle in blue ink surrounds the paragraph talking about my aunts—and not my father.

So Jack noticed it too.

Even if the article just said, *Thankfully, the youngest Hart, Lewis (14), wasn't home at the time, and did not have to witness this terrible tragedy,* that would make sense to me. So why doesn't it say at least that?

I stare at the photos included in the article. The burned Bone House. My three aunts, golden-haired. Grandma and Grandpa standing behind them with their hands on my aunts' shoulders. Grandpa's face is blank. Grandma's smile is gentle and sad. It looks, I think, just like someone should look if they are being photographed after something awful has happened.

Dad may not be in this article, but he has to know about the fire.

And if that is the case, why has he never told me about it?

Even with everything that happened, and his huge fight with Grandma, it seems strange that he would have been able to resist telling such a dramatic story for eleven years.

He is hiding something from me. They all are—my aunts, my grandparents.

I am going to find out what.

We sneak out after dinner to meet with the Baileys. Avery is covering for us again, but I don't think she's happy about it. This time Dex, Ruth, and Bennett are coming with us.

Gretchen is making notes on her map of the Everwood, which she does every time we're outside.

Jack has a backpack crammed full of cleaning supplies.

So do I. And so does Kennedy.

We are quite serious about cleaning tonight. I have insisted upon it. The Bone House needs us.

I raided the pantry and the garage, sneaking things back up to my room while the adults were busy.

I am a thief.

It feels good.

I try to think about that feeling instead of the article, or the fire, or my father.

Gretchen and Kennedy are arguing about something, hissing back and forth. The sounds become wrapped up in the whispering trees until I cannot tell the two apart.

Ahead of them Cole is herding Dex, Ruth, and Bennett like cattle.

So back here it is just me and Jack. I like that.

I think I have a crush on Jack.

This is not the first crush I've had. Last fall, when Dad was working on an important journal article and Mom was wrapped up in a huge house renovation, we ordered cheap pizza all the time. The delivery boy was freckled and a teenager and had shaggy, sandy-colored hair. He smiled at me and remembered my name.

I quickly fell in love with him. At least I think it was love. I have read about falling in love, and I have watched movies in which people fall in love. Whenever the delivery boy came to the door, I could feel myself becoming silly, like I might start either laughing or crying at any moment.

After a couple of weeks, he stopped delivering pizza to us.

At this point in my life I like to think he got a better job or went on vacation. But at the time I feared he had sensed my love and had run as fast as he could in the other direction.

I did not eat pizza after that, even though refusing pizza and requesting Chinese instead made Dad cranky. The sight and smell of pizza had become too painful. Every time I even thought of it, my throat clenched up and my stomach flipped over, and I wished the world would swallow me up so I wouldn't have to feel that way ever again.

If that is what falling in and out of love is like, it is no wonder Mom and Dad don't want me around this summer.

(It occurs to me that this is the first time I have accepted the possibility that Mom and Dad are not in love anymore.)

(It sort of feels like I am noticing this about someone else's parents. I'm like a doctor observing something strange about my patients, who are nice, but I don't have to be friends with them or anything.)

"*Arrrrrrr* you okay?" Jack asks, his finger crooked into a pirate's hook. "You look kind of intense."

Jack absolutely cannot know I have been thinking about love and crushes and other delicate subjects. Instead I say the first thing that comes into my head:

"So, what's up with your dad?"

Right. Because Geoffrey Bailey, the drunk driver, is not a delicate subject at all.

Jack freezes for a second. "What? What do you mean?"

(Do not say you have been secretly researching his family, Finley. Whatever you do.)

"Just wondering. You never talk about him. Or your mom."

Jack starts walking again, his hands in his pockets. His arms are so skinny, they are mostly elbow. "Well, my parents are being held captive too, of course."

"By the troll."

"Right."

I take a deep breath and concentrate on the sensation of my legs taking a step, a step, another step.

"You're weird tonight, Finley," Jack informs me. "What's going on in that orphan-girl brain of yours?"

(Grandma missing Dad. Does he miss her?)

(Geoffrey Bailey being arrested for drunk driving.)

(The dying Everwood trees, and newspaper articles, and blond heroines, and a dead child named Cynthia Travers.)

(How Jack smells like dirt and sweat, which is not as disgusting a smell as you might think.)

But I do not want to scare Jack away. I will not tolerate another pizza-delivery-boy disaster.

"I don't know," I say. "Random stuff."

"*Super* random," Jack agrees. "But it's okay. I like random."

We have reached the Bone House. The dry grass of the Wasteland makes strange, scratchy noises, and the open air makes me feel lonely, although I am surrounded by people.

It is a feeling I am used to.

Kennedy figures we can be away from Hart House for an hour without the adults getting suspicious. Currently, as is their custom, they are gathered at the dining room table playing dominos and drinking after-dinner cocktails and probably not thinking about us at all, but you cannot be too careful.

So we move fast.

We pull on thick gardening gloves from Grandpa's workbench and take pieces of rotting wood and scraps of ruined furniture outside.

Jack and Gretchen sweep dirt and leaves out of the kitchen, into the living room, and out the open side of the house into the field.

Kennedy and Cole scrub the countertops. I gather trash into big garbage bags. Dex, Ruth, and Bennett work on the floor, although it is so badly damaged that I am not sure it will ever be clean. It will take us many trips to make a noticeable difference here.

But we will make this house look something like a home again, little by little.

We owe it to the Travers family.

I take a garbage bag outside and, with Gretchen's help, lift it into the bed of the old pickup truck. Everything stinks; I almost gag at the smell. But Gretchen looks completely unaffected, so I try to look that way too.

### WHAT IT MEANS TO BE A HART

- You look pretty even after sprinting across a forest.
- You look completely unaffected even when you are up to your eyeballs in garbage that smells like feet and rotten eggs.

Back inside the kitchen, Gretchen stops and makes a horrible face.

"Oh, gross. Do you think they're, like, *into* each other?"

I follow Gretchen's glare to the sink, where Kennedy and Cole are having a dirty paper towel fight.

The more Kennedy giggles, the darker Gretchen's expression becomes.

"So what if they are?" I say. "Once I had a huge crush on this pizza delivery boy—"

"That's different," Gretchen whispers. "She can like all the pizza delivery boys she wants. But Cole is a Bailey."

"Gretchen, you don't know anything about them."

"I know Grandma and Grandpa hate their guts. That's enough for me."

"What does that matter? We've been hanging out with them for days now."

Gretchen blows hair out of her face. "I have my eye on him, is all I'm saying."

Jack shows up out of nowhere and grabs another bag of trash to take outside.

Gretchen scowls and stalks away, and I follow Jack into the backyard. We are quiet for a few minutes, going back and forth between the kitchen and the truck with whatever trash we can carry.

I start to worry that I should be saying something. Most of the time I think I could be perfectly content without saying a single word, but no one else seems to function that way. There is so much talking in the world, and so much expectation to talk, even if you do not feel like talking.

I find it overwhelming.

"Sorry about Gretchen," I say.

"Whatever. I'm not worried about her." Jack squints one eye shut and jumps onto the truck's open tailgate. "*Arrr*, I am wise in the ways of the world, orphan girl. I have sailed across many seas, and made port in many lands. One knight is not enough to scare me!"

I laugh, and Jack jumps down beside me, grinning. "Come on," he says, "let's go visit them."

I do not have to ask who he is talking about. How wonderful a thing that is, to understand someone else without even trying to.

We crawl through the big oak tree's branches and sit on the dirt by the Travers family's gravestones. Jack's knee bumps against mine.

My thoughts are a whirl of . . . well, to be honest, I am not quite sure, so I take a second to organize a list in my mind.

### ABOUT JACK BAILEY

- Jack does a great pirate accent.
- When he says my name, it sounds beautiful.
- When he smiles at me, I cannot help smiling back.
- Jack is a *Bailey*.

The evening is still and hot around us, but under this tree we are in a cocoon of cool mud and night noises and shifting leaves with a thousand different voices. My shirt is sticky from all the cleaning, and when the wind trickles past us, I shiver.

"Do you think it hurt them?" Jack asks quietly. "You know, when they died?"

"Yes."

Jack looks at me. "That doesn't freak you out?"

"What doesn't?"

"Dying."

"I guess. Other things freak me out more." I hesitate, but Jack seems interested.

"Like what?" he asks.

I should not have said anything. "I don't know. Stupid stuff."

"I'll tell you what I'm scared of."

"Yeah?"

"Totally. Let's see." Jack settles back on his arms and watches the leaves move overhead. "Tornados. Comets, like, flying off course and crashing into Earth. Dolls."

I crack up. "Dolls?"

"Yep. Dolls. Hey, don't laugh! They have these tiny little demon faces. Like if you look away, they'll jump on you and suck out your soul. You know?"

"I think that might just be you."

"Fine, fine, believe what you want. But when the dolls rise up, you'll think about this moment and wish you'd listened to me."

I lean back against a branch. The tree sways ever so slightly in the wind, and I let it rock me.

"So what are you afraid of, Finley?" Jack asks. "I told you mine."

### WHAT I AM AFRAID OF

- What Mom and Dad are talking about while I am gone.
- That I will never be a real Hart.
- My blue days, when I feel like I am stuck underwater, where everything is slow and cold.

- When I lose myself, and my brain speeds up, and
  my heartbeat speeds up, and everything inside me
  comes crashing down until I can hardly remember
  what it feels like to breathe without a hundred stones
  stacked on my chest.
- That I will feel this way for the rest of my life.

"Jack?"

"Yeah?"

Looking at the gravestone of Frank Travers, I think about
how the Bone House must have looked when they were all
alive—two solid stories, maybe three solid bedrooms; whole
and breathing and warm with light. Strong, like a house
should be.

(Like I am not.)

"Can I tell you later?" I ask Jack.

"When?"

"Sometime. I promise."

Jack yawns. "Okay. Deal."

### ABOUT JACK BAILEY

- When you promise him something, he'll believe you.
  No questions asked.

Before we leave, we construct a tiny shrine to the Travers
family under the stairs that lead up to the second floor.

We find this chair with a stained, frayed cushion and

wobbly legs, and on the chair we arrange the framed picture of the Travers family, along with one of the coffee cups we found in the kitchen, a couple of books from the living room, and one of Cynthia Travers's stuffed animals—a purple dog with one ear and one eye. But it is still smiling hopefully.

Even Ruth is quiet while we stand by the shrine, listening to the wind move through the house. A train horn sounds, and the spell is broken.

"Good night," Kennedy says, waving at the Travers family photo. "See you soon."

Everyone files out after her and does the same thing, saying good-bye to the Travers family like they are real people instead of ghosts. I am the last one out, and as I step onto the porch, I notice Cole giving Kennedy our stolen box of dues. I had forgotten all about it.

I search for the proper word to describe the expression on his face: *Adoring. Soft. Bashful. Nervous.*

None of those quite work; his expression is all of those things at once, and more.

The best way to describe it is this:

Mom and Dad used to look at each other like that.

# 21

MY AUNTS HAVE TO DRAG my cousins out of the house on Tuesday morning—literally, in Dex and Ruth's case. Not even Kennedy's sweet-talking can console them.

I help Aunt Bridget get Dex and Ruth settled in the car. They will not sit still until I remind them of their impending knighthood, at which point they turn into statues.

Once they are buckled in, Aunt Bridget closes the door and lets out a huge sigh. "Thank you, Finley."

"You're welcome."

"I tell you, I've never seen them like this. Coming over here for days and days at a time. That's certainly never happened before. They usually think Grandma's house is so boring. 'There's nothing to *do* here.' 'She'll make us *clean*.' 'Can we go *home* yet?' But now? You'd think taking them for two short days is the end of the world."

Aunt Bridget looks like she cannot decide if she wants to smile. She brushes hair out of my eyes, and her fingers are warm against my skin, like Mom's. I try not to lean in to her, but I think I might a little bit.

"You're working some kind of magic on them, Finley."

Avery passes by on her way to the garage, wearing her

orange paint shorts, a Led Zeppelin T-shirt, and a crooked smile. "Black magic, you mean."

Aunt Bridget rolls her eyes. "Don't mind Avery. She's a teenager. She can't help being obnoxious."

I laugh, which feels strange; this is sharp and shiny Aunt Bridget, after all. I know she is angry at Dad. I always wonder if she is angry at me, too.

But then Aunt Bridget holds me close and kisses the top of my head. I hear her heartbeat, and I wonder, since we are Harts, if mine sounds just like hers.

"I'm glad you're here," she whispers, and instead of answering, I press my cheek harder against her chest.

When they leave, I run after their car down the long driveway, waving back at Dex and Ruth, until I can no longer keep up.

Mom calls at 7:57 on Thursday. She has not called in a few days, and I was not expecting her to tonight, but I guess she felt brave enough to conquer her phone fear today. When her picture pops up on the screen—her freckled face kissing my freckled face—I smile. It's impossible to look at that picture without smiling. Our faces are so squashed and happy in it.

If someone found my notebook and read what I have written about my mother, they might think I don't like her very much:

> Mom snapped at me tonight when I messed
> up her stack of papers. Then Dad snapped

*at her for snapping at me, and now they are downstairs yelling at each other. I hate her.*

*Mom's yelling again. I hate it when she's like this. She gets so stressed. I don't know how to talk to her.*

*Mom didn't let me take my notebook with me when we ran errands today. She doesn't get me at all, and I don't get her, and I don't want to.*

*I wonder if Mom is where I get my blue days from. They have to come from somewhere, don't they?*

I am not sure which idea is more terrifying: that my blue days come from my mother, or that they don't come from anywhere in particular. That they are these toxic clouds floating through the universe, and they thought I was worth latching on to.

But when I am with Mom, and she is happy, I feel like I am not simply myself but a piece of something bigger and stronger.

"Finley!" Even through the phone connection Mom's voice is a clear, crisp bell. "Oh, sweetie. I'm sorry it's been days, I really am. I've been so busy."

I sneak downstairs and out onto the Green. Grandma has the kitchen windows open while she bakes, and a Jimmy Reed song drifts across the yard with the dragonflies. The freshly cut grass is warm and scratchy on my bare feet.

"I really feel rotten, baby. But you know how crazy this time of year gets."

With Mom, every time of year is a crazy time of year. How are she and Dad possibly talking about anything important if all they do is work?

I curl my toes into the grass. It's almost like I can feel the green color seep up through the bottoms of my feet, sleepy and slow, like drinking a glass of water on a hot day. "I know, Mom. It's okay."

"So, tell me everything. How's it going?"

Mom asks me this whenever we talk, but this time I am not sure how to answer her. My summer has, over the past week, become much more complicated than I anticipated.

"Fine," I say.

(But there was a fire, and no one talks about it. No big deal.)

I hear Mom typing on her computer. "And how is everyone?" she asks.

How best to describe the mood at Hart House tonight?

From here I can see inside the big living room windows. Dex and Ruth are galloping around on their hands and knees, probably pretending to be unicorns, which is Dex's favorite game. Gretchen is running back and forth between the kitchen and the living room; each time she comes back, she holds a fresh cookie. Kennedy is braiding Avery's hair, who is braiding Aunt Dee's hair. Stick and Aunt Bridget are dancing to Grandma's music. Aunt Bridget holds a drink; Stick is wearing a glittery paper pirate hat that Ruth made.

Uncle Nelson and Grandpa sit in the big leather chairs, trying to watch TV, but I can't imagine they can actually hear it.

I grin, watching them. "Same as always. Loud."

Mom laughs—her real laugh. It is this great big guffaw she tries to hide when she speaks with clients because she thinks it sounds unprofessional.

Whenever I make her laugh her real laugh, I feel like I will never have a blue day again.

"Your dad said Hart House was always a bit of a zoo," she says. "I guess that hasn't changed, huh? What else? I feel like . . . What else?"

"You feel like what?"

"I just . . . I miss you so much. I feel like I haven't seen you in months, and it's only been, what? Five weeks?"

I sit down in one of the swings and push myself back and forth, trying not to think of what the past month has been like for my parents. Did they send me to Grandma's to protect me from whatever is happening at home?

Or did they send me away because I was making things worse?

"Four weeks. Ish."

"Well. Feels longer to me. How are you? Really."

"I'm okay. Really."

"You would tell me, right? If you were miserable?"

"Yes," I lie. I don't lie about many things, but I always lie about that. There is enough going on in my parents' lives. They don't need to worry about me.

(I am fine.)

(I should be happy, so I will be.)

Mom sighs. "I'm just checking, is all."

"I'm having fun. Mostly."

"Oh, honey. You're not still scared of Avery, are you?"

"*Mom.* I'm not scared of her, but she's seventeen. We have nothing to talk about. And she's so pretty."

"So are you, Finley."

I roll my eyes. "You're my mom. That doesn't count."

"It does too. It counts double."

"You sound like Ruth. She thinks she and Dex should get double votes, double ice cream, double everything. She says since they're twins, they have special powers, so we have to keep them happy or else they'll turn to the dark side. She's . . . a little nuts."

Mom chuckles. "Remind me again. That's Bridget's daughter, right?"

It still feels strange to hear Mom say Aunt Bridget's name. "Yeah."

I wonder: If we had been a normal family all this time, would Mom and Bridget be friends?

"Are you still going on drives with your grandfather?"

"Sometimes." And then I am thinking about the article, and Grandpa's face as he read it—like it was an article not about a fire but about the end of the world.

Does Mom know about the Travers fire?

The question begs to be let out, but I don't allow myself to ask it. Not tonight. Who knows when Mom will call again?

I dig my toes into the ground so hard, I feel dirt wedge beneath my nails.

(Act normal, Finley.)

(Nothing is wrong here. Nothing at all.)

"Did you know Grandpa does crossword puzzles too?" I ask her. "And Uncle Nelson, but he's not as good at them as Dad is."

"No one's as good at crossword puzzles as your dad. Except for maybe you. But don't tell him I said that."

Hearing Mom talk about Dad like everything is the same, like we are at home sneaking pepperonis off Dad's slices of pizza and trying not to burst out laughing—it makes me feel light inside, like I am made of wings, flying up and up.

"Sometimes I go with Stick when she runs," I continue, "but just part of the way."

"I'm so glad you're getting to spend time with your aunts. What about Dee?"

"Aunt Dee . . . I don't know. She's nice, but sometimes I think she's afraid to talk to me. She looks at me like . . ."

"What is it? What do you mean?"

"Like she feels bad for me. Or she wants to say something but then she decides not to."

"Ah. I see."

I pause, drawing circles in the dirt with my toe. "She told me she loves Dad. That she always will."

Mom goes quiet. "I'm sure that's true."

My wings slip away from me. I am losing her.

"Grandpa likes Beethoven," I say quickly. I squeeze my eyes shut. Great. Beethoven. One more thing to remind Mom about Dad. Why can I not think of safer things to say?

But Mom just laughs and says, "Don't you mean Beethoven?"

I relax against the swing. "Yeah. We listen to that a lot and talk about random stuff. There are a ton of cows out where we drive. He's really funny, actually. He's always making these comments, like he always has really good comebacks. But then he can get really serious, too. The other day he and Gretchen were playing chess, and I literally saw Gretchen *sweating*, she was so nervous. He's intense."

That makes Mom laugh again. "I've heard that your grandfather has always been a formidable man."

"He wears nice pants and shirts *every day*. Even when he's sitting around the house or whatever."

"Your dad once told me that when he was growing up, they had to change for dinner," Mom says. "You couldn't wear sweats or pajamas. You had to put on nice, clean clothes. Dresses for the girls. Slacks for your father."

I think of my typical dinner uniform at home—my pajamas. Curled up on the couch. A plate on my lap, and Dad behind me at his desk, and Mom to my left in the kitchen, and something deep in my chest shifts, aching.

I push myself back and forth on the swing. "That's insane. I'm so glad they don't still do that."

"It was your grandmother's thing, apparently."

"She loves things to look nice."

Mom pauses. "Yes, she certainly does."

"I think . . . She kind of scares me."

"Goodness, why is that?"

Because she almost fainted in the kitchen last week.

Because she does not like to talk about *upsetting topics*.

Because most of the time I cannot see past her smile—but when I do, I see someone who is angry and sad and tired. And I am afraid it is somehow because of me. I am afraid I remind her of Dad, and whatever he did.

"Because," I say, "I don't know. She wears these pearls all the time, and she's constantly cleaning. She makes us clean too, every day. Not normal cleaning. Major cleaning. Like the president's coming over or something. She cooks *every meal*, and she does all this volunteer stuff—this clinic and the library and backpacks for kids. And did you know she and Grandpa gave a bunch of money to the city? Like, to the library and the parks and all that."

Another pause, longer this time.

"I did know that," Mom says. "Yes, of course. They got to meet the mayor and everything. I didn't know your dad yet, but . . . yes. I remember him telling me about that. Isn't it great of them, Finley, to get involved in their community?"

Mom has started using her work voice—light and fake and professional, and not Mom at all.

I am tired of adults with secrets in their voices.

"Yeah," I say. "It's great."

It is like someone has inserted a glass wall between us so we cannot touch each other, and I don't know where it came from, and I hate it.

"So," Mom says, after a minute, "Finley. There's something I wanted to talk to you about, before we say good night."

I twist the swing's ropes; the rough fibers bite into my palms.

I bet I know what she wants to talk about.

Her. Dad. Her and Dad, and me, and our house, and our things, and our family, and what will happen next. The fake smiles. The future. I'm not an idiot.

I will not listen to one word of it.

Behind me a door slams. I turn and see someone running down the hill from the Bailey house to the cluster of trees hiding the Post Office.

Jack.

I wave at him. Mom is talking, but I am not listening. I hear words—*your father*, *trying really hard*, *not working*—but I am not listening. I will not, I *cannot*.

I wave and wave at Jack. Jack, Jack, please see me.

He whistles like a mourning dove, which is the signal we use when we can't shout, to keep Grandma and Grandpa from hearing. He waves at me to come down, and I can see his smile even in the dark.

This late, the Everwood crawls with shapes and shadows, but I am not afraid of them. Those shadows belong to me. I know just how they feel on my skin and in my hair and under my bare feet.

My Everwood may have secrets, but it never lies. Not to me.

"Mom, I have to go," I say, and hang up without waiting for an answer.

ATE ONE NIGHT THE ORPHAN *girl awoke to find herself being blindfolded.*

*"Who's there?" she demanded. "What are your intentions?"*

*"You'll see," came the voice of the lady knight.*

*As she was led through the Everwood, the orphan girl heard others—the champion, the young squires, the three Rotters.*

*"Are you scared?" asked the pirate captain, laughter in his voice.*

*"It will take much more than a blindfold to frighten me," said the orphan girl boldly, and she felt pleased when the captain replied, "I know."*

*When the blindfold was removed, the orphan girl found herself in the Wasteland, the Bone House a crooked shadow looming overhead.*

*The captain helped the orphan girl onto a large stump. The others gathered around her in a circle.*

*"Orphan girl," the pirate said, "we have brought you here tonight to thank you for your bravery, your kindness, and your leadership. Without you, we would not have begun our adventures, and the Rotters would no doubt still be an object of scorn."*

*"We have a crown!" cried the youngest pirate, who was immediately silenced by the young lady squire, who tackled him to the ground for talking out of turn. The champion, acting quickly, separated them, and then scolded the lady squire*

*for acting so undignified on such an important occasion.*

*"We do indeed have a crown," continued the captain, once the moment of chaos had passed. "For you, orphan girl, deserve a grander title. You are not simply an orphan girl. You are our queen."*

*Overcome, the orphan girl knelt on her throne. The young squires and the youngest pirate adorned her in necklaces made of paper flowers.*

*The pirate captain gave her a crown. A circle of twigs tied together with vines, it was a perfect fit for the orphan girl's head.*

*But she was an orphan girl no longer. She was a queen.*

*"I accept this crown," the queen of the Everwood declared, "and pledge to you, my loyal subjects, that I will do everything in my power to protect you, and our Everwood, from whatever evil may lurk in the world."*

*The knight blessed the queen's shoulders with her sword. The Rotters crowed their jubilation to the skies. The champion led a dance around the queen's throne.*

*Afterward the queen told them stories of the Everwood, from the lonely days when she still traveled on her own.*

*The dagger in her pocket shifted, sharpened. The queen felt the prick of its blade.*

*But she ignored it and what it might mean.*

*For the queen, as you can imagine, had never been happier than she was at this moment.*

*She even began to think her great sadness would now, at long last, disappear.*

# 22

No.

No.

*No.*

It is happening again.

I wake up, unable to move, pinned to my bed by something I cannot name.

My sheets are wet with sweat, and so am I.

My heart is racing, and so is my mind.

I imagine a spool of thread falling from Mom's hands as she sews a button back onto a tufted sofa cushion. The spool rolls away and away, down the stairs, its thread spinning loose faster and faster . . .

That is me right now.

I am so close to losing myself.

I cannot breathe very well; there is a giant clamp on my chest.

I lie still and try to think of what happened on Friday night:

My coronation.

My cousins surrounding me, dancing in my honor, and Jack, placing the crown on my head.

Think of that, Finley. Think of that.

Focus on those memories.

You were happy then, weren't you? You were, you were.

So why not now? Why do you feel so heavy *now*?

You are not the Travers family, dead and buried. You are not the Bone House, broken and alone.

You live in a mansion, with rooms full of people who have declared you to be their queen.

BUT.

(My brain screams this.)

BUT . . .

You will never be as pretty as Avery, or as brave as Gretchen, or as kind as Kennedy, or as funny and wild as Jack.

You are small and strange.

You are far from home.

You can't stop feeling sad. You are *wrong*. You are *weak*.

Your parents are getting a—

They are getting a—

A train horn howls in the distance. There are tracks near Hart House, somewhere through the woods. I keep hearing the horn, but I have not yet found the tracks. I imagine that I can hear the train's wheels turning, churning, chugging, and then the train's wheels are my heartbeat, and then . . .

I hurry toward the bathroom at the end of the hallway, the one I share with Avery.

I throw open the toilet-seat lid and kneel in front of it. Maybe I need to throw up.

But that's not it.

I do not know what *it* is.

I know I should be happy, and sleeping, but instead I feel like I do not fit in my own body.

A door opens.

Avery.

"Finley?"

Oh, Avery, why did you have to wake up? I do not want you to see me right now.

You cannot know. You cannot understand.

*I* do not understand.

"Finley." She sits beside me on the floor. "Are you sick?"

I shake my head.

"What's wrong?"

I whisper, "I don't know. I feel . . ."

How to finish that sentence?

I feel sad.

I feel heavy.

I feel itchy, and afraid, and out of breath, and like my brain is on fire, and nervous, and guilty for being nervous, and like I am about to cry.

Will I be like this forever?

I will, I will, I won't, I *can't*. Please.

Are you listening, whoever is in charge of such things? Please, do not do this to me.

I shake my head.

"What's going on here? Avery?"

A new voice. Grandma's voice.

Oh no. Grandma, in her peach silk robe, her hair clean and neat and white.

(So perfect, even at night? *How?*)

If Avery wouldn't understand, then Grandma . . . she might hate me.

She might be afraid of me, if she knew.

If she knew *what?* What *is* this? What is wrong with me?

She might make me leave, separate me from my cousins. From Aunt Bridget, with a heartbeat like mine.

"Finley's got a tummy ache," says Avery. "Probably from all those cookies after dinner."

Thank you, Avery. Thank you, thank you.

"Yeah." I put a hand on my stomach. "I think I had, like, ten? At *least.*"

Grandma does not look convinced. She stares at me like I am a spot on her spotless white floor.

She is trying to hide it, but I can see. I am not a Hart, not to her, not ever.

Harts do not freak out for no reason in the middle of the night.

"Would you like some medicine?" asks Grandma. "Something to calm your stomach?"

"No, that's okay. I'm fine. I'll be fine."

She fills a cup with water, gives it to me, feels my forehead, frowns, wipes her fingers on a hand towel, tries to hide the wiping, fails. I see, and I know what that means.

I do not blame her.

I would not want to be contaminated by me either.

"Drink up," she says. "I'm sure you'll feel better in the morning."

No, I won't.

"Okay."

I never feel better.

(Not even now that I am queen.)

"Thanks, Grandma. Sorry to wake you up."

"It isn't any trouble. Wake me if you have trouble getting back to sleep, all right?"

(As if I would ever bother her like that.)

Once Grandma has gone back to bed, everything is quiet. I can feel Avery looking at me, but I ignore her because I am so humiliated, I want to melt into the floor.

And I still cannot breathe quite right. I am still sweating, and still shaking, and I know what I look like right now because I have often examined myself in the mirror during such moments.

I look pale. Sick. Hollowed out.

Avery does not seem to care that I am ignoring her.

She scoots closer and pulls me into her arms, and even though I am sweaty, even when I start to cry, she holds on tight.

# 23

WHAT DO YOU DO WHEN you wake up in the middle of the night, in a house that is not yours, and lose yourself to the strange sadness and fear inside you worse than you ever have before, and humiliate yourself in front of your most terrifying family members?

If you are me, you sleep.

A lot.

On Sunday, I think maybe around lunchtime, Gretchen tiptoes into my dark room.

"Finley?" She sits on the bed, where I lie under a mountain of blankets. "Are you okay? Grandma said you got sick last night."

If only it *were* some kind of sickness. Maybe I could take medicine or undergo a radical, experimental surgery.

Something to cut the sickness out.

But it isn't that.

It is sadness.

No reason to be sad. So many rational, listable reasons to not be sad.

(I know; I have listed them.)

And yet it remains inside me.

"Yeah," I mumble. "Too many cookies."

"Oh, I've *totally* done that before. Grandma's cookies are so good and yet so very evil. I think the more of them you eat, the more of them you have to keep on eating. Like a curse. Maybe she got the recipe from one of the Everwood witches. That sounds like something they would do. Right? Or maybe *Grandma* is a witch."

"She's not a witch," I say into my pillow. "She's too clean."

Gretchen scoots closer to me. "Hey. Really, are you okay? Do you need me to bring you something?"

More blankets? A sadness extractor, freshly sharpened?

"Do you ever have bad days?" I ask her.

"Sure. Mom says that's when you get up on the wrong side of the bed."

"So you feel sad?"

"Yeah, I guess. But I just go outside or run around or Mom does something doofy, and I feel better."

Ah. I see.

Then our bad days are not the same.

On my bad days, running around or going outside or being doofy changes nothing.

My sadness still sticks in me like a sword.

Gretchen pokes me. "You think you'll be okay for the fireworks tomorrow?"

The Fourth of July. My summer here is half over. "Yeah. I'm just tired."

"Jack left a note at the Post Office. Says he wants to go to the Bone House tonight. He says he likes cleaning. He's incredibly weird."

I know I should want to go too. After all, I am the queen. It was my idea to start cleaning up the Bone House, to make it back into a home. I found the photograph. I led myself and Gretchen into the Wasteland, that first day.

I have a responsibility to my forest, to my people.

And part of me does want to go, truly.

But the rest of me sinks lower into the mattress at the thought of having to get out from under these covers. The idea of even moving my hand to touch Gretchen is overwhelming.

It is much, much easier to stay still.

Until I have recovered from last night is all. Just until then.

As Mom would say after a particularly stressful day, I need more time to "recover my equilibrium."

There isn't anything wrong with that, is there?

"You'll feel better by then, right?" asks Gretchen.

"Maybe," I say. "I'll try. I'm going to nap for a while."

"Well, we'll be outside. Dex wants to paint the walls inside the Tower, and I think we should let him so Kennedy doesn't pull her hair out. That's okay with you?"

"The painting, or Kennedy pulling her hair out?"

Gretchen snorts. "Now that's funny. Feel better, okay?"

(I think that might not be an option for me.)

"I will." I pretend to yawn. "Thanks, Gretchen."

Then she is gone, and I am alone, which is what I wanted—but it doesn't make me feel any better.

I wake up later and dig out my phone from underneath my pillows.

I find Dad in my recent contacts. My thumb hovers over the call button.

But what would I say?

*Dad, I am freaking out for no reason.*

*Dad, I am pretending I am sick today so I don't have to talk to anyone.*

*Dad, I hurt, and I don't know why.*

But then what? Then he would come and get me, and I would have to be at home, with him and Mom and their problems.

(Am I one of their problems?)

(I cannot be one of their problems. I will not allow it.)

I slide the phone underneath the pillows and wrap myself back in my blankets.

It will go away on its own, whatever this is. It has to.

I will *make* it go away.

Even sad people have to eventually leave their beds for the most basic reason: hunger.

I have missed lunch, but there are sandwiches in the refrigerator.

I eat only because I know I must eat.

But it isn't like I want to die.

I have heard of such things as "suicidal thoughts." Sometimes I have even examined my sadness with that in mind:

*Are these suicidal thoughts? Do I want to die?*

No.

*Do I want to hurt myself?*

No. I am simply sad.

So it isn't that.

But when I eat this ham-and-cheese sandwich, I am eating it like a car consumes gasoline. I am not sure I actually taste it.

There is bread, cheese, ham, mayonnaise.

I am a machine obeying my programming.

(Chew, chew, chew, swallow.)

The house is quiet. Afternoon light pours in through the sunroom and warms my toes.

I hear someone moving around in the garage and peek out the window.

Avery, painting, earbuds in, bandana tied around her head.

I cannot ever tell what she is painting. They aren't pictures, really; they are more like the floating things you see when you close your eyes. Colors and shapes, and thick brushstrokes that cut the whole thing in two.

My hand rests on the doorknob.

Should I apologize for what happened last night?

*Sorry for crying all over your shirt.*

*Sorry for being gross and sweaty. Sorry you lied for me.*

*Sorry for being such a freak, Avery.*

I cannot do it; I am too frightened.

So I wander.

I could go outside; every now and then I hear one of my cousins shouting.

But . . . shouting. And sunshine, and having to talk, and answering questions: *How are you feeling? Are you okay? Did you eat something? Did you throw up?*

The prospect is overwhelming.

So I wander through the quiet, cool house.

The carpet is white. The walls are dark. The furniture is polished.

The piano, in the corner of the living room, is old.

I press my fingers to random keys. I don't know the first thing about playing music, but it seems like the keys I press make a song anyway, which makes me feel a little better.

I even start to think that maybe I *will* go apologize to Avery. She would understand, right? She seemed to understand last night.

But then I hear a strange sound—like someone crying out in pain.

It is coming from the hallway leading to Grandma and Grandpa's bedroom.

I have never been to that part of the house, but concern for my grandmother—as much as she terrifies me—pushes me forward.

I don't think Grandpa is home. He has probably gone for one of his drives.

What if something is wrong with Grandma? I am the only one around.

I sneak down the hallway. It is colder and darker than the rest of the house. Family pictures line the walls, but I don't see Dad in any of them. They are all of my aunts, their husbands, their children.

I feel like a shadow in this dark hallway, like I do not entirely exist.

Maybe this moment will change things.

I will save Grandma from whatever is distressing her, and prove myself worthy of her.

She will no longer look at me like I am a spot to be cleaned.

She will take pictures of me, and add them to this wall, right beside my cousins.

I feel a tiny tug of happiness inside me.

Then I step into her bedroom, and I see—

Grandma, sitting at her vanity, her eyes red.

Grandpa, holding a syringe to her arm.

*Injecting her.*

Grandma, adjusting her hair—which *moves*, all in one piece, sliding across her scalp.

And I understand: That is not her real hair.

It is a wig.

Medicine.

A wig, clean and white and smooth.

I was not supposed to see this.

They turn and stare at me. I must have made a sound.

"I—"

Grandpa sits on the bed and rubs a hand over his face. "Oh, Finley."

Grandma stares at me, her lips drawn tight.

I was not supposed to see this. Was not, was not.

"I'm sorry," I whisper, and turn and run.

# 24

I RUN OUTSIDE, BECAUSE IT is the only safe place I can think of to go.

My cousins. They will know what to do.

They can explain to me what I have just seen.

I bypass the stone steps and slide down the dirt wall of the pit.

The Tower—there it is. There they are, painting.

Ruth and Bennett have green, Dex-sized handprints in the center of their faces. They grin at me from their spot in the dirt.

Kennedy has blue paint in her hair and looks exasperated—but less so when Cole puts his hand on hers.

Gretchen is trying to explain to Dex how the spaceship he has painted *cannot* be as big as the sun Gretchen has painted. It is technologically impossible. Kennedy says, "He can paint whatever he wants, you weirdo."

And Jack . . . Jack is staring over my shoulder, a paintbrush in his hand.

Someone is following me.

I turn.

Grandpa—hurrying down the stone steps with storm

clouds on his face. Staring at Jack. Staring at Cole, holding Kennedy's hand.

*Baileys.* My dad's words return to me.

*The Baileys—their dad, I mean—he wasn't a good kid. He did . . . bad things. He's not safe to be around, and if he has kids now, I bet they're not much different.*

*I wouldn't trust them for anything. Okay?*

(But you're wrong, Dad.)

(I'd trust Jack in a heartbeat.)

*Okay? Finley?*

"Finley?" Grandpa is speaking. "Finley!"

I flinch. Grandpa's voice sounds even sharper than it did in the car, when he threw the article out the window.

"Yes?"

"You and Kennedy take your cousins back to the house."

Gretchen protests. "But, Grandpa, we were—"

"I don't want to hear it. Get back in the house, right now."

Dex begins to cry. Kennedy hurries away with him and Ruth. After a second Gretchen goes with them.

I cannot leave.

I am afraid for Cole and Bennett. And for Jack.

I have never seen Grandpa look like this. He is red in the face, and his eyes are made of metal. Where is my grandpa who loves Beethoven? Where is my grandpa who looks like Dad and builds tree patios and knows how to pick out the perfect batch of strawberries?

"What the hell do you think you're doing?" he spits at the

Baileys. "You know you are to never—*never*—come near this house, this property, or any of my grandchildren."

Hearing Grandpa say *hell* is like hearing a clap of thunder.

"Sir," Jack says, "let me explain—"

"I don't want an explanation. I want you to get home. Now."

Bennett bursts into tears, but this changes nothing. Grandpa's face is made of stone.

"Grandpa, please, it was my fault," I say. "I invited them over."

Grandpa whirls around, his arm raised, and for an instant I think he is going to hit me.

Jack runs over and shoves Grandpa away from me.

Grandpa pauses, staring at me like he can't believe what is happening. His eyes are wide; he is breathing hard. He lowers his hand, looks at it like it is not his own.

I grab Jack's hand and put myself in front of him. Grandpa won't hit me, he won't hit me, he won't.

"Grandpa, please," I say. "I'm sorry. They'll go home. Okay?"

I squeeze Jack's hand.

He squeezes mine back.

"Get out of here," Grandpa says quietly.

None of us move.

"Get out!"

The Baileys run, Bennett crying in Cole's arms. Jack looks back once, over his shoulder.

Now it is just me and Grandpa and the empty Tower.

Grandpa stares at it for a long time, and then rips down the Everwood banner. Cole's signature is obvious in the bottom corner.

"I'm sorry—"

"Hush, Finley. You've done enough. "

"But they didn't do anything—"

"You don't know *anything* about those boys, or their family. They're not the kind of people we associate with." Grandpa stares at the Bailey house for a long time, and I recognize the look on his face. I have seen it many times on my own.

(Grandpa, why are you afraid?)

I cannot believe he would hurt me.

But would he have hurt my friends?

(Not *my* grandpa, not him, not him.)

"Get yourself back inside," he says, "and don't you tell anyone—*anyone*—what you saw today. I mean it, Finley. Do not test me on that."

He does not have to be more specific.

I will never forget what I saw in his and Grandma's bedroom, and what it could mean.

Avery stands at the top of the pit. She must have heard the noise. She watches me as I hurry up the stone steps and rush into the house, but she doesn't say anything.

I am glad. There are too many terrible things I could say, if I had to open my mouth and answer her.

*Grandma is sick.*

*I hate Grandpa.*

*There are no pictures of me on the wall outside their bedroom.*

*To them, I do not really exist.*


No one makes me come down for dinner.

Perhaps they do not want me there.

Fine. That is just fine with me.

I will lie here in my bed with the window open and listen to the trees talking to me, and they will tell me everyone's secrets, and when I finally go downstairs, I will know everything there is to know, and no one will be able to frighten me.

Not even Grandpa. Not even Grandma.

No one.

I cuddle my pillow, the one I brought from home. It smells like our apartment.

Someone knocks on my door. I do not answer.

"Finley?"

It is Grandpa. My heart pounds itself back to life, but I do not move. He cracks open the door and steps inside.

"I owe you an apology," he says quietly. "I'm sorry I frightened you. I frightened *me*."

I do not answer.

"But you can't see those boys anymore. All right, Finley? I won't budge on that, and neither will your grandmother."

The clock on my nightstand ticks, ticks, ticks. "If I do—"

"You won't," Grandpa interrupts.

"If I do—"

"*Finley.*"

"Will you make everyone stop talking to me, like Grandma did to Dad?"

*Tick, tick.*

*Tick, tick.*

"Good night, Finley," says Grandpa. His voice is a closed door.

When he's gone, I close my eyes and listen to the trees talking.

*What do I do?* I ask them.

*What do I do?*

*What do I do now?*

Then I lie very still and wait for an answer.

**O**NE MORNING THE QUEEN OF *the Everwood awoke to a dark sky.*

*The trees around her were completely bare.*

*She lay on a nest of brittle, gray leaves. Everything she touched crumbled to ash.*

*She drew her cloak about her and shivered.*

*Someone, somewhere was watching her.*

*"Hello?" she called out into the gloom.*

*"Your friends are not here," came a low voice. There was a fluttering of wings, a soft, cold breeze against the queen's skin.*

*A crow landed on a nearby branch, its feathers as sharp as its black beak.*

*The queen reached for the pocket where she kept the dagger.*

*It was empty.*

*The crow watched coldly.*

*"What do you want?" asked the queen.*

*"I want you to leave here," replied the crow, "and never come back."*

*"Leave? Leave the Everwood?"*

*The crow inclined its shining head.*

*"But why? I am the queen."*

*"Queen?" The crow let out a small, rough laugh. "A crown does not make a queen."*

*"But they chose me."*

"Who did? Your friends? Of course they did. They don't know what you carry inside you."

The queen bristled. "And you do?"

"Only you can truly know."

"Then what are you doing here? If you're not going to help me, leave."

Howls, hungry and fierce, made the queen whirl. She expected to see bared teeth and glowing eyes, but she saw only trees bending in the wind. Gray leaves fell; the air smelled of smoke.

The crow perched on the queen's knee. "Child," it said, "they are coming."

"Who? How can I stop them?"

With its beak the crow pulled aside the queen's collar.

There, over her heart, beneath her skin, roiled a shifting darkness.

The queen recoiled. "What is that?"

"You know better than I do," said the crow. Then it pecked her chest, and with each strike it drew out strings of darkness like tar from a pool.

The queen shuddered to look at this thing inside herself. She hated the sight of it.

When the crow began to gasp and heave, she shoved it away. Its feathers cut her fingers.

"It's hurting you," said the queen. "Please, stop."

"It hurts me only because you are fighting me," explained the crow. "Do not be afraid of yourself. We are all both light and dark. We are both joy and—"

"This darkness is not me," snapped the queen. "You know not of what you speak."

The crow regarded her calmly, and the pity on its face was too much for the queen to bear. She turned away. "Leave me, I said. You know nothing."

"I know we might already be too late," said the crow, and it glided away into the night.

# 25

### WHAT IT MEANS TO BE A HART

- You look pretty even after sprinting across a forest.
- You look completely unaffected even when you are up to your eyeballs in garbage that smells like feet and rotten eggs.
- If something is wrong with you, it must be fixed.

ON THE FOURTH OF JULY, Dex cracks under pressure.

Upon questioning him, Aunt Bridget discovers that, on top of befriending the Baileys, we have also been visiting the Bone House.

When she tells Grandma and Grandpa, I am standing right there in front of them.

Aunt Bridget shoots me concerned looks I can see out of the corner of my eye, but I do not look back at her.

Traitor. I thought she loved me, and here she is, ruining everything.

Walking in on Grandma's shot was bad, but this is worse. Grandma does not get angry or make threats. She smooths down her shirt and says, "I'm so disappointed in you that I can hardly think, Finley."

"Candace, hold on," Grandpa begins. "She doesn't know—"

"Go upstairs to your room, right now." Grandma turns away, as though she cannot stand looking at me. "We'll speak about this later."

But we don't speak about it. Not that night, watching the fireworks in town.

(Everyone laughing, everyone gasping and pointing—except for me. Except for Grandma and Grandpa.)

Not the next night either.

## WHAT IT MEANS TO BE A HART

- If something is wrong with you, it must be fixed. Quietly.

It has been decided that, considering recent events, something really ought to be done about me.

It's not that I am a bad kid.

But I am problematic.

I hear Grandma say so. Over the next couple of days, Hart House is full of whispers:

*Before Finley came, our grandchildren never—never—associated with white trash like the Bailey boys. They would never have even thought of it.*

*Before Finley came, our grandchildren would never have wandered off into those dangerous woods. All the way back to That House, can you believe it?*

"That House" is obviously the Bone House. For some reason Grandma and Grandpa speak about it in code words, but it's obvious what they mean.

(But why wouldn't they just say the Travers house?)

(Why do they not speak about my heroic aunts? The Hart girls: Wonder Woman times three!)

*Did you know? I found Finley in the bathroom the other night, crouching in front of the toilet. She said it was a stomachache, but I don't believe her.*

*How can you believe someone who has been sneaking her cousins off into the woods like a bunch of delinquents?*

*Do you think she got into the liquor? Those Bailey boys might have put her up to it. I wouldn't put it past them.*

*That notebook of hers . . . if she's not dragging her cousins through the woods, she's making lists in her notebook. She has pages and pages of them.*

*Isn't that a bit obsessive?*

*Doesn't she strike you as somewhat . . . troubled? Gretchen says Finley writes in her notebook to keep from being sad.*

*What does that mean? Sad about what? Has she said anything to you? Why doesn't she say anything?*

*She's so different from us.*

*Lewis was always quiet too, and look what happened with him. He left us. He was never like the rest of us.*

*I think it would be best if—*

*Plus, it would get her out of her head—*

*And we should keep the other kids away from her, for a while—*

*Don't you think?*

*It's for the best.*

"It" is meeting with a children's psychologist once a week.

All I know about psychologists is that they treat people who have something wrong with their brains.

(Twelve-letter word for "Freud, for example.")

On Thursday, Grandma sits in Grandpa's office and tells Dad about the situation over the phone.

I sit in the hallway outside the closed glass doors and watch her, trying to read her lips.

I hope this makes her uncomfortable.

After ten minutes Grandma opens the door. "Your father wants to speak with you."

I take the phone. "Dad?"

"Fin. Finley, sweetheart, what were you thinking?"

My eyes fill up with tears. "What do you mean?"

"The Baileys, Fin. I told you not to be friends with them. I told you your grandparents wouldn't like it."

I can practically hear him running his hand through his hair, over and over.

"Dad, I'm sorry, but we didn't do anything wrong. We were playing."

"And taking your cousins to some strange house late at night?"

"The Bone House isn't strange. It's just lonely."

There is a pause so long and heavy that I feel it against my skin.

"I know, Fin," Dad says at last. "I know."

"Grandma and Grandpa think I should go see a psychologist."

Another sigh. "Yeah. She told me. Do you think that would help?"

"Help what?"

"Your mom and I will drive down and come with you."

No.

(I am not broken.)

*No.*

(I am not one of their problems.)

I start pacing. I want to kick Grandpa's books off the shelves. "There's nothing wrong with me."

"Nobody's saying that. But maybe talking to someone will help you figure out some things. We've been thinking for some time now that it might be a good idea for all of us to go, together. Maybe this is some kind of sign."

"Like what? Help me figure out what things?"

"Like your notebook."

"What's wrong with my notebook?"

"Your grandma says you write it in constantly."

"Not that much. And it's not like she watches me 24/7."

(I bet she will now.)

"You can also talk to the counselor about me and your mom. Anything you might be feeling in that regard. We can all talk together."

"Stop using your professor voice, Dad."

"We can drive down next week—"

*No.* All of a sudden my heart goes wild with panic.

I won't listen to what they have to say. They won't come here. They *can't*. Because that might mean they are done talking. That they have worked out everything they could work out.

Because that will mean . . .

"If you come down here," I tell him, "I won't go. I swear I won't."

Dad switches off like a radio. I stare out the office window at the Everwood trees. They pull at me. I tap the glass. *Hello, trees.*

"Your mom and I think it might help," Dad says quietly. "We'll let you go alone, if that's what you want, but when you come home, maybe we can go with you. What do you say? I know this is a hard summer, for all of us—"

"Not for me. I'm having tons of fun."

Then I hang up.

# 26

THE DAY OF MY FIRST appointment arrives. I will have one every Tuesday afternoon at three o'clock.

Last night, instead of sleeping, I looked up Dr. Bristow's patient reviews online.

I had to sneak down to the computer in Grandpa's office, because Grandma took my phone from me. I am not allowed to use it except for my nightly calls with Mom and Dad.

Grandma says the Internet is toxic.

Instead I should help her clean these pans.

Let's bake. We have run out of cookies.

(We must be normal now.)

Dr. Bristow's ratings are high.

I do not think my grandparents would associate with a doctor who had bad reviews.

Before we leave, Grandma presents me with a sundress to wear to my appointment. Her fingernails are a pale, polished pink.

"You always wear those baggy T-shirts," she says to me. "I thought this would be a nice change."

The dress is pretty—white with pale blue stripes—but it is inappropriate for the Everwood.

The only queens who wear gowns are queens who live in palaces and hold court in shining halls.

Queens who live in forests and run wild with pirates must choose more practical attire—for combat, for exploration.

But what do queens do when everything has been taken from them, when their world is changing?

Queens hold their heads high.

When I am dressed, Grandma stands behind me and sweeps my hair up into a knot. Together we look in the mirror.

"You look lovely, Finley," she says. "You even look a little bit like me, when I was your age."

(When she was my age—in a house with not very much love, not very much money.)

(Now *there* is a reason to be sad.)

I stare at our reflection. I wonder if Grandma is erasing the old image of Finley Hart in her mind and replacing it with this Finley, in the sundress, who is trying her best to achieve a magazine smile, who is seeing a psychologist because she is a spot who must be cleaned.

Who looks like her grandmother once did.

The dress feels stiff around me, like I'm wearing folded cardboard, but I sit quietly in the car while Grandma drives me. *Grandma*, driving me. She is skipping her afternoon nap to take me to this place. She looks very thin in the driver's seat.

I suppose it is tiring, to be sick, to be hiding your sick.

It is certainly tiring to hide what's happening from my cousins.

They know nothing about my appointments, and I would prefer to keep it that way. They think the adults have decided we need more structure to our summer, and that's why we have basically been grounded from playing outside.

That's why my cousins haven't been coming over to Hart House as much over the past few days, only showing up for a dinner or lunch here and there.

So we don't run off and do things like befriend pirates and explore dangerous old houses.

So we can be Harts. Harts, who follow rules. Harts, who do not associate with people like the Baileys.

(If my cousins find out what's really going on, what will they think of me?)

(I am not a liar, and yet here I am, lying.)

(I will lie forever if I have to. My cousins and the Baileys can never, ever know the truth.)

How do I feel about all of this?

I feel . . . nothing.

I feel like I have been in a very hard sleep, and now I am stumbling around trying to wake up.

(WAKE UP, FINLEY!)

(Be normal now.)

We pass the road that leads to the farm stand where Grandpa and I buy our strawberries. My heart tears open.

"I'm so proud of you, Finley," Grandma tells me. "I think this will be good for you."

I am not sure how to respond. "It will?"

"Absolutely. This will get everything back to normal, you see? A normal summer."

(Because we mustn't be anything but normal, we Harts.)

She cleans a crumb off my cheek.

How do I feel?

Angry.

Alone.

Small.

Stiff.

Have either of my grandparents talked to me about what I witnessed in their bedroom?

They have not, and I have been too afraid to ask.

## WHAT IT MEANS TO BE A HART

- If something terrible is going on, you must try to not ever talk about it.

Grandma and I step into the waiting room. Pale green walls, stacks of magazines, soft piano music playing in the background. The room is full of kids—some older than me, some younger; some with parents, some without.

Some look happy, some don't.

But then, I know very well about the lies you can find on people's faces.

Grandma fills out forms, and we sit and wait. I hook my

feet around the legs of my chair. Beside me Grandma is motionless except for one finger, tapping on her knee. Her dress is covered in tiny flowers.

She clears her throat. "I hope you have a good time today."

"A . . . good time?"

"I only mean, I hope it's helpful."

I stare at the floor. The carpet is made up of a million different shades of blue. "Thanks."

(I don't need help.)

"I hope so too."

(I don't need help.)

(There is nothing here to help.)

(I have fixed it.)

(I will fix it.)

"We're lucky," Grandma says, "that we can afford to bring you here." She rearranges the folds of her dress. "Have you thought about that?"

"Yes," I say quietly, which is true. When I looked up Dr. Bristow on the Internet, I saw how much it costs to come here. I hear the news; I see things in the newspaper that aren't crossword puzzles. I don't understand everything, but I understand some things. Not everyone could come to this place. A lot of people could not.

(What a lucky girl you are, Finley Hart.)

(How lucky we are, to be able to afford this place, this food, these clothes.)

(So get it together, Finley.)

Grandma folds my hand into both of hers, and we wait together. The air-conditioning is on so high, my skin is covered in goose bumps. I feel a little sick. The *Pastoral* Symphony cycles through my head. I almost beg her to return to the car. Can't we listen to Beethoven instead?

(Beeth-oven. It's funnier that way.)

"It's okay," Grandma says quietly. "Everything is fine, now."

Is she talking to herself or to me?

"The Baileys are our friends, that's all," I whisper.

Grandma doesn't answer. She says, "Maybe we'll go shopping tomorrow. What do you think?"

"Finley Hart?"

A smiling woman enters the room. She is dressed sensibly and has dark, curly hair. I recognize her from the pictures I found online: Dr. Bristow.

She waves at me. "You ready to come on in?"

"I guess."

We stand. Grandma says, "Avery will pick you up in an hour."

"Oh, please join us, Mrs. Hart," suggests Dr. Bristow. "We recommend—"

"If it's all right, we'd like to let Finley speak with you alone today. Just to get things started." Grandma places her soft hands on my shoulders, warming me up. "If that's all right."

This does not surprise me. I heard what Grandma said the other night, in the kitchen, once she thought I had gone to sleep:

*Finley has made such a mess of things.*

I suppose I am responsible for cleaning it up.


The couch frightens me.

I know what it means. I have seen enough television shows.

I am supposed to sit on this couch and tell Dr. Bristow about what's troubling me.

But if I do that—

If I do that—

Besides, there are too many things troubling me.

Where would I even begin?

I can't begin.

No one can know about the blue days. They are mine. They are my secret—mine and my notebook's.

(No one can know. No one can ever know.)

If anyone found out . . . what would they say?

I know:

*Oh, but you should feel lucky to live in that beautiful house with those beautiful people!*

*Did you know your grandparents gave lots of money to the town of Billington? The library wouldn't even be here without their contribution.*

*Such wonderful people.*

*You don't seem to be at all like them.*

(Just breathe, Finley. Don't let them see.)

"Finley?"

I blink.

Dr. Bristow is sitting on the edge of her desk, sipping at a cup of coffee. "Do you want to sit down? You don't have to, of course. But I promise you this—it's a freakishly comfortable couch. A patient actually fell asleep on it once."

All right. I can handle sitting down.

But every step I take fills my body with crashing waves of fear, building

building

*building*—

(A hundred Finleys screaming through a hundred different megaphones.)

I perch on the edge of the couch, ready to run, if necessary.

Dr. Bristow smiles. "I'm so glad you've decided to sit. Because if you didn't, I'd stay standing too, and my feet are *killing* me." She slides into her chair and then pops right back up. "Oh! Do you want something to drink? I've got water in my fridge over here."

The idea of drinking water right now nauseates me.

I shake my head. I cannot possibly open my mouth, not even to say a simple "No."

I must keep myself held tightly together, straight up and down, like someone has stuffed me into a too-small bag and zipped me up.

If I move too much, or say even one word, the zipper will burst open and I will fall out.

No one wants to see that.

"It won't bother you if I drink my coffee, will it?"

I shake my head again. Dr. Bristow takes another long sip of coffee, and I examine her: Perhaps Mom's age. Eyes as dark as her hair.

"Do you like it here in Billington?" Dr. Bristow says.

(I didn't think I would, but I did. For a while.)

I say nothing and shrug.

Dr. Bristow sorts through files on the table beside her. She does not seem to be in a hurry.

"I like it all right, but I've got to confess something: If it weren't for my husband, no way would I live in a small town like this. I'm a city girl. I've lived in Billington ten years now, and the quiet still freaks me out."

(I'm from the city too. I live in an apartment with my parents.)

(For now.)

I stare at the floor.

"But that's what happens when you fall in love, I guess. You end up doing stupid things like spending too much on wedding cake and moving out to the middle of nowhere."

(Please don't talk about love.)

(My parents . . .)

I stare at my shoes. They are freckled with Everwood mud. Then I cannot see the mud anymore and realize my tears are blurring everything out.

Dr. Bristow sets down her coffee mug. "Hey. Finley?"

I am not afraid. (I am afraid.) I am not sad. (I am full of sadness.)

(But I do not understand why.)

I will push and push on these thoughts until they are nothing.

Dr. Bristow never has to know.

I think of Grandma—Grandma, her wig sliding. Hiding in the bedroom. Sleeping for hours. Getting injections.

### WHAT IT MEANS TO BE A HART
• You are excellent at keeping secrets.

"You know, I've got lots of work to do," says Dr. Bristow, from a great distance. "If you want to sit there and relax for a while, we can try to talk again in a few minutes. You're in the driver's seat here."

How unexpected. I'm sure that is not how this is supposed to work. Right?

Dr. Bristow smiles at me. "Promise. Okay?"

But this is not how you clean up a mess. It cannot be.

I should be saying something to her.

Grandma and Grandpa and Mom and Dad are paying Dr. Bristow to fix me.

But it can't be so bad to sit here, just for today. Can it?

Dr. Bristow winks at me. "Comfiest couch in the world."

I do not smile; I am still afraid of moving too much.

But I can sit, and breathe. Fine.

Dr. Bristow moves to her desk and begins to type on her computer.

Five minutes pass before I feel comfortable enough to relax my shoulders, and when I do, they ache as though someone has been driving hot needles into my bones.

I find the clock on the wall, watch the second hand, and wait.

*Tick, tick.*

*Tick, tick.*

HE QUEEN EXPLORED THE WHITE *halls of the Great Castle, gliding from gallery to ballroom to terrace.*

*She drifted into a strange museum, somewhere in the heart of the castle. In this museum people gazed at priceless artifacts kept in pillars of glass. The people wore jewels and thick white powder on their faces.*

*Whispers followed the queen wherever she went.*

*The museum people stared after her. The queen's skin crawled with fear.*

*"What do you suppose went wrong?" they whispered. "I thought this orphan girl was to become queen and save us."*

*"I must have read the signs wrong," came a cold voice. "For this girl is nothing like what I thought."*

*The queen whirled to find the voice. The smooth white statue she had passed only moments ago turned its creaking head. Its blank white eyes turned blue and dazzling.*

*Despite her fear, the queen held her head high. "Who are you?"*

*"I am one of the ancient guardians of the Everwood."*

*The queen wanted to flee, but she did not. "I am the queen of the Everwood."*

*"Not anymore," said the ancient guardian. The curve of her stone head melted into a fall of white hair that reached the ground, and in her hand she held an ancient brass key.*

The queen ran until she entered a hall of mirrors, and soon she got turned around. Everywhere she looked, she saw reflections of herself—but they were all wrong.

She saw a blinking light and thought it might point the way to freedom. Turning corner after glass corner, she followed the light for hours.

When she at last stumbled into a dark room with one small window, she realized that the light was merely a flickering candle in a dim corner.

She turned to flee, but the path of mirrors had disappeared.

Instead she saw a heavy wooden door, and she heard in its lock the turn of a key.

# 27

NOW PLAYING: SUPERVISED MOVIE NIGHT!

I imagine the words flashing over the front door of Hart House in bright lights, like at an old-fashioned movie theater.

It has been twelve days since Grandpa found us with the Baileys.

(Twelve days since I saw Grandma crying while Grandpa injected her with a syringe.)

I peek out the curtains to watch my aunts' cars pull around the circular driveway.

Do they orchestrate such things, or are they so in sync that they arrive together without even trying?

## WHAT IT MEANS TO BE A HART

- You know instinctively when you are supposed to do something, especially when it involves other Harts.

Approximately fifteen seconds after Stick parks her car, Gretchen barrels into my room, jumps onto my bed, and yanks me into a hug.

"So. These past couple of weeks?

"Yeah?"

"They've su*cked*."

"Agreed."

Gretchen releases me and sits up. "So what's been going on?"

"What do you mean?"

"I mean what have you been *doing* without us around? Almost two whole weeks without the Everwood? Ugh. I miss the darn trees. And, wow, never thought I'd say *that* sentence. Anyway, I've been dying of boredom, in case you're interested. But I complained about it so much that Mom decided we needed a project, and now the kitchen is painted. So, yippee."

I say nothing about my appointment with Dr. Bristow. "I don't know. I didn't do much, really. Helped at the clinic a couple of times. Went shopping with Grandma. Got some new dresses."

"Uh-oh. Where are they?"

I nod at the closet. "Like, six of them."

Gretchen takes one look at the dresses and scowls. "Barf. What are you, some chick from the fifties?"

"Grandma said I looked like her. I actually kind of like dresses, you know."

"Yeah, but you can't wear dresses in the Everwood. She should have gotten you hiking boots. Or a safari hat!"

"I don't think we can go to the Everwood anymore."

"Well, this whole grounded thing, blah blah blah, it's not, like, *forever*. They're just being stupid about the Baileys. But after tonight, I bet—"

"Seriously, Gretchen. They don't want us back there anymore. Grandpa told me this is for real."

Gretchen stares at me. "Not even in the Tower?"

"Maybe. But I mean, they'll be watching us from now on. We can't go wandering off anymore."

"They'll think we've abandoned them."

"Who?" (I know who.)

"Frank and Joy and Cynthia? The Travers family, come on."

I try to care about what Gretchen is saying, but I am so tired. Maybe now she and my cousins can care about the Everwood for me. They never seem to get tired like I do. "Maybe we should abandon them. We could leave them to rest in peace."

Gretchen's face hardens. "Finley Hart, you don't mean that. We're not finished cleaning the house yet!"

*The queen did not want to abandon the lonely wizard ghost and his family.*

*But with the Everwood so changed, with the unending howls coming at night, the queen knew that whatever came next, it could not involve her friends. They were safer without her.*

*She could not risk the ancient guardians' wrath.*

*So the queen held her head high and endured her dark prison.*

*"Queens," she told herself, "are not afraid of sacrifice."*

"Finley? Hello? *Finley.*"

I jump when Gretchen flicks my knee. "Huh?"

"Space cadet. I said we can't let the Baileys clean everything on their own."

I wonder what Jack has been doing since Grandpa yelled at him, what he has been thinking. Does he understand that none of this is our fault?

I hear movement on the stairs and jam my notebook under my pillows.

Grandma can dress me and watch my every move, but she will never get her hands on my notebook.

Dex and Ruth race into my room and start jumping up and down.

"*Free Willy! Free Willy!*" they scream.

"Oh God. Have mercy, ye tyrants." Gretchen collapses into a heap on the floor. "They've started this whole whale obsession thing. To torture me. Obviously." She lifts her head up and growls at the twins. "What about *Peter Pan*? Or *The Great Mouse Detective*? Or, I don't know, *any other movie in the world*?"

Ruth crouches down and shouts in Gretchen's face: "WHALES."

"Hey-ooo, kiddos!" Uncle Nelson yells up the stairs. "Rug rats! Little rascals! Snot faces!"

"Ewwwww!" Dex and Ruth squeal.

"Come on, we're starting the movie!"

"This is cruel and unusual punishment," Gretchen complains. "I'm starting to see this movie in my *dreams*!"

"And what do you think you'd see in your dreams if

Grandpa made you clean the toilets with a toothbrush?"
Uncle Nelson calls back.

"Poop dreams!" Ruth shrieks.

Dex tugs us toward the door. "Hurry, hurry, hurry, hurry."

As Gretchen stomps down the stairs, she whispers to me, "We are not finished talking about this, Finley. Meet me in the kitchen at nine thirty. Say you need a glass of water or something. We'll discuss."

I nod. "Okay, sure."

But I already know I will not.

At nine o'clock I claim to have a headache and am allowed to escape to my bedroom.

All the way to the stairs I can feel Gretchen watching me. She probably feels betrayed; I cannot blame her.

But she will see soon enough that it is safer for me to stay away from her, from all of them.

I am a bad influence.

I am a stubborn stain on a white rug.

Besides, I really do have a headache. I have had one all week.

(Instead of sleeping, I listen to it pound and I count the booms.)

*(Tick, tick.)*

*(Tick, tick.)*

HE QUEEN SAT, LOCKED AWAY.

The poison inside her was spreading, and she worried it would never stop.

A crow-shaped shadow darkened her window, but when she went to look, all she could see was fog, thick and deadly like smoke.

It seeped through the walls of the Great Castle and settled in the queen's blood. It sat heavily on the branches of the Everwood trees, and coated the abandoned watchtower with gray slime.

The air in the Everwood turned rancid and sour. With every breath she took, the queen's lungs burned.

Whatever wickedness lay at the heart of the Everwood, whatever had been turning the trees gray and drying out their leaves, was getting worse.

The queen peered out her window. She sifted through the fog with her fingers, as if she could push it out of the way.

"I must find the source of this cloud," said the queen. "I can clear the Everwood. I can heal it. I can."

But the more desperately the queen clawed through the air, the more a sharpness in her chest tugged, sending spikes of pain through her body.

She looked down, gasping, and saw thin spools of darkness seeping out of the place over her heart.

The darkness unfurled into the fog, twisting, growing.

*And the imprisoned queen understood: This fog was not natural, nor was it evil magic.*

*It was her.*

*The darkness inside her had escaped. It was no longer a secret, and it would never be again.*

*She looked out at the dying trees and remembered the snake's words, so long ago:* The Everwood is not as strong as it once was; your darkness will bring out its own.

*As the crow had warned her, she was too late.*

# 28

WHILE GRANDMA IS NAPPING ON Sunday, I hear the call of Jack's mourning dove and casually make my way to the living room windows, even though my heart is now a wild drum.

Jack is across the river, mostly hidden by the trees. He waits a minute, then makes the mourning dove call again, then runs back to his house.

Avery agrees to cover for me, and while she's talking to Grandpa about her latest painting, I sneak outside to check the Post Office.

Inside, just like I hoped, I find a note from Jack:

*My queen—*

*Don't worry. I was careful by the Post Office. No one saw me.*

*How are you? Not to be weird, but I've been watching your house from over here. Seems like no one's coming over as much as they did before.*

*Cole and Bennett and me, we've been working on the Bone House when we can, but it's not the same without y'all. We used to go over there by ourselves all the time, but everything's different now.*

*Meet me at the Bridge tonight. Midnight. You need to get
out of the house.*

*Don't be scared. But I know you won't be.*

*ARRRRRR,*

*Jack*


At eleven forty-five Hart House is quiet and still. I sneak
outside, pull on my sneakers, and listen to the leaves whispering, the train horn in the distance—and the call of a mourning dove.

I squint into the darkness. A figure stands at the other end
of the Bridge, waving at me.

Once I cross, Jack throws his arms around me.


### ABOUT JACK BAILEY

• Jack gives wonderful hugs, *real* hugs, like Mom's and
  Dad's hugs, like he never wants to let me go.


My heartbeat is officially out of control. Somehow I speak.

"Uh . . . what are you doing?"

(Of course, I do not manage to say anything intelligent.)

Jack gives me a look. "Hugging you? It's a thing friends do?"

"But . . . *why* are you hugging me?"

"Because I missed you."

He does not seem embarrassed to say this. He says it like
it is a plain and simple fact.

"You did?"

"Yeah. Without you, trees are kind of boring now."

The Everwood, boring? "How dare you."

"No offense. So, you escaped."

We begin walking through the Everwood toward the Wasteland. "Barely. I kept thinking I would knock something over and wake everyone up."

"Nah. You're better at stealth than you think. Hey, let's take the long way."

"Why?"

"Because I want to talk to you, that's why."

"Where's the long way?"

He points toward the part of the Everwood between his house and the Wasteland. "By the train tracks."

"I keep hearing a train at night."

"Yeah. It used to scare me when I was little."

We crawl between a gap in an old fence at the eastern end of the Wasteland. The grass is taller here, and it tickles my legs.

"Why did it scare you?"

"I thought it was a monster," Jack says, rolling his eyes, "and that it was coming to get me. I thought it roared because I'd done something to make it angry."

"Like what?"

"I don't know. Dad always tells me I'm doing something wrong."

I want more than anything to ask him about his dad, and why he never talks about him. I want to know about Mrs.

Bailey. I want to know about the loud noises that come from the Bailey house on quiet nights.

But I do not want to ruin this moment with Jack.

We walk in silence through another stretch of woods until we reach the train tracks. Jack helps me up onto the wooden fence running alongside them, and we gaze down the dark stretch of railroad.

A train horn whistles, down the tracks to our right, and Jack says, "When I figured out it wasn't a monster, that it was just a train, I started coming out to these tracks all the time."

"Why?"

"To get out of the house. I sit and watch the tracks and imagine following them until I get somewhere else."

"Where?"

Jack shrugs. "Anywhere but here, I guess."

"Would you take Cole and Bennett with you?"

"Maybe. I don't think they'd make it, on the road. Bennett's too little, and Cole's too nice. He acts like he's tough, but he's not. What if we had to do bad things to survive? I don't think he'd be able to."

*Bad things.*

*The Baileys—their dad, I mean—he wasn't a good kid. He did . . . bad things.*

*I wouldn't trust them for anything.*

The train horn sounds again. I feel cold, even though it is warm out.

Jack looks at me. "Do you ever think about running away?"

"Not really. I don't want to leave my parents."

"They're nice?"

"Yeah. They're always busy, and they're kind of weird, but I love them."

Down the tracks a tiny white light grows larger.

"That's cool, to have nice parents," Jack says. "You're lucky. I wish I could meet them."

I am lucky. I know that.

I am aware of the children across the world—even in my own city—who are poor, or sick, or hurt, or orphans.

Pretending to be a poor orphan girl is one thing; I would not actually want to be one.

But Jack does not understand.

I have nice parents. Yes, that is true. But I am full of sadness, and I wish I weren't, and I feel bad that I am.

And my parents are getting a—

They might be getting a—

(But I wouldn't have to say the word. Jack would understand.)

I wonder if Jack is mad at me for having nice parents, since I assume he does not.

It does not seem particularly fair for him to be mad at me for that.

It also is not fair that the Travers family is dead, that my world is filled with blue days, and that Jack seems to be hiding an unhappy secret too.

The train is coming. I feel its approach in the fence; the

wood vibrates against the bottoms of my sneakers.

I get an idea—something to make Jack smile. Something to shake off the heaviness I can feel settling onto my shoulders and weaving into my chest.

(Go away, go away, *go away*!)

I jump off the fence. "Come on. Let's run for it."

"What?"

"The train. It'll be here soon. Let's outrun it."

"You're crazy."

(Possibly.)

The horn sounds again, louder this time. Jack sits on the fence, watching the train approach.

I shrug. "Fine. I'm faster than you, and you're too chicken to admit it. I get it."

Jack jumps down. "No way is a queen faster than a pirate. You'll trip over your gown."

"*You'll* trip over your wooden leg."

The train is almost on top of us; the horn is so loud that I want to cover my ears, but I don't. The chugging wheels make my bones shake.

"In about five seconds you're going to be so embarrassed," Jack shouts over the noise.

"We'll see about that," I shout back, and as the train rushes past, I take off running.

All I can see is the open dark path in front of me—train on one side, forest on the other. I imagine following the tracks for days, finding what lies at the end of them.

By the time I got there, maybe I would have outrun my sadness, forever.

No more blue days.

No more fear.

The thought makes me dizzy—or maybe I am out of breath already.

Jack shoots past me.

I assumed he would beat me; his legs are longer than mine, and I am not an athlete like Kennedy. But I did not realize just how fast he would be.

My lungs are on fire. I am pumping my arms through the air and pushing my legs faster than they have ever gone before. Still, I am not fast enough to catch Jack.

He races on, and I think I see him reaching for the train.

He will grab hold, jump on board, and leave this place behind forever, like he has always dreamed.

But then the train pulls ahead, and Jack falls behind. He throws up his arms to the sky and shouts.

Gasping for breath, I stop beside him. "I thought you were going to do it. I thought you'd leave, like you said."

Jack looks after the train. It has disappeared into the darkness, but the sound of its horn floats back to us, reminding us it is there.

Then he looks at me. "Not without you," he says, and grins the Jack grin I know.

# 29

AFTER THAT, THINGS ARE QUIET between me and Jack, like
we traded all our words for running power and now have
nothing left.

Strangely, I do not feel the need to try to fill the silence
with talking. Not this time.

We walk back through the woods toward his house. Cicadas sing from the trees, and the sky is dusted with a million
stars. My fingers brush against the tall grass, and once I think
I feel Jack's fingers touch mine, but I am too nervous to look
down and check.

When we get back into the woods, everything is velvet: the
sky, the still air, the soft earth. The trees blot out the moon.
Jack holds back branches for me, and I do the same for him.
He touches my hand again—I know it is real this time—and
I hold on. I cannot look at him, but I don't let go, not even
while we climb up the hill to his house.

"Well," Jack says when we get to the top.

"Yeah," I answer, and I'm probably supposed to go home
now, but that seems unthinkable.

(Eleven-letter word for "no way I am doing that.")

"Jack? Is that you?"

Jack lets go of my hand. *"Dad?"*

I turn and squint, see a man sitting in a lawn chair a little ways from the Bailey house. The flickering porch light buzzes.

So this is Mr. Bailey. He does not *look* like a troll.

Jack steps toward him cautiously. "What's up?"

"Enjoying the night," says Mr. Bailey. He takes a sip from a bottle of root beer. I recognize the orange label. "Who's your friend?"

Jack relaxes, stuffs his hands in his pockets. "This is Finley. We were just talking."

"Hey, Finley. Hart, isn't it?"

I nod.

"Nice night, don't you think?"

I glance at Jack. How are we not in trouble right now? Why is Mr. Bailey not marching Jack to bed this instant? "Yes, sir."

"So polite. But then you Harts always were."

Jack sits on the ground by his dad and waves me over. "Can Finley stay for a while?"

Mr. Bailey laughs a little, raises his bottle in the direction of Hart House. "Sure. Why not? No one's awake to see."

I sit beside Jack and bring my knees to my chin. Dad's words keep coming back to me—*I wouldn't trust them for anything, he did bad things, he did bad things*—but Jack is leaning against his dad's leg, and Mr. Bailey puts his hand on Jack's shoulder, and I do not see how this could be a bad man.

Or why Jack would call him a troll.

"I love the woods best at night," Mr. Bailey says, after a while. "It's like you can hear the trees thinking."

Jack nudges me. "Tell him a story."

"What?"

"One of the Everwood stories." Then Jack says, louder, "Finley's a good writer. She has a whole notebook full of stories at her house."

"Really?" Mr. Bailey actually sounds interested. "What are they about?"

I stare at the ground. "They're not very good."

"Shut up," Jack says. "They're amazing."

I glare at him.

(Jack thinks my stories are amazing!)

"This is embarrassing," I mumble.

"No it isn't. Come on, do your thing."

Jack thinks it is so easy to just *do* things: to steal your neighbors' property so they will chase you. To hug your friend because you missed her.

Mr. Bailey takes another drink. "You don't have to, if you're scared."

"Finley's not scared of anything," Jack says. "She's the queen."

"Is that right?" Mr. Bailey laughs a little. "Of course she is. All those Hart girls are queens, didn't you know?"

Something about Mr. Bailey's words stings, like I have stepped into those pale green prickers hiding beneath the grass in the Wasteland.

*Those Hart girls* are my aunts, my cousins, my grand-mother. We share blood. What does Mr. Bailey know about anything?

"Fine," I say sharply. "I have a story about how the Ever-wood was first made, when the world was very young and full of magic. Would you like to hear that?"

Mr. Bailey throws his empty bottle into the weeds. "Sure thing. Can't sleep tonight anyway. Maybe this'll help."

"He means that in a good way," Jack explains, lying back in the dirt. "Reading relaxes him. I've been reading *Tom Sawyer* to him sometimes. You like that, right?"

"I like it when you do their voices." Mr. Bailey reaches down to Jack, and Jack grabs his hand and squeezes. "You're good at making me laugh."

Jack smiles up at him.

I take a deep breath, and begin.

# 30

APPARENTLY DR. BRISTOW DOES NOT want to sit in silence this week.

She talks to me for about five minutes straight once my second appointment begins—about her husband (the principal at the local middle school), her dog (a mutt of questionable origins with a fondness for shoes), and her taste in movies (a lot of science fiction).

Then she leans back in her chair and sips her coffee. "Am I terribly boring?"

I am shocked into speech. "No."

"Aha! You can talk! I was starting to get worried."

"Sorry."

"No, no, no—don't apologize. There's nothing to be sorry for. I just thought, with me rambling on and on, you must have found me very boring and decided to keep quiet so maybe I would eventually stop talking."

"No, it's not that. It's—"

I stop before I can say anything I will regret.

How can I explain to her the truth?

That I am sitting here not talking because I am afraid she will dig deep inside my thoughts and discover all my secrets—

and maybe even more than that. Maybe things I don't want to know.

Definitely things I don't want Grandma to know.

(I am not broken.)

I glance up at Dr. Bristow. She smiles and gives me a little nod.

"It's nothing. Really."

"Finley, I'm going to be frank with you. I like honesty, and I think sometimes adults decide not to be honest with children because they think doing so will protect them, but I don't agree with that philosophy."

Every adult in my life seems to be keeping some kind of secret right now. The idea that there could be one who isn't is astonishing. "Really?"

"Really. Is that okay with you?"

"Yeah. But . . ."

"You don't have to be honest with me back. I understand you don't know me very well yet. It's okay. I probably wouldn't trust me either."

I relax, and I realize I have been digging my fingers into the couch.

"Okay."

"Okay. So, as part of me being honest, I have to ask you something. Do you know why your parents and your grand-parents decided to make you these appointments with me?"

Because I am not what they want me to be.

Because I am a bad influence.

Because they do not understand me. I am quiet, and obsessive, and I like spending time alone.

(If only they knew there was even more to it than that.)

I am not certain my grandparents could understand the concept of blue days, of fear that comes over you in waves and wakes you up in the middle of the night, of heaviness that seems to grow from somewhere deep inside the universe.

I think if I sat my grandparents down and tried to explain these things to them, they would say something like:

*You're feeling a little out of sorts because of this nasty business with your parents.*

*You're going through a phase. Everyone goes through phases.*

*You're not making any sense, Finley.*

To maintain a sense of calm, I think of sitting in the cool dark with Jack and Mr. Bailey, telling stories about the Everwood.

And I tell Dr. Bristow, "No," and shrug. "I don't know why."

"Your grandparents told me you're staying with them this summer because your parents are having some trouble. They're worried about you. They say you've gotten your cousins playing some dangerous games in the woods—"

"They're not dangerous," I blurt out. "The . . . games. They're not dangerous. We're just playing."

"What do you play?"

I imagine explaining the Everwood to Dr. Bristow and almost laugh. "You wouldn't understand."

"That's probably true. It'd be like when my husband tries

to explain football to me. I know that's a terrible cliché, but it's true—he starts talking safeties and offsides and all the different kinds of penalties, and my eyes just kind of glaze over."

Her effort to cheer me up is admirable, but it doesn't help. I am clamped tight again, like I was during my first appointment.

Dr. Bristow wouldn't understand.

My grandparents think she would—maybe they even think *they* would—but they are wrong.

The Everwood and the Bone House and the train tracks and the fire and the three lonely gravestones—these are things for me and my cousins and the Baileys. No one else.

It is not my place to tell the group's secrets to this stranger, no matter how kind she may appear to be.

So even though it makes me intensely uncomfortable, I stare at the floor and refuse to acknowledge Dr. Bristow for the rest of my appointment.

After a few minutes she stops trying to talk to me, refills her coffee, and starts working on her computer, humming under her breath.

For at least one more session I am saved.

# 31

AVERY HAS BEEN DESIGNATED MY official psychologist chauffeur.

I am not happy she knows about this situation, but I will not complain, because that is something stains do. Spots and messes and non-Harts.

*The queen held her head high.*

"How'd it go today?" Avery asks as I slide into the passenger seat of her tiny car.

A faded bumper sticker on the back of the car says THE CLOSER YOU GET, THE SLOWER I'LL DRIVE.

"I don't know," I say. "It was fine."

Avery pops her gum, pulls down her enormous sunglasses from the top of her head, and drives out of the clinic's parking lot.

At first Avery and I ride in silence, and I am happy to stay that way. We have not said much to each other since that night in the bathroom, except for when I ask her to help me sneak down to the Post Office, or at least check it for me.

But then Avery starts flipping through radio stations. "So what kind of music do you like?"

*Beeth-oven,* I want to say. "I don't know . . . Kiss FM, I guess?"

Avery makes a horrible face. "You're kidding, right?"

"Uh . . . no?"

"Finley, please. You can lose brain cells listening to that stuff." Avery presses a button on her stereo. "How about this?"

A song begins—a man singing by himself, and a piano. The man has an English accent.

"What is this?" I ask.

"You're *kidding* me."

"No."

*"Finley."* We come to a stoplight, and Avery tilts her head back against the headrest.

"Avery? Are you okay?"

"Listen to the song. It's the freaking *Beatles*, Finley. They were only, you know, revolutionary. It's inexcusable that you don't know this song."

"I'm sorry—"

"Don't be. Just listen."

Avery rolls down the windows and turns up the volume.

What started out as a man and a piano grows to a couple of men, a tambourine, some drums. Although I do not usually listen too closely to song lyrics, I make an effort to listen to these, because I get the feeling Avery expects me to.

I like these lyrics. They are a little sad, about a lonely boy who does not think he is worth much. A boy with sadness. A boy who is afraid.

Avery begins to sing along. We turn off the main road onto

a farm road, and the sunlight hits us square in the face. I squint, and Avery looks like she is made of gold.

The song escalates in volume, and the singer begins to scream. So does Avery, banging on the steering wheel.

"Come on, Finley, this part's easy," shouts Avery over the song and the wind. "It's the same thing over and over."

But I cannot possibly do such a thing. If I tried, I would not look cool and wild, like Avery does, slapping her steering wheel like she is the best drummer in the world.

When the song is over, Avery turns down the volume. "I'm kind of obsessed with that song right now. What do you think?"

"It's . . . long."

"Pffft. It's exactly as long as it needs to be. Do you feel wiser now? You should. It's the start of your education on actual good music. I'm going to start playing you new stuff every week."

"Okay."

Avery continues singing the song to herself, and I listen closely, because I want her to turn the song back on but am too nervous to ask her. So I focus on the thin sound of her voice and try tapping out the song's drumbeat on the side of the seat, where she cannot see.

When we turn onto Redbrook Road, Avery pulls the car over and parks beneath a tree.

For a minute she stares out the window in silence, her skin marked with clusters of sunlight. A grasshopper snaps past the window.

Before I can ask her what's going on, she says, "Look, I know you know about Grandma."

"I . . ." I close my mouth, open it, close it again. "Okay. Yeah."

"I assume they told you not to tell anyone?"

"Grandpa said not to. Grandma hasn't said anything to me about it. At all."

Avery snorts. "Yeah, not surprising."

"But, um, I actually don't know much. I saw Grandpa giving her a shot. I saw her wig. But they didn't tell me anything. I don't really know what any of that means."

Avery pushes her sunglasses on top of her head and looks at me. "She has advanced multiple myeloma. It's this really bad cancer. She's on a short break from chemo and radiation treatments, but she's about to start back up with chemo. She hides it really well: 'Oh, I'm busy with this and that,' and 'Your grandfather and I are visiting friends in the city this weekend'—you know, that kind of thing. The injection you saw Grandpa giving her is this medicine the doctor thinks will help prevent more of the bad cells from forming."

Avery takes a shaky-sounding breath. "I've known about this for weeks. They had to tell me because Grandpa is losing it. Seeing her like this, he gets so upset, only you could never tell, of course. Anyway, he needs someone around to help him take care of Grandma when she's feeling sick. But they won't let me tell anyone. Or, I guess I *could* tell everyone, but they told me that if I kept their secret, they'd pay for my tuition to the Rigby Institute next year."

This is a lot of information to process.

Grandpa is losing it? Like he did when he found us with the Baileys, except the exact opposite. Shaking, maybe, but not with anger.

Imagining him upset about Grandma, and what that might look like, makes me feel very small.

Would he cry?

I have never heard Avery say so many words. She grips the steering wheel like we are on the run from the police.

"The bad cells?" I say.

"Cancer cells. The ones that grow tumors."

"Oh. What's the Rigby Institute?"

Avery glares at the dashboard. "It's this prestigious art school on the East Coast. It's basically my dream school, but Mom and Dad can't afford to send me there. They act like they could, but they can't. Mom goes to the city twice a week to shop for clothes she shouldn't buy. Did you know that? I love her, but she's an idiot sometimes. They think I don't hear them talking when I'm at home. Don't they get that my bedroom is right above theirs?"

"Adults don't ever think we're listening."

"If I ever have kids, I will never delude myself into thinking they're as stupid as my parents think I am."

"I don't think they think you're stupid. They probably don't want to admit they can't afford that school. Maybe they're embarrassed."

Avery looks at me long and hard. "Well, maybe. Anyway,

so I'm keeping Grandma and Grandpa's secret so I can go to my dream school. Is that terrible of me? I think it's pretty terrible. But you don't see me telling anyone, do you? So I guess I've made up my mind."

Avery's eyes are bright. She bites her lip and slams her sunglasses back down.

"Whatever." She starts the car back up. "I should be sorry they told you. It's cruel that they told you. You're eleven years old. You don't need to be keeping secrets like this. You should be keeping stupid, pointless secrets, like who your crush is and that you stuffed your bra when you went to the movies the other night. You know? But whatever. God forbid we talk about things like real people, you know? 'Oh, sweetie. Oh, Avery. You can't tell anyone. It'll upset your aunts, your mother. They'll be devastated.' Like, no freaking kidding? I couldn't have guessed that."

Avery shoves a strand of hair behind her ear. "And you know what's even more terrible? I'm glad they told you, because now I have someone I can talk to about it."

Avery punches the gas, and the car squeals back into the road.

This does not help my spinning head. I clutch the seat.

"Avery?"

"What?" she snaps.

"Why would I stuff my bra?"

Her mouth twitches. "I'm kind of glad you don't know the answer to that yet."

When we pull into the driveway, we do not get out immediately. I feel like stepping out of the car will ruin the little world we've created in here, Avery and me.

Avery fiddles with her car keys. "I'm sorry I went off like that. I shouldn't have—"

"It's okay," I say quickly. "I liked it. I thought . . ."

"What?"

"I thought you didn't like me that much."

"I've been kind of a jerk to you, haven't I?"

"No, just . . ."

"Distant?"

"Yeah."

Avery nods, looks in the mirror, yanks her hair into a ponytail. "I'm jealous of you, Finley."

I stare at her. *"Why?"*

"Because you got away. You didn't have to grow up here, with everyone breathing down your neck, everyone expecting . . ."

I hold my breath until I can't anymore. "Expecting what?"

"Expecting you to fit in, and be the perfect Hart. 'Oh, your grandparents.' 'Oh, your adorable little cousins.' 'Oh, the *Hart* family, aren't you lucky to be one of them?'" Avery moves the armrest up and down. "It's exhausting."

I feel a desperate urge for my notebook. I want to write down this conversation and read it over and over until I know everything Avery has said by heart.

"Avery?"

"Yeah."

"Do you know why I never visited before this summer? Do you know why everyone's mad at my dad?"

"No. I really don't. Sorry."

I want to ask her about the fire. I decide I will someday. But not today. Avery thinks I am cool, like she can trust me with her secrets.

That is not a feeling I am willing to lose.

"No one will tell me. Grandma says Dad is an upsetting topic." I pause. "She says she misses him. Grandpa does too."

Avery lets out a long breath. "Well, good luck with that. If a Hart doesn't want you to know something, chances are you'll never find out."

"Hi, you two!" calls Aunt Dee, standing by the garage and waving a spoon. "Hurry up! Grandma's icing cookies!"

"Of course," Avery says grimly. She gets out of the car, slams the door shut, and goes to hug her mother.

If you looked at her smiling face, you would never guess she was about to cry a few minutes ago.

FTER SEVERAL DAYS IN HER *lonely prison tower, the queen awoke to familiar, eerie howls. Fear slithered through her bones.*

*She looked out her tiny window. The fog had worsened. The world was dark.*

*Through the fog the queen heard the howls continuing their fearsome song, but worse than that were the sounds of death.*

*Muffled though they were, they were unmistakable: trees crashing to the ground, animals crying out in pain.*

*The air smelled like the underside of things—things that should not see the sunlight and yet had somehow been unearthed.*

*"Because of me," said the queen, her heart full of shame.*

*She ripped a piece of cloth from her hem and tied it around her face, shielding her nose and mouth. She donned her ruined cloak and climbed out her window, down the slick castle wall.*

*It was a risk. If the ancient guardians realized she had escaped, their wrath would be terrible, the queen knew.*

*But the Everwood needed her. No one else loved it as she did.*

*The distant howls bled on—ravenous, impatient.*

*"You will not destroy my forest," the queen told the darkness. She jumped from the wall onto the sodden ground, and her palms turned black with wet ash. "I will find you, whatever you are, and I will make this world right again."*

*Then the queen struck out into the dying trees, parting the fog like curtains of shadow.*

# 32

ON FRIDAY AFTERNOON EVERYONE COMES over to Hart
House, and Grandma tells us kids we have to clean the attic
before dinner.

At this pronouncement Gretchen groans and throws herself onto the floor. Ruth whispers something to Dex, and then
they do the same.

"*Why?*" Gretchen whines.

Grandma snaps on her pink rubber gloves. "Because it's
filthy, that's why, and we've been putting it off for too long.
Stand up. Acting childish is not attractive."

"I *am* a child," Gretchen mutters under her breath.

Avery smirks at Gretchen. "I don't think anyone but you
cares about the state of the attic, Grandma."

"And isn't that a shame? Come on, Harts. Snap to it."

The staircase to the attic is narrow and tall, and the steps
creak beneath our feet. Kennedy has a twin in each hand.
"Isn't this fun, you guys?" she says. "It's like going on an
adventure."

Beside me Gretchen crosses her eyes and sticks out her
tongue at Kennedy. The attic is gigantic, the size of Hart
House. The ceiling is low, with thick wooden rafters. Three

small, round windows on each wall let in sunlight that paints the room in bright streaks and dust clouds.

There is a mannequin wearing a ratty hat, a huge mirror half-covered with a sheet. A collection of old bicycles. A smell of dust. One corner of the attic is decorated with faded paper shapes nailed to the wall and colored with crayons. Boxes crowd the floor: plastic boxes, cardboard boxes, old wooden chests and crates.

"Avery, you and Dex take that wall." Grandma points to the piles nearest us. "Kennedy and Ruth, start cleaning the windows. Gretchen, you and your grandfather will start over there, and Finley?" Grandma touches my shoulder. "You'll stick with me."

My grandmother's hand is warm and feels as light as a sigh against my skin. When Grandpa passes her, she plants a kiss on his cheek.

(Four people in a house of twelve know what is inside her, and I am one of them.)

(I wish I were not.)

Gretchen drags herself over to Grandpa. "Shouldn't our parents have to clean too?"

"By all means, keep whining," says Grandpa calmly, "and I'll make you clean this entire attic by yourself."

"You wouldn't!"

Grandpa raises one bushy gray eyebrow. "Try me, grand-daughter of mine."

Gretchen shuts up.

We sweep away dirt and cobwebs, dust windowsills, and sort through boxes. Grandma arranges three piles: toss, keep, donate. There are boxes labeled KITCHEN, CHRISTMAS, TOOLS.

BRIDGET. DEE. STICK (THE GREATEST).

LEWIS.

I see my father's box before Grandma does and tug it around the corner behind the covered Christmas tree so she cannot see it. I grab Grandpa's knife when he is not looking and slice open the box.

Inside is a bag of marbles, an old model car. Books, ribbons for school writing contests, award certificates. A story titled "The Not-So-Great Gatsby" written on yellowed, lined paper.

Photos of Dad as a boy, making faces for the camera, flexing nonexistent muscles.

Dad with my aunts. My age. Avery's age. Arms linked.

I run my fingers across their faces, imagining I can feel cheekbones, noses, ears. Aunt Bridget is the tallest; her smile squishes her eyes. Dad's ears are too big for his face. Stick has crossed her eyes and stuck out her tongue. Dee is making a kissy face.

Grandma has called my aunts upstairs. I hear them exclaiming over their own boxes.

I tuck the photo of them and Dad into my pocket. It does not deserve to be stuck in a box.

Then I find a note, wedged between a high school yearbook and a spelling bee trophy.

Dad's handwriting has not changed much; I immediately recognize the messy letters:

*Mom:*

*I'm leaving.*

*By the time you find this, I'll be gone.*

*I already told Dad. Don't get mad at him. I made him swear not to tell you.*

*This is your fault. Don't think for one second that it isn't.*

"Finley, where did you go? Come help me with this bag of clothes. We can donate most of them, I think."

I jump at the sound of Grandma's voice. The letter falls from my hands.

"Whatever is the matter with you?" Grandma feels my forehead. "You look flushed."

I jerk away from her, grab the letter, and hurry across the attic toward the door. "I . . . have to go to the bathroom."

"Wait. Stop right there."

Grandma's voice cuts the room in half. Everyone stops cleaning to stare at us. She must have seen Dad's box. "What do you have in your hand?"

"Nothing." I try to stuff the letter into my pocket, but Grandma is too quick. She grabs the letter, and I pull away. It rips in half.

"Give that to me." She holds out her hand for my piece, her mouth thin. "That is not for you."

Gretchen jumps down from her step stool. "What is that?"

I back away from Grandma and start to read. "'Mom: I'm leaving. By the time you find this, I'll be gone.'"

"Finley, don't." Grandma's voice is steady, like she is trying not to frighten a wild animal. "Give that to me, now."

"'I already told Dad. Don't get mad at him. I made him swear not to tell you.'"

Aunt Dee gasps. Aunt Bridget says, "Dad," in a strained voice.

"Come on, Finley-boo." Stick smiles at me, like we are all playing a game. "Let's not make a big deal out of this."

Grandpa stares at the letter, his shoulders slumped.

"I thought I told you to throw that away," Grandma tells him quietly.

"I couldn't, Candace," Grandpa says. "I thought it was important to remember."

"Remember what? That our son left us? That he wants nothing to do with us?" Grandma catches me by surprise, grabs my wrist, tears my piece of the letter from my hand.

I am too shocked to move. "Give it back. It's mine."

"It isn't," she says calmly, tearing both pieces of the letter into halves, quarters, eighths. "It's nothing."

Stick hugs me from behind, kisses my cheek. "Finley, how about you and me go downstairs and find some music, huh? We'll turn it up real loud, fill the whole house."

I yell at Grandma, "You don't love him. None of you love him. *I* love him. It's mine. You're a thief!"

Dex starts to cry. Avery holds him close, shushes him. I cannot look at her. I do not like hearing Dex cry. Everyone is watching me. What are they thinking?

"We don't have time for this," Grandma says. "Let's get back to work. All right? Chop-chop." There is nothing in her voice—no anger, no sadness. A blank canvas as white as her hair.

(Fake, fake, fake.)

I break free of Stick's arms and run downstairs.

Gretchen sneaks into my room and sits beside me on the bed, swinging her legs. "You really freaked out my mom earlier."

"I don't care what she thinks." I am facing away from her, staring out the window, not seeing anything but the memory of that letter in my hands.

*This is your fault. Don't think for one second that it isn't.*

"You freaked *me* out, yelling at Grandma like that."

I ignore her. "What did you think of the letter?"

"God, Finley, I don't know. Can't we forget about it?"

I sit up and face her. "Don't be a coward, Lady Gretchen."

"Quit it with the Everwood crap, okay, Finley? This isn't about some game. It's about our family."

"It isn't a game. It's real."

"It *is* a game. It was our game, and it's over now. Okay?" Gretchen looks away and wipes her eyes. "You're so weird. Why are you being like this?"

I don't know what to say to her. This is not my Gretchen; this is an impostor. I do not cry in front of impostors.

"I found this." I hand her the photo of her mom, my dad, our aunts—all four of them blond and tan with summer.

Gretchen examines it for a long time. I hear Stick calling for her downstairs. They're not staying for the night, even though I know they normally would.

Once again I have ruined everything.

"Don't let Grandma see it." Gretchen hands the photo back to me. "It's a good picture."

"Gretchen?" I call out.

She stops at the door. "Yeah?"

"I love you. I'm sorry I freaked you out."

Gretchen hurries back and hugs me. When I am ready to let go, she doesn't.

"Why do you think he wrote it?" she whispers. "Why did he leave?"

Her breath smells like Grandma's homemade icing, and my eyes fill up. My Gretchen.

"I don't know yet," I admit. "But maybe the Everwood will tell me."

"My mom might tell us. We could ask her over and over until she gives in. I'm really good at being annoying. I know her weaknesses."

"No. Not yet. I need time to think. Okay? Promise me you won't ask your mom, or talk to her about any of this. Okay? Please, Gretchen."

(If I ask too many questions, I am afraid of what Grandma and Grandpa might do to me.)

262 / CLAIRE LEGRAND

(Will they make me leave too?)

"Okay, okay."

"Gretchen?" Stick knocks on my door. "Now. I mean it."

Gretchen squeezes me tight and kisses my cheek. When she is gone, I look for a specific list in my notebook.

### WHY MY DAD LEFT THE FAMILY

- ~~Because he was called away on an adventure that required him to sacrifice all personal ties.~~
  - ~~But then he got married, so that can't be it.~~
    - ~~Unless . . . am I part of some secret international plot? (Unlikely.)~~
- ~~Because they wanted him to take over Grandpa's business with Uncle Reed, but he didn't want to. (But why would that be a secret?)~~
- ~~Because he was different. (Like me.)~~
- Because of Grandma.

HE QUEEN FOLLOWED THE HOWLS *through the Everwood.*

*Above her the crow's dark wings slashed through the fog, leaving trails of light behind.*

*The light vanished quickly.*

*"Hurry," hissed the snake, winding through the brittle grass.*

*"Hurry," urged the fox, nipping at the queen's ankles.*

*"You go too quickly!" gasped the queen. "I cannot breathe in this darkness!"*

*But the crow, the snake, and the fox did not slow. There was no time left for pity.*

*They cut through a clearing and took a trail alongside the river—and here the queen stopped.*

*She felt the weight of malevolent eyes upon her.*

*She realized that the howls had stopped.*

*All around her was a thick quiet, heavy with danger.*

*"Crow?" she whispered. "Fox? Snake?"*

*They did not answer her.*

*But someone else did.*

# 33

I HAVE DECIDED THAT PEOPLE do not come to your rescue, like they do in the movies. If they did, I would not feel this way right now.

(Even though I have Jack, Gretchen, the Everwood?)

(Yes, even so.)

Perhaps I have to rescue myself.

Which is difficult to do, when you are as tired as I am.

When you wake up to a bedroom full of morning sunshine and feel like crying for no particular reason.

When you are weighed down by something you do not understand.

(Breathe, Finley.)

(Don't let them see.)

Unfortunately, I cannot remain in bed today.

Grandma, Stick, and Aunt Dee are taking me, Kennedy, and Gretchen to a farmers' market Grandma organized for the WIC clinic. We are to wear bright name tags and man the information table and talk to people about healthy eating.

I protest, claiming I have come down with the flu, but Grandma does not believe me.

She marches into my bedroom at eight o'clock on Saturday morning, throws open my curtains, and flings my quilt off me.

I barely manage to slip my notebook under my pillow before the sunlight hits me.

I am sure I look terrible; I slept for perhaps a total of one hour. Not that it matters. I wrote three Everwood stories, and creative expression is salubrious.

(Ten-letter word: "healthy, beneficial, invigorating.")

"Rise and shine, Finley! We need to be downtown by ten."

Grandma searches through my collection of new dresses until she finds one that satisfies her: a long sundress with a white top and a yellow skirt. She lays it out on my bed.

"Get dressed, sweet girl. We have to pick up your aunts, and I won't be late."

"Grandma," I croak, "I really don't feel well."

"Nothing a little work and conversation can't fix!" Grandma finds a pair of suitable shoes. "Here, these will do. Come, get up. You'll love the market. Lots of fresh air, fresh food, nice people, and sunshine. Tell me that doesn't sound just marvelous."

She pauses at the door, smiling.

When I look more closely, I realize her hand is gripping the door, hard. She is leaning on the door frame.

Her makeup is flawless, but I see a strip of sweat along her hairline.

I peel her smile away and see . . .

What must it feel like to have a poisonous disease growing inside you, eating you up bit by bit?

Surely it feels a lot worse than feeling sad.

Sadness is for people who lose their families in a house fire.

Sadness is for people who have cancer.

"Okay." My head is swimming and aching; moving is like trying to run through water.

"I hope you're feeling better than you were yesterday. No allergies from the dust, I hope?"

### WHAT IT MEANS TO BE A HART

- If you have a fight in the attic in front of everyone, if you freak out your aunts, if you make your cousins cry, you don't talk about it the next day. *Obviously*.
- Acting so childish is not attractive.
- We are grown-ups here. We are normal.

I imagine carving a smile onto my face from the inside out. I will not say anything about that letter from my father. In this clean, white bedroom it does not exist.

Perhaps it is my imagination, but Grandma seems to stand up straighter once she sees me smile. She comes over and hugs me, kisses my hair, tells me that we will have a lovely day together and that everything will be fine.

So I know I am doing the right thing.

. . .

The farmers' market is in the square downtown. Rows of covered tables hold boxes of fruits and vegetables, local cheeses, fresh flowers.

Grandma and I sit at a table near the front of the market, wearing our name tags and pointing people where they need to go. Gretchen, Kennedy, Stick, and Aunt Dee drift through the crowd, handing out flyers about WIC services.

I could stand up and call out their names, and they would all turn to me—but I nevertheless feel very far away from them, like we are separated by hundreds of miles.

"Candace, good to see you! Great turnout, don't you think?" It is Roxann Bates, who was at the 10K race earlier this summer. She bustles by, carrying bushels of basil.

That race seems like it happened in another life. I was a different Finley then. I knew nothing about fires or sick grandmothers or boys named Jack.

"Absolutely!" Grandma calls out. "Those mailers did the trick! Couldn't have done it without you."

Roxann Bates salutes Grandma. "You're the mastermind! I'm just good at stuffing envelopes. Ha!"

Roxann Bates hurries off, waving at someone else and calling out, "Wait! Mark, don't put the tomatoes *there*!"

When Roxann is gone, Grandma touches my arm. Her face is pale, sweaty, splotchy. Her eyelids flutter. "Will you excuse me, Finley? I need to use the ladies' room."

"Are you okay?"

"Nothing to worry about. If you need help while I'm gone, get Stick, all right?"

"But, Grandma—"

"Finley, please. Everything is fine." Then Grandma squeezes my hand and leaves.

I sit very still and count to thirty, which is all I can handle. I find Aunt Dee and wave her over.

Her face is flushed with the sun. Her eyes sparkle. This is what a healthy person looks like.

"I have to go to the bathroom," I tell her. "Can you watch the table?"

Aunt Dee adjusts the visor I am wearing—one of Grandma's, as white as her fake, fake hair. "Where's your grandmother?"

"Talking to anyone she can find."

Aunt Dee laughs. "Of course. Sure, go on. The library's letting us use their restrooms."

I weave through a forest of people. The sun is too bright, reflecting off everyone's shoes and bags and sunglasses. Flashes of light blind me. There are tons of kids here, little ones. They're laughing and screaming and talking and crying, and my heart is a drumroll, and I need to find Grandma *now*.

It is quiet and cool inside the library. Pam the librarian waves at me from her desk. I wave back and go the other direction.

(Grandma, please be okay.)

In the women's restroom someone is getting sick in the farthest stall. I hurry inside another one and sit on the toilet and pull my feet up so I become invisible.

It's Grandma, in the farthest stall. Grandma, getting sick.

It goes on for way too long, and I make myself listen instead of covering my ears, because if she has to feel that, then someone else should have to hear it. It is too lonely otherwise.

I want to open the door and hug her until she stops, but I cannot move. I sit there, invisible, and wait until she is finished. I listen to her breathing get back to normal. I watch through the crack in my door as she rinses her mouth and washes her hands and pats her face with a paper towel.

Then she fixes her hair and practices smiling in the mirror.

"All right, then," she says to herself, and tugs her shirt straight, and leaves.

I count to ten and sneak out after her, following her bright white hair back through the market until we return to the table where Aunt Dee waits with Kennedy.

"Mom, you okay?" Aunt Dee lets Grandma have her chair back. "You look a little out of sorts."

"Why, thank you, Deirdre," Grandma says lightly. "I'll try not to take offense at that. I'm perfectly fine, only a little overheated. Would you get me some water, Kennedy, darling?"

Kennedy leaves, and Aunt Dee gets pulled away by a mother with two kids who wants to apply for WIC services.

I slip back into my seat.

"Where did you run off to?" Grandma asks.

I take a deep breath. "Bathroom."

Grandma goes very still. Then she says, "Ah."

I feel like we are playing the Quiet Game. When you're tired of playing and want to shout out all the words you've been keeping inside you, but you absolutely cannot lose.

So instead you sit, and bite down on everything screaming inside you, and wait.

"ELLO, LITTLE QUEEN."

They were shaped like humans, but with no eyes and no noses—only gaping mouths. Their bodies were made of shadow. Their horns curved like scythes.

They were three.

"The Dark Ones," the queen whispered.

The Dark Ones howled, the same sound that had haunted the queen's dreams for weeks.

"She knows us! The queen knows us! What an honor!" The Dark Ones bowed low, stretching toward the queen's feet.

The queen reached into her pocket, thinking of her knife—but withdrew only a single black feather.

The Dark Ones cackled. "She fights with feathers!" one cried.

"She fights with fur!" This Dark One held out its hand. Clenched inside was the terrified fox.

"She fights with slithery, slippery scales!" The third Dark One wrapped the struggling snake around its neck and pulled tight.

"Leave them alone!" cried the queen.

But the Dark Ones only laughed and laughed.

The crow dove out of the trees with a piercing cry and pecked at the Dark Ones where their eyes should have been.

The tallest grabbed the bird by the neck, opened a hole in its own dark chest, and stuffed the bird inside.

"Stop it! Stop it!" The queen searched for weapons and

*found none. She threw herself upon the Dark Ones, tugged them to the ground, stomped on them, tore at them with her teeth—but still they howled and screeched.*

*"You can't hurt us," they jeered. "We are you, and you are us."*

*"I am nothing like you. I am a queen."*

*"And you carry darkness inside you." The Dark Ones stroked the queen's cheeks with six clawed hands. "And we know nothing of light."*

*"If you release my friends," said the queen, "I'll allow you to have me instead."*

*"Oh, she'll allow it, she'll allow us," laughed the Dark Ones. "The mighty, mighty queen!"*

*"Well? Have we a bargain?"*

*The Dark Ones fell silent. "You would give yourself to us?"*

*"How can I not? You are me, and I am you. We are the same. We are one."*

*The Dark Ones licked their lips. Their fangs dripped black. "We will do this thing, little queen."*

*So the queen held her head high and closed her eyes.*

*The Dark Ones latched on to her, digging their shadowed claws into her shoulders, wrapping their arms around her throat.*

*When the queen opened her eyes, she saw the world through a cloudy black veil.*

*She staggered to the river, and in the water's reflection she found only her own image.*

But she knew the Dark Ones were there, heavy on her back.

She felt their claws.

She smelled their rotten breath.

"Run," she told the snake, the fox, the crow. "There is nothing left for you here. Run!"

The snake fled first, then the fox, and last, with a soft, sad cry, the crow.

The queen was alone.

On her back the Dark Ones crooned, "You will never be alone again."

# 34

IT IS THE NINTH THURSDAY I have spent at Hart House.

Everyone is downstairs. I hear a movie playing. Aunt Bridget brought out the board games after dinner, and there is a full-blown tournament underway.

I did not eat dinner with everyone else, claiming I felt sick.

*The Dark Ones stroked the queen's head, their fingernails digging into the queen's scalp, pressing hard against her skull. Her body throbbed with pain.*

I decide it is safe to take out my notebook from underneath my pillow.

(I do feel sick, but not in the way my family thinks.)

Later I try to sleep, but I cannot. Recently I have been finding it difficult to stop my racing thoughts.

*"No sleep for the little queen," crooned the Dark Ones, pressing against her pounding head. "Not now, not ever."*

Someone is pushing a piece of paper beneath my door. I see shadows in the hallway and hear footsteps down the stairs.

The front door opens and shuts; Grandma calls out good-bye. She will watch the procession of cars down the driveway, waving until she cannot see them anymore.

I retrieve the note and read it:

*Gma & Gpa going to city this wknd,* the note says, in Gretchen's handwriting.

Gretchen. Kennedy. Dex. Ruth.

As I picture each of their faces, it becomes harder to breathe.

I could have gone downstairs tonight to see them; I could have.

*"Could have, could have," sang the Dark Ones mockingly. They ground their heels into the queen's shoulders until her knees buckled and she fell. "What good is 'could have'? Too late for 'could have.'"*

I read the note again: *Gma & Gpa going to city this wknd.* And then: *FYI.*

I stand in the hallway outside Avery's bedroom door for five minutes before I decide I really should just knock.

This week on the way to and from Dr. Bristow's office, she introduced me to the Clash and the Violent Femmes. So I suppose we are mostly friends now.

But what I am about to ask her is a big deal. Possibly too big.

I bounce on my toes, thinking.

Avery opens the door. "Okay, you win. I was going to let you stand out here all night, but it turns out I'm not that patient."

"You knew I was out here?"

Avery gives me this look like, *Please, you amateur.* "So, what is it?"

I follow her inside. "Well . . . it's complicated."

She sits on the floor and resumes painting her toenails a bright orange. "Spit it out, Fin."

"I wasn't really sick tonight. Or I was, kind of, but not like everyone thinks."

"Okay . . ."

How to put it? "I was feeling stressed."

Avery looks up, her perfectly shaped eyebrows furrowed. "About your parents?"

My throat clenches up. I cannot look at her. "I guess. It's fine, though." I am lucky to be safe and alive. I have no bills to pay. I have my Everwood.

(So stop complaining, Finley!)

(A divorce won't kill you.)

Avery nudges my foot with hers. "Hey. I'm sorry. We don't have to talk about that." She holds out her bottle of orange polish. It's called Orange You Glad?

Sure, why not? This will give me something to do with my hands. I pull off my socks and go to town.

"So, anything else on your mind?" Avery asks. "You don't have to tell me, but maybe it'll help?"

Lots of other things are on my mind. Particularly the Dark Ones on my back.

Sometimes when I look in the mirror, I think I can see them, even though I am fully aware that they are figments of my imagination.

I try not to let myself think about them, but my brain is disobedient.

Avery is watching me, frowning.

"Lots of things," I answer, trying to sound breezy. "You know, the usual stuff."

". . . Right."

"Anyway, I think I would feel better if everyone came over Saturday night and we had a giant party while Grandma and Grandpa are in the city."

"Okay. . . . For some reason I thought you were going to tell me something a lot worse. You looked all dramatic and Finleyish when you came in."

"What does *Finleyish* mean?"

"Way too serious for an eleven-year-old. Like you have a million thoughts to overthink."

I laugh a little because I am not sure what else to do. I love that Avery feels like she knows me well enough to turn my name into an adjective. I cradle the word *Finleyish* in my heart like it is a bird with a broken wing.

"The thing is, I'd like it to be a secret," I say.

"You'd like what to be a secret?"

"The party. I want you to drive me to everyone's houses and help me sneak them out while the adults are asleep, and then I want us to come back here and have a secret party. I want us all to be able to go in the Everwood without anyone finding out."

I finish my right foot. My toenails look like tiny, bright traffic cones.

"Are you serious?" Avery says.

"Completely. I promise I'm not high on nail polish or anything."

Avery's eyebrows shoot up. "What do you know about being high?"

"Nothing other than what I hear on television."

Avery shakes her head, smiling. "You're crazy, you know that?"

"Sometimes I think I might be."

Avery goes quiet and faces me. "Look. I shouldn't have said that. I've got to be more careful about what I say around you."

"No, you don't. Then it'll be like with Grandma, and no one will say anything real around me, and everyone will be pretending."

"Finley—"

I bend down and blow on my toenails until I regain control of myself. "So will you do it?"

"Seeing a psychologist doesn't mean you're crazy," Avery says. "Lots of people see psychologists. I probably will someday. If you grow up in this family, it's kind of inevitable. And what does *crazy* even mean, anyway? It means 'different from normal,' I guess, but what does *that* mean? I don't think it means anything, because there are too many possible definitions of *normal*, which means *crazy* doesn't mean anything either."

I do not say a word because my eyes still feel hot and wobbly. I am not sure I can convincingly blow on my toenails for much longer.

Avery sighs. "All right. I'll do it."

"Really?"

"Really."

"Why?"

"Because you're my cousin, and I know this will make you happy. And Kennedy misses you tons. She texts me constantly for updates."

I sit back and stare at my toenails. "They miss me." Saying it out loud sends a soft wave of warmth through my entire body. "They miss *me*."

"Of course they do. If you ask me, I think this whole situation is a load of . . . well, of you-know-what. Grandma and Grandpa should let you guys run wild in the forest as much as you like. Who freaking cares? You're eleven."

"They don't like the Baileys."

"They're snobs, and they need to get over it." She tosses a clear bottle at me. "Here, I forgot. Top coat."

"I think it's more than that," I say. "Something happened when they were all teenagers. The aunts, I mean, and my dad. Mr. Bailey, too. Something nobody wants to talk about.

I think it's why Dad wrote that letter. He and Grandma got into a big fight."

"Maybe he was being eighteen and dramatic. It happens."

"Maybe. Did you know there was a fire back in the woods when they were teenagers?"

"The Travers fire? Sure."

"Did you know your mom and all the aunts, they tried to save the family, but they couldn't?"

Avery frowns. "Really?"

"Yeah. And no one talks about it. That's strange, right?"

Avery shakes her head. "Aren't you a little young for conspiracy theories?"

"Yeah, I guess."

We are quiet for a couple of minutes as we paint over our toenails with the top coat.

Then Avery clears her throat. "So, you know Grandma and Grandpa aren't going to the city for fun, right?"

"Then why are they?"

"That's where Grandma's doctor is. She's starting up her chemo treatments again."

I stop applying the top coat. "Oh."

"It's not a big deal," Avery says, not looking at me.

"Yes, it is."

Avery sniffles and looks up at the ceiling. "God. I hate this."

I scoot closer; her leg is warm against mine.

Avery puts her arm around me. "Okay. Okay. We're doing it. We're having a party."

"We don't have to—"

"No. We do. We're not going to *not* do it just because Grandma's sick. She doesn't want anyone to treat her any differently? She wants to keep it a secret? Fine. We're going to have a great time without her. Everything is normal, and what's more normal than a party, right?"

Avery glares over at me, her eyes still wet, and I nod.

"Okay," I say, "we're going to have a great time."

UEEN SHE IS.”

    “Queen she's not.”

    “Ours she is.”

    “Free she's not!”

As the queen stumbled through the Everwood, the Dark Ones sang, taunting her. When they hungered, they clawed darkness from her heart and slurped it down.

“Child, you carry a great burden.”

The queen looked up, dazed, and found that she had walked into the humble hut of a seer.

The seer's eyes were white and blind. They fixed on the Dark Ones hunched on the queen's back, though the creatures were invisible to everyone but the queen herself.

“Forgive me,” said the queen hoarsely. “I have lost my way.”

The seer knelt before the queen and took her chin in one bony hand. “You do not know how true that is, child. I can help you.”

“No.”

“I will ask you for nothing in return. Consider it a gift. I want to help you.”

The queen struggled to her feet. “I am the queen of the Everwood. I do not need your help. I must find my way out of this forest and bring my burden with me. Only then can the Everwood be saved.”

"So brave," said the seer, "and so foolish. Take this, please." She folded wrapped food into the queen's hands.

The Dark Ones slapped it away.

"The queen is hungry! The queen needs to eat!" They tore chunks of fog from the air and spooned it into the queen's mouth. She ate greedily.

They clawed at her heart, drew out fresh spools of darkness, and devoured it. The queen lost her footing and struggled to breathe.

The seer watched, unblinking.

"We feed her; she feeds us!" the Dark Ones cried. "A queen, a queen, a delicious queen!"

"Thank you for your kindness," gasped the queen, and left the hut, her head held high.

# 35

*Dear Jack,*
*Meet us at the Tower tomorrow night at 11:45.*
*The ancient guardians are away.*
*We will be having a midnight revel.*
*All pirates are required to attend.*
*Your friend,*
*Finley*

First we liberate Gretchen.

Avery inches her car down Stick's cul-de-sac with the head-lights turned off. She is chewing gum and looks supremely bored, but I don't buy it.

From the backseat I text Gretchen; five seconds later her window inches open. She pops out her screen, pulls the window closed, and sneaks across her yard and into Avery's car through the door I am holding open for her.

I am impressed that she manages to restrain herself until we've left Stick's street.

That is when she explodes.

"Oh my *God*," she shrieks, yanking me into a painful hug. "This is the best night of my life. Can we do this every weekend? I feel like I could run a marathon, or maybe punch someone. I seriously could."

Avery snorts. "I'd like to see that."

We drive across town to pick up Kennedy and the twins from Avery's house. It is not as palatial as Hart House but still large enough to fit, I estimate, ten of my apartments inside it.

Kennedy convinced Aunt Bridget to let the twins sleep over tonight, so she could help them sneak out. Avery, Gretchen, and I all hold our breaths from the moment I text Kennedy to the moment she, Dex, and Ruth join us in the car.

(I realize that is physically impossible, but that's what it feels like.)

In the front seat Kennedy lets out a huge sigh and slumps. Ruth and Dex bounce between me and Gretchen, singing, "Par-ty! Par-ty!"

Gretchen punches Kennedy's arm. "You okay there, beautiful?"

Kennedy bursts into giggles. "I have never snuck out before. *Never.*"

"Oh, Little Miss Perfect. We're rebels now. Let's get tattoos!" Gretchen says.

*"No."* Avery glances over. "Kennedy, are you wearing lip gloss?"

Kennedy freezes, her eyes huge. "What? No."

"You totally are."

"Please tell me you aren't wearing lip gloss for Cole Bailey,"

Gretchen moans. "I will literally puke my guts up if you're wearing lip gloss for Cole Bailey."

"Don't even think about it." Avery glares at us in the rearview mirror. "Puking is strictly forbidden in my car."

As we make our way back to Hart House, I listen to Gretchen rant about Cole Bailey. Kennedy defends him. Avery plays peacemaker.

The sounds of their voices fold me into a warm feeling that reminds me of home.

Here, in this car, I fit. I am one of them.

Here I am a Hart.

## WHAT IT MEANS TO BE A HART

- You don't need anyone but each other to throw a really good party.

The Everwood is different in the dark.

Tonight there is no moon. Clouds hide the stars. All we have to help us find our way through the trees is a flashlight.

Right now my forest seems like a living, breathing creature with a mind of its own.

Any minute now the Everwood's shadows will shift and stretch, and the mud underneath our feet will transform into a huge beast that will carry us away.

I do not think I would mind being taken away to a strange land with only my cousins for company.

We have arranged lanterns around the Tower. Avery found strings of lights in the garage and has hooked them up to an extension cord. It looks like we are surrounded by tiny fairies.

(The good kind, not the Everwood kind that set traps.)

Kennedy has pulled up the radio on her phone, but one of Avery's requirements for allowing this party is that she gets to choose the music.

So now we are listening to Marvin Gaye. Kennedy is dancing with Dex, Gretchen is setting up snacks, and Ruth is running around in her monster mask, roaring at the top of her lungs.

*The queen startled, looking through the trees and the ever-present fog. Was that a chimera, a creature of the Everwood deep, approaching in the gloom?*

*"She sees things that are," whispered the Dark Ones. "She sees things that aren't."*

Ruth latches on to my leg, roaring through her paper-bag teeth.

"What else?" Avery puts her hands on her hips. "This looks pretty good so far, right?"

When I look up at Avery, my heart expands to fill my entire body. I worried it would be weird, having her here. She is new to the Everwood. I would not blame her for thinking we are childish.

But she doesn't look like that at all. She is laughing, letting herself be dragged by Ruth to the Tower, because Ruth insists that Avery add her artwork to our painted collage.

Avery belongs here—in the Everwood—like we do.

I put on my crown and make a fallen tree my throne.

I have this horrible feeling that Jack never got my note, or that he has forgotten about me since we stopped coming out to the woods.

But then a chorus of shouts fills the air. Ruth leaps out of the Tower and puts up her fists.

"Attack mode!" she shrieks.

Gretchen rolls her eyes. "It's just the *Baileys*."

*Just* the Baileys. And Gretchen says it like it means nothing, when it really means everything.

### WHAT HAS CHANGED THIS SUMMER

- Jack, Cole, and Bennett are *just* the Baileys.
- The Bone House is clean(er).
- I am no longer afraid to talk to Avery. (Mostly.)
  - Related: I have developed an appreciation for classic rock.
- My cousins are no longer strangers who happen to resemble me.
  - They have become more than that.
  - They are inside me now, pieces of myself I never realized were missing.

- Now that I have found them, I will never let them go.
- I have developed my first crush on an age-appropriate boy.


Here he is, bowing to me, wearing an eye patch Dex assembled out of construction paper and bright green finger paint.

I try not to laugh. "Should you have wet paint so close to your eye?"

Jack shrugs, grinning. "Girls wear mascara."

"I don't wear mascara."

"You can try some of mine, if you want." Avery plops down beside me. "So, you're Jack, huh?"

Jack springs to his feet. "Arrrr, the one and only, matey!"

"Matey?"

"He's a pirate," I explain. "All the Baileys are."

Gretchen is lying flat on her back nearby, looking for stars through the Baileys' telescope. "Once they were notorious, but they've been redeemed."

Avery nods sagely. "Oh, I see."

"And you must be the artist," Jack says.

"Avery."

"Finley says you're really talented. She says you could get into any school you wanted."

My face flushes. What do I know about art, anyway?

But Avery kisses my cheek and whispers, "Thanks, Fin."

With her beside me, everything is okay. Our shared secret knowledge sits between us, invisible, tying us together.

It does not seem so terrible that Grandma has cancer, that Dad is not here. Everything feels beatable and not quite real, like I am watching the world unfold on a television screen.

Cole is painting vines onto Kennedy's arms with dark green paint.

Ruth is burying Dex in leaves.

Gretchen is blindfolded, playing Marco Polo with Bennett and Jack. Kennedy yells a warning every time someone gets too close to the river.

There is no reason for me to be afraid. The night spins on and on, like it was made for us. We are wild Everwood creatures, and this is our kingdom.

Then I hear Cole yell, "Stop it!"

At the sound of his shout I turn around and see Gretchen trying to start a fire.

She has made a circle out of stones from the riverbed, with twigs piled in the middle of it. Kennedy hands her the skinny lighter from the kitchen.

"It's not a big deal," Gretchen says. "It'll be a little one. How else are we supposed to toast the marshmallows?"

Cole slaps the lighter out of her hand.

Gretchen stares at him. I think it's the first time I've seen her speechless.

Avery steps out of the Tower, paintbrush in hand. "Hey, chill out! What's your problem?"

"My *problem* is that it's dangerous," Cole replies. "Do you want to explain to your grandparents how their backyard got burned down?"

"It's fine. I'm watching her. We've got a garden hose."

"Right. Have you ever *seen* a forest fire?"

"No. Have you?"

"On TV. It's summer. It hasn't been raining. Do you get that this place is covered in dry leaves? Do you know how fast a 'little fire' could grow out of control?"

Bennett looks out from behind the mask Ruth helped him make. "But, Cole, I want s'mores!"

"Dad told us to never make a fire back here, not even a little one," Cole says. "*Never.* You know that."

Jack laughs. "Since when did you start caring what Dad thinks?"

"Shut up, Jack. You don't get it. You're not the oldest."

"Aw, you're right." Jack pouts and bats his eyelashes. "Please, Big Brother, will you protect me?"

Cole shoves him. "I said, shut up."

"Guys, stop it," Kennedy says. "You're freaking out Dex. Let's just eat the marshmallows uncooked."

Gretchen crosses her arms over her chest. "What kind of s'mores have *uncooked* marshmallows?"

Jack retrieves the fallen lighter and flips it on. "Seriously, Cole. What kind of pirate are you?"

In the next few seconds a million different things seem to happen at once:

Jack successfully lights the pile of twigs on fire.

The fire catches and grows, quickly—still within the circle of stones, but even Gretchen backs away.

Cole screams, "Put it out!" and kicks dirt onto the fire.

Jack shoves him, Cole shoves back, and I am not sure who tackles who, but soon they are wrestling in the mud and leaves, punching each other.

"Whoa," Ruth whispers, staring wide-eyed.

"Stop it!" Kennedy shrieks. "Somebody's going to get hurt!"

Avery grabs Jack's shoulders. "Cut it out! If you want to fight, go home and do it. Not here."

I am impressed by Avery's Mom voice. Jack and Cole glare at each other, panting. I think everything might be okay now—but then Gretchen lights the fire once more.

"It's *not* a big deal," she insists.

"Fine," Cole says, "light your stupid fire. I'm going to go tell Dad."

Gretchen snorts. "Yeah, like he'll actually stop drinking long enough to leave the house."

Cole steps back, looking like Jack has punched him all over again.

Everything is quiet except for the crackling fire and the radio.

"What?" Gretchen crosses her arms and glares at the ground. "Everyone knows about that. People at school say—"

"Shut up, Gretchen." Jack holds his cheek. "You don't know anything."

"Gretchen, don't be a jerk, and put out that fire," says Avery.

"But Cole—"

"I don't care. *I'm* telling you to put it out."

But it is too late. Cole is already running toward the Bailey house.

I take off after him.

Avery yells at me to come back.

"Finley!" Jack calls. I hear him running after me. "Don't! Stop!"

But I will not stop. If Cole tells his father about our party, about the fire, Mr. Bailey will probably tell Grandma and Grandpa, too—and then what?

*"The queen in her forest, far from home," the Dark Ones chanted, grabbing on to the queen's shoulders and twisting, twisting. "The queen in her forest, all alone."*

Cole must have really hurt Jack, because I am outrunning him, chasing Cole up the steep hill to his house on all fours, pulling myself up by the roots of a gnarled tree.

"Finley, please, stop!" Jack shouts. "Don't go inside!"

I follow Cole across the Baileys' run-down wooden porch and through a swinging front door with the screen broken. He stops at the entryway to a dark living room with peeling wallpaper, lit up by a television.

I am dizzy and out of breath. "Please, Cole, don't tell your dad. Grandma will—"

"Who are you?"

A woman stands in front of me, thin and tired-looking. Her mouth is hard; her eyes are harder.

"I'm . . . Finley. Finley Hart."

"Hart? What do you want? Don't you know how to knock? Or are you too good for that?"

Cole hurries over. "Mom, leave her alone—"

*Mom?*

"I'm sorry," I say. "I was trying to talk to Cole—"

"You're friends with my boys?" The woman steps toward me. "Stay away from them, all right? They don't need to get mixed up with you people on top of everything else."

"Are you still here?" bellows a voice from another room. "I told you to get out!"

The woman yells back, "Don't worry, you won't see me again for a *long* time." Then she looks back at me. "Seriously, girl. Don't stick around here. Baileys have bad blood." She grins. It is not a friendly smile. "But I guess you know all about that, huh?"

Then she shoves past me and out the door, car keys in hand.

Cole watches the woman leave. The headlights of her car make his face look frightened and small. "Finley, get out of here, seriously—"

Something crashes in the other room, like a chair falling over.

Jack barrels in from outside. "Please, Finley, just go."

Jack is crying.

Jack is *crying*.

I stare at him. "Jack?"

"Who is that?"

We all freeze at the sound of Mr. Bailey's voice. He stumbles out of the living room toward us.

*The queen stepped back in horror. Here, at last, was the infamous Fellfolk troll.*

*His lair was a festering pile of waste—a once-grand castle now fallen to ruin.*

*Curled on her back, the Dark Ones cheered. "Run, little queen! Or he'll pound you and smash you and grind you to bits!"*

I do not run.

"It's nobody, Dad," says Cole. "You can sit down and watch—"

Mr. Bailey ignores Cole. His face is pale and thin, his dark hair greasy. Like that night two weeks ago when we watched the stars, I think he looks like Jack—but this time it is all wrong. He reeks—like Aunt Bridget's drinks, but so much worse—and he cannot keep his balance.

"Hello, sir." I will not run. I will not run. "It's Finley." When he does not answer, I add, "Remember? I told you the story about the Everwood?"

Mr. Bailey points at the door. "Get out of here. No Harts allowed on this property."

But I am afraid to move, even though Jack is tugging on my hand. "Leave, Finley, *leave*."

"Get out, I said!" Mr. Bailey yells. He looks like he either wants to throw something or cry. "Get off my property!"

My ears ring with the horrible things he proceeds to say about my family: We are snobs. We are criminals. We don't deserve what we have. I run out onto the porch and to the edge of the hill that leads down to the river.

Someone approaches the hill with a flashlight—Avery, holding Bennett's hand.

Jack catches up with me. I could reach out and touch his arm, but I have never felt so far away from another person.

"Jack," I whisper, "I'm really sorry."

"It's fine."

"You kept telling me to stop and I wouldn't—"

"You should have. You weren't supposed to see them. He's not always like this. You saw him that one night. Mostly he's fine."

I cannot see Jack's face, but I can hear him crying. Jack is not supposed to cry. Jack is supposed to smile and make jokes and talk like a pirate.

"That was your mom?" I ask. "That woman who left? Where did she go?"

Jack won't look at me. "Away. Like usual. I guess I don't blame her."

"What do you mean?"

"Just leave, Finley. Get out of here."

"Not until I know you're okay."

"I know how to handle him."

"Maybe you can stay with us tonight, until your dad calms down."

"We're fine, okay? He won't hurt us. He'll fall asleep and wake up and not remember anything."

"But, Jack—"

"Did you not get it? I told you to leave!"

Then Jack shoves me—not hard enough to make me fall, but hard enough to break something inside me.

Jack has never looked at me like this before, like we are worse than strangers. Like he wants nothing to do with me.

"Jack, I'm sorry—"

"Get out of here, Finley. And don't come back."

As Jack helps Bennett up the hill, I stand there, shaking. Jack leads Bennett inside and slams the broken screen door closed. Bennett presses his face against the screen and waves at me. His cheeks are painted yellow and orange.

At the bottom of the hill Avery waits with her flashlight. "You okay?"

"No." I feel like I am going to cry, but nothing comes out.

"Are *they* okay?"

"I think so. I hope so."

Avery takes my hand. "It was a good party, for a while."

I do not answer her, but she is correct.

I suppose most things in a person's life are good for a while, even if that doesn't last very long.

Maybe that is why, even after something has gone wrong, we spend so much time trying to fix it.

Because we remember when it wasn't broken.

# 36

AFTER THE PARTY, AVERY AND I take everyone home and help them sneak back into their houses. Then we return to Hart House and get rid of any evidence of the party. Avery insists on making me pancakes at four in the morning. I can only swallow a couple of bites.

The hollow place inside me that once held my friendship with Jack has been cut open and is bleeding into the rest of me.

Now it is nine in the morning. Ten. Twelve. Grandma and Grandpa will be home soon. I should shower; my hands and arms are covered in dots of paint. Looking at them makes me remember how excited I felt yesterday.

How naïve that Finley was.

(Five-letter word for "gullible, childish, lacking in worldly wisdom.")

At two o'clock I hear the wheels of Grandpa's car crunch on the gravel driveway. I sneak out onto the stairs and listen as Grandma walks across the house, goes straight to her room, and shuts the door.

When I find Grandpa, he is in his office, sitting at his desk and staring at his blank computer screen.

"Grandpa?" I inch inside. "Are you okay?"

He blinks and smiles tiredly at me, and I do not realize until that moment how lost and small he looked before, sitting there all alone.

"Fine. I'm fine." He waves me over to the window seat.

"Grandma's okay?"

"She's very tired, but she'll feel better after some rest."

I fold my arms across my chest. I cannot possibly sit down. "Are you scared?"

Grandpa nods. "Yes."

"Is Grandma?"

His smile is soft. "Your grandmother isn't scared of anything."

"Do you want to go on a drive?"

"Not today. Too much driving this weekend. But, actually, I wanted to tell you something." He folds his hands in his lap and clears his throat. "Your parents are coming by this evening."

"My . . ." I sit down. "Dad's coming?"

"Yes, and your mother. For dinner. They wanted to surprise you, but I . . . I thought you might want to know ahead of time."

There is a thrumming sound in my ears. The rest of the world goes quiet. I cannot think of a reason why my parents would want to show up here to surprise me, except for—

"Okay," I say. I cannot look at Grandpa. If I see his face, it will tell me everything I need to know.

Mom and Dad arrive at five o'clock.

Grandma is still shut away in her bedroom and shows no signs of coming out.

It is probably better that way.

Part of me hugs Mom and Dad; the other part of me is hiding deep inside myself and does not notice much of what is going on around me.

(Are they really here? I do not want to know.)

Grandpa dishes out leftovers, and we all sit around the kitchen table trying to eat. I manage five forkfuls of pasta salad with Avery sitting across from me, watching me, before I cannot take it anymore.

"Why are you here?" I ask.

Everyone is quiet. "We wanted to see you," Mom says, and her smile is so thin and flips my stomach.

"I don't believe you."

Grandpa sets down his fork and wipes his mouth. "Avery, why don't we let them have the room to themselves?"

After Grandpa and Avery leave, I am left stuck between my parents.

(Avery, please come back.)

"So!" Dad tries to sound cheerful. "You know Donovan in 4C?"

"Yeah."

"Mr. Finch got him his first car last week."

"No way."

"Way. Donovan Finch is now officially a driver."

"That's disturbing."

"I agree," says Mom. "They should raise the driver's license age to eighteen."

"Or twenty-five," Dad suggests. "Or never."

Mom laughs, kind of. Silence fills the kitchen like a cloud.

Dad blows out a breath. "So, Finley, we've got something we need to tell you, and it's not going to be an easy thing for us to say, or for you to hear."

"You might not want to talk to us about it at first," Mom says, "not for a while, and that's okay."

"Mom?"

She reaches across the table for my hand. "Yeah, sweetie?"

I am right between okay and freaking out. "What is it? What's wrong?"

(I know exactly what, but I cannot admit it yet, not even to myself, not in these last few seconds before everything changes.)

Then they tell me.

The colors and sounds of the kitchen fade away into static—except for certain words. They buzz around my brain like flies:

*We'll always love each other . . . just not in the same way we used to.*

*Your dad and I . . . we just want to be happy. And we aren't anymore.*

*Sometimes you can love someone, very much, and then things change.*

*This is not because of you. Okay, Fin?*

(No, no, no, no.)

". . . so we think it'd be a good idea if you came home with us," Dad is saying, "instead of waiting a couple more weeks. Then we can start figuring out some things together, and we can talk through what comes next. There'll be a lot of big changes, but—"

"I'm not leaving."

They stare at me. "Sweetie," Mom says, "I know this is hard, but—"

"If you make me leave, I'll hate you forever."

Dad tries to hug me, but I jerk away and go to the other side of the room. "I'm having fun, okay? I'm going to stay until the middle of August like we said I would. I shouldn't have to leave because of your problems."

Mom starts to cry, but I really couldn't care less. I am alone in my static-filled world where sounds cannot hurt me and words cannot hurt me and my parents cannot hurt me.

"Fin, we need to start tackling this as a family," Dad says, "and it'll be easier if you're home with us."

"Home? What home? What family? We're not a family anymore. That's what you just said, isn't it?" I point down the hall toward the rest of the house. I don't even know what I am saying. My voice pinches and cracks, and I hate it. "This is my family. *This* is my home. You brought me here, you made me come here, and I'm going to stay. Isn't that what you wanted? I'm staying. You can leave. *You* can leave."

Then I walk away, past Grandpa standing at the door to his office, and up the stairs, and I shut myself into my room, and I lie very still on my bed, and I breathe, and breathe, and breathe.

Avery comes into my room before bed. "Hey. Your parents left, huh?"

If I open my mouth to answer her, I will begin crying and never stop.

"You want to watch a movie in my room?"

The only safe thing to do is remain perfectly still, right here in my bed, with my notebook.

Avery sits down beside me. "Fin, talk to me."

I find myself wishing I were Jack, even for ten seconds, even though he hates me now, so I could say exactly what I am feeling with no problem.

I find a clean page in my notebook and write it instead:

*D-I-V-O-R-C-E.*

(Seven-letter word for "a family, split in half.")

Avery does not say anything. She is getting pretty good at reading me.

Instead she lies down beside me and pulls the blankets up to our chins, which is just how I like it. With your blanket pulled up that high, it is easy to pretend the rest of the world doesn't exist.

# 37

THEY SAY BAD THINGS HAPPEN in threes, and that seems to be true:

1. Jack got mad at me.
2. D-I-V-O-R-C-E.
3. The twins got poison ivy.

Aunt Bridget brought them over after breakfast, and their legs are red and itchy.

Grandma kneels in front of Dex. "Dexter. Look at me. How did this happen, sweetheart?"

"I have no idea when they were exposed," says Aunt Bridget. "They haven't been anywhere near poison ivy this weekend. It makes no sense."

Dex does not look at Grandma. He looks right at me.

"It was a witch's curse," he says, smiling proudly. "We helped the queen fight."

"These are battle scars," Ruth explains, as if Grandma and Aunt Bridget are three years old. "It's not a big deal, Mom. It was just a party. Haven't you ever snuck out of the house before?"

The room turns cold.

Ruth looks nervous all of a sudden. She looks at me, at Avery. "I was just kidding," she says quietly. "It's not a big deal. Really."

Grandma stands up. "I see."

(Am I the only one who sees her wince, like moving hurts?)

Aunt Bridget frowns. "A witch's curse? What is that supposed to mean? Is this part of your game? Dex, tell me what happened. Right now. What party?"

With everyone staring at him, Dex bursts into tears and tells the whole story, wailing and snotting his face. I stand there, unable to move. This is not what was supposed to happen. It was just a party; it was *our* party. Nothing happened. We were safe.

When Dex is done, Grandma heads for the stairs. I am so afraid that it feels like the rest of the world has stopped moving and is frozen on ice!

"Mom?" asks Aunt Bridget. "Where are you going?"

"I'm putting a stop to this."

I hear the door to my room open, and I understand.

No.

No.

*No.*

"Grandma?" I run up the stairs after her. "What are you doing?"

Avery follows me up the stairs. She is saying something to me, to Grandma. About the party, about everything. She is sorry. She takes full responsibility.

But I don't care. My legs aren't moving quickly enough.

Grandma is in my bedroom. Lifting up my pillow. Shaking my notebook out of the pillowcase.

I do not think. I run at her, grab my notebook, and pull. "Put it back! Stop it! That's mine, it's *mine*!"

Strong arms come around me.

"Finley, it's okay," Grandpa says. "We're not going to throw it away. It's only for a little while, sweetheart."

"Where are you taking it? Please, give it back!" I kick the air, kick Grandpa. I see Avery, in the corner. "Avery! Get it, Avery! Make her stop!"

Avery sounds like she might start crying. "Fin, it'll be okay. I'm so sorry, Grandma, this is my fault. The party was my idea, okay? I swear. Finley didn't do anything."

Grandma tucks my quilt and pillows back into place. "Avery, I never imagined you would do something so irresponsible. Sneaking your eight-year-old cousins out of the house in the middle of the night?"

"I know, it was stupid—"

Aunt Bridget stands at the door, the twins behind her. "What on earth is going on?"

"Bridget," says Grandpa, "take Dex and Ruth downstairs. You'll upset them."

With Grandpa distracted, I wiggle loose and grab my notebook, but Grandma has a good grip on it.

"Please, Grandma, give it back!"

"Finley, I'm trying to help you," Grandma says soothingly.

"You've been spending too much time in this made-up world of yours. It isn't healthy, don't you see? It's confusing your cousins and you, too. We'll all have dinner tonight, and you'll stay downstairs with us. We'll play some card games. Doesn't that sound fun?"

I am crying so hard, I lose hold of my notebook. I can't find it.

Where is it?

*Where is it?*

Grandma gathers me into a tight hug.

"Let go!" I try to get loose, but she is strong. She sits on the bed with me in her lap.

"Shh, Finley, shh," she whispers, but I will not listen, not to her, not to any of them.

I shut my eyes and twist and push. "Give it back. Please. Please."

"Sit here with me for a while." Then she says, so soft, "You're going to be fine. We've got you. We've all got you."

"My parents," I whisper. "They're getting a . . ."

(*D-I-V-O-R-C-E.*)

Grandma hugs me even closer, and I am angry at her, but I never want her to let me go. She is warm, and she is sick, and she is mine.

"I know, darling," she says to me. "It's all right. You can cry. I'm here now. Breathe, sweet girl."

I shake my head. Breathing is too hard. I grab on to Grandma's shirt.

Grandma starts to rock me. She smells like cookies and perfume and clean sheets.

"Finley girl, Finley girl, what does she see?" Grandma begins to sing. "I see a birdie, flying so free."

No one sings to me except Mom, during storms. I press my face into Grandma's sleeve. I am so tired.

(*D-I-V-O-R-C-E*.)

"Finley girl, Finley girl, what does she see? I see a butterfly, sweet as can be."

My head hurts. If I could lie down, I would feel better. Grandma's arms rock and rock. Her voice floats like feathers.

"Finley girl, Finley girl, what does she see?" Grandma kisses my head. "I see a house, and a tall green tree."

"Please," I whisper, "give it back. It's mine."

(A family, split in half.)

Grandma's arms tighten around me. "I'm so sorry, Finley girl . . ."


*The Dark Ones whispered, "What do you see, little queen?"*

*"I see nothing," answered the queen, and laid her head in the dirt.*


When I wake up, afternoon sunlight fills the room with gold.

Grandma is sleeping beside me.

Her wig sits crookedly on her head. Her eyelids are thin, and her hands curl around the pillow.

She took my notebook.

She took my Everwood.

But she looks like a child, sleeping like this. She snores like Dad.

I put my hand on her arm. Warm, small, delicate. Her makeup has rubbed off, and I see the wrinkles of her skin.

Finley girl, Finley girl, what do you see?

I see a Hart, and she looks like me.

# 38

WITH GRANDMA ASLEEP, AVERY IN her room, and Grandpa nowhere to be found, I sneak outside and hurry through the pit, across the Bridge, and into the Everwood.

*"No matter where you try to run," taunted the Dark Ones, pounding on her shoulders, "you'll be left behind by everyone!"*

*"A pretty family, split in half," began one of them.*

*"It's almost enough to make you . . . laugh!"*

*The Dark Ones' cackles beat against the queen's head like fists.*

When I see the Bone House rising up out of the field like a lonely monster, my lungs feel too full for my body.

I climb the porch and step inside. "Hello? Jack? Anyone home?"

I wait, afraid to move. Maybe Jack is cleaning somewhere. Maybe he is out back visiting the Travers family. Maybe he will crash into me with a hug.

But the Bone House is silent today. I am alone.

I find the Travers family shrine under the stairs and sit in front of it, staring at the ruined photograph.

"What do I do?" I ask them.

*"There you are," said the ghost of the wizard, floating through the cold castle walls. "I thought you'd forgotten about me."*

*"Never," said the queen, her voice faint, for the Dark Ones had stolen so much of it away. "I have been on a hunt for . . ." The queen paused. It was difficult to think with these weights on her back. "I cannot remember."*

*"We don't like ghosts," complained one of the Dark Ones. "Make it go away."*

*"You don't want to talk to him," hissed another. "He's got nasty ghost warts and vile ghost breath."*

*"Thank you for finding my family, girl queen," said the wizard's ghost. "The castle is not so empty now, and we are not so alone."*

*"Have you happened to see," whispered the queen, "a pirate boy here?"*

*"Why, as a matter of fact I have. But not for some time. Listen now. Listen."*

*The wizard's ghost pointed out toward the Everwood. "The trees are whispering something."*

*"Trees can't talk," spat the Dark Ones. "Ghosts only tell lies."*

*"Go find him." The ghostly hand on the queen's shoulder*

*dripped through her like cold rain. "No one in the Everwood*
*should be alone. That's what the trees say."*

I wander the house, seeing what the Baileys have done in
my absence. Some leaves have blown in to scatter the floor,
but if you ignore the missing half of the house, and the black
marks we cannot scrub away, it almost looks like a family's
home again. There are plastic cups and paper plates. Someone has stacked old blankets in the corner of the living room.

On a wall in the kitchen I find a mural. The colors are
bright and new. There are four boys and four girls. Dark
heads and golden heads.

One of the girls isn't painted as well as the others, but I
love it the best. It is me. I look wild and have freckles and am
holding a notebook.

I am wearing a crown.

When I get to the Baileys' house, I am so nervous, I almost
turn around—but I have to tell Jack that I am sorry, that my
parents are splitting me into pieces, that I miss him.

I have to explain how I know that Cole painted the mural in
the Bone House—except for the picture of me. Jack painted
me; it's obvious and messy, and mine, and his.

But when I get to the front door, I hear voices around the
house.

One of them is Grandpa's.

I tiptoe past the creaking wooden porch and peek around

the corner to see the dirt driveway, Grandpa, and Mr. Bailey. They're arguing.

Grandpa hands Mr. Bailey an envelope. "Please take it, Geoffrey."

"I'm tired of your money," Mr. Bailey says. "Go home to your castle and leave us alone. I won't say anything to anyone, you know that."

"And what'll you do for your boys?" asks Grandpa sternly. "School's coming up. They'll need clothes, and supplies—"

"Oh, don't play stupid. The other day my youngest found three backpacks with ribbons tied on, sitting on the porch. Stuffed full of school supplies. Wonder where they got those, huh?"

*A Pack for Every Back,* I think. Grandma gave the Bailey boys backpacks? But she hates the Baileys.

(They're a blight on the town.)

"Somebody's got to do it," says Grandpa.

"I can take care of my own kids," insists Mr. Bailey.

"Some days you can. Other days . . ."

"You know, maybe things wouldn't be so bad if your family hadn't—"

"Don't even start with that," Grandpa says, his voice low and dangerous. "You had problems long before the fire, and you know it."

My blood runs slow and heavy at the word *fire.* What fire? Not *the* fire?

Everything is quiet. Mr. Bailey looks angry, like he's about to yell at Grandpa, then he stops, and looks away into the woods.

Grandpa seems like he might be about to say something too, but instead he pats Mr. Bailey gently on the shoulder, presses the envelope into Mr. Bailey's hands, and leaves.

I wait, listening to the fading sound of his tires crunching on the dirt road. I am thinking hard, trying to sort through what I have heard, when Mr. Bailey comes around the porch and finds me.

We stare at each other.

"I can't escape you Harts today." He grabs a half-empty bottle from the porch rail and takes a big sip. "What do you want, Finley?"

I do not know what to say. I wonder if he even remembers how he yelled at me the other night.

"What's the matter? Need some money?" Mr. Bailey takes a stack of bills out of the envelope and shakes them out across the floor. "Your grandpa gives me tons."

I stand, shaking a one-hundred-dollar bill off my foot. Mr. Bailey's breath smells today; I should probably go, but the sight of all that money spilled across the wood keeps me in place. It looks wrong there, rude and ugly.

"Why?" I ask.

"Well, once upon a time," he says, taking another sip and then tossing his empty bottle into the trees. "Isn't that how those stories you write start? Once upon a time there was a family of snobs who lived in a castle and didn't want anyone to know about the bad things they did. So they paid the lazy bum across the river to make sure he never told anyone their deepest, darkest, most terrible secret."

Mr. Bailey watches me. "Do you get it?"

"The family of snobs is my family," I whisper. "And the lazy bum is . . ."

"Yep, that's me. King of the bums." Mr. Bailey's smile is made of razor blades and mean jokes. "And the secret is this, Miss Finley Hart: There was a fire back in these woods, a long time ago. And your family started it."

I back away from him. The world pounds in rhythm with my heart. "You're lying."

He shakes his head. "Girl, I wish I was."

"Dad?" Jack's voice calls out from inside. "Who are you talking to?"

Before Jack can see me, I jump off the money-covered porch and run.

# 39

AT TWO THIRTY THE NEXT afternoon, Avery does not drive me to Dr. Bristow's office.

Grandpa does.

We do not speak.

This is all right with me. Since yesterday my mind has been a dark and dangerous maze, like the forest I once thought the Everwood to be.

Mr. Bailey was lying. He had to be lying.

And yet it makes sense.

My aunts were heroes, but no one in my family has ever talked about it.

The fire took place twenty-two years ago. Dad was fourteen. Eventually he left, and he never looked back.

He had an argument with Grandma.

Pieces fit together, but many are still missing.

I cannot believe this is true, because if it is, that means—

I glance at Grandpa.

He looks exactly as he has since coming home on Sunday—tired and red-eyed and like his skin no longer fits quite right.

The radio is on, but he is not singing.

(Not my Grandpa. He couldn't. He *wouldn't*.)

I almost tell him I heard him talking to Mr. Bailey; the words are *right there*, ready to jump.

But if I tell him, if I ask him for the truth—

I grab Grandpa's hand, and he holds on tight.

I do not want to know the truth. Not now. Not yet.

Not ever.


When Dr. Bristow joins me in her office, she is her familiar, cheerful self.

"Hey there, Finley," she says, heading for her minifridge. "Want something to drink? I've got juice today. That pretentious, overpriced kind you get at coffee shops. Decided to splurge this morning, and I've felt guilty about it all day."

"Sure."

"So." Dr. Bristow settles in with her coffee. "You had an eventful weekend, I hear."

Ah. So we are getting right to it. Fine.

I sip my juice and shrug, keeping my eyes on the floor.

"Do you want to talk to me about it?"

"Not really."

"You know, I snuck out of the house quite a few times when I was your age," Dr. Bristow says. "Never for anything illicit. Just messing around with the neighbor kids, like you did, having fun."

Illicit. Seven-letter word for "against the law."

(Like starting fires and not telling anyone about it?)

(It cannot be true.)

Dr. Bristow sits back. "I'm glad you befriended the Bailey boys. They need it."

"You know them?"

"Sure. My husband's the principal at the middle school, remember? Cole and Jack. Smart kids, and sweet."

I follow the weaving path of my shoelaces. Under, over. Under, over.

"Jack's about your age, right? Maybe a little older."

Hearing someone else say his name is like a hand around my throat. "I think so."

"They were hanging out with you and your cousins, right?"

I nod.

"Why do you think your grandparents have a problem with that?"

Because Mr. Bailey knows their secret. It all makes so much sense now.

(But he's lying, he has to be!)

I shrug.

"Finley. Hey, can you look at me for a sec?"


*The queen found herself transfixed by the seer's milky white eyes.*

*The seer smiled. "Hello, child. There you are. It is nice to see your face."*

*On the queen's back the Dark Ones shrieked at the invasion of the seer's magic. They dug harder into the queen's back, pressing her lower to the ground.*

*"Resist," they hissed. "Resist her."*

*"Child," said the seer kindly, "I only want to help you. You know that, don't you? I only want to help you regain your crown."*

*Then the seer moved closer and said, "The ancient guardians need you, my queen. The Everwood needs you."*

The phone on Dr. Bristow's desk rings, and she goes to answer it.

I am so tired, I feel dizzy.

"Finley, I'm sorry," says Dr. Bristow, "but I have to go talk to another patient for a couple of minutes. I never do this, but it's kind of an emergency." She puts her hand on my shoulder. "Is that okay? I'll be right back."

I stare at her shoes and nod.

(Do not look into her eyes, Finley, whatever you do.)

(Her eyes will ensnare you; she will see right into your soul.)

Once Dr. Bristow is out of the room, everything is quiet—except for the sound of birds singing in the tree outside her open window.

*Her open window.*

I stare at it, and I form a plan. My heart pounds out the steps like the bullet points of a list.

I don't know how long psychologist emergencies take to resolve. There is no time for me to debate this.

I hurry toward the window and climb out. It was not

particularly wise of Dr. Bristow to leave her window open. I cannot be the only kid who sits in her office desperate for escape.

I doubt she will leave the window open after this.

I pull the window shut behind me and crawl through the row of hedges outside, scraping up my arms and legs. Once I have cleared them, I pause to get my bearings.

Dr. Bristow could stick her head out the window any moment now. I peek back through the hedges to check, and catch my reflection in the glass.

*The queen stared at her reflection, and all at once everything became clear.*

*She saw what she truly was, what she had always been before arriving at the Everwood, and what she would always be: an orphan girl, sad and lonely. Obsessive. Troubled. Different. The daughter of a ruined family.*

*Her adventures in the Everwood had been nothing but a great pretend.*

*She had discovered the secret of the Everwood, and it was unthinkable.*

*The Dark Ones jeered. "Finley girl, Finley girl, what do you see? I see a queen who will never be free!"*

*And the queen knew they were right.*

*She had tried to do the noble thing. She had tried to leave the Everwood, to rid it of her own poison.*

*But she could never leave. At last she accepted that horrible truth.*

*The Everwood was the only place left to her that she understood. It was a place where she could live in peace with the Dark Ones on her back. It was a place she could control.*

*She would be alone, but that was for the best. She had always been alone, and when you are alone, you cannot love, and the secrets of others cannot hurt you.*

*So she tore the crown from her head and ran west as fast as her legs could carry her.*

# 40

I THINK I MIGHT BE lost.

I am following the route to Dr. Bristow's office in reverse, keeping to the trees at the side of the road.

*The queen clawed her way deeper into the forest, raising welts on her skin.*

I am trudging through a cornfield when it begins to rain. I assume the storm has been building all day, but I have not been paying attention.

*The sky opened up and unleashed a storm. The rain fell in icy sheets, and the lightning flashed. But not even the roiling storm clouds were as dark as the creatures on the queen's back.*

*"Run away and hide," they whispered. "We'll hide in the Everwood, where the monsters go. We'll sleep when we want to sleep, and hide when we want to hide, and no one will tell us what to do, and no one will have any secrets."*

It is dark out now, and the rain isn't stopping. My clothes are plastered to my skin.

When I find the train tracks, I follow them. I will follow them to wherever Jack once dreamed of going. I will go into the deepest parts of the Everwood that no one has yet explored—where no one lies, and everything is truth.

*"What was that?" cried the Dark Ones. "There, in the trees—is that your little pirate friend?"*

I whirl to face the woods, but I see only a misshapen tree, its branches whipping about.

The wind is beginning to howl. Mom once told me that the sound of a tornado is like the sound of an oncoming train.

I run down the tracks.

At a crossing, a simple farm road, I hear laughter, shouts, and turn to see—

*A trio of witches, riding armored steeds, flew out of the sodden woods, shrieking in glee, for witches thrive in the chaos of storms.*

*As they raced by the queen, they flung out their arms and scraped her skin raw.*

*The queen fell.*

I am dizzy for a moment, and lie there catching my breath.

When I sit up, I can barely make out the three teenage boys on their bicycles, speeding away from me.

One of them circles back. "Guys! Come back, it's some kid!"

No. You are not welcome here.

(And you should be glad. People who meet me are bound to end up disappointed.)

(My family is infected with lies. If you touch me, you might catch them.)

I get up and keep running, the train tracks to my right. I will run faster than Jack ever could.

*The queen ran for miles, though every bone in her body ached. Her head swam with hunger. When she thought she could run no longer, she heard a voice in the wind, calling her name.*

"Finley?"

I stop, wiping hair from my eyes.

Jack slams into me, wrapping me in a rain-soaked hug. He says nothing; he is breathless from running. His fingers dig into my shoulders. His body is bony and strong.

"What are you doing out here?" He steps away, yelling over the rain. "Everyone's out looking for you."

It takes me a minute to understand what he's saying. "What?"

"It's been hours. It's almost seven. People are freaking out! God, Fin, where have you been?"

I point down the tracks. "I'm leaving, like we talked about."

"Why? Are you nuts? We were just *talking*."

"I don't want to be with my family anymore."

"But you love your family!"

"My grandparents hate me."

"No way. It's impossible to hate you."

"They are concerned about me."

"Why? There's nothing wrong with you."

"Yes, there is."

"But—"

I whirl to face him. "You don't know me, Jack. You have no idea about anything."

A crash of thunder makes us both jump. Without saying a word, we head for the Bone House, walking back along the tracks side by side, our heads down in the wind. The wet field grass clings to our legs. Once we're inside the Bone House, Jack gets us blankets from the living room. We huddle inside them under the card table. The closed kitchen door rattles in the wind.

Jack's hair lies flat against his head in dark pieces. This might be the cleanest I have ever seen him.

"Look," he says, "I didn't mean to make you mad out there. It's just, I think you're great. Anyone who says there's something wrong with you, they're the wrong ones."

More thunder; the house groans and shakes. How am I supposed to explain to him what I mean? I cannot scare him away and lose him, not again.

"My parents are getting a divorce," I tell him, because though it is awful, it is the easiest thing to say. "They told me on Sunday."

"Aw, Fin." Jack shakes his head. "I'm sorry. That really sucks."

"Yeah. I know."

"You okay?"

"No. But that's not the worst part."

"There's worse?"

I tell him what his dad told me—about my family and the Travers fire. He looks as shocked as I felt.

"But . . . why would they do that?" he asks. "You don't think they did it on purpose, do you?"

"I don't know what I think. But I don't want to go back. If it's true, then what does that mean? Can I still love them? I don't know if I can."

Jack is quiet for a long time. "I still love my dad, and he's done bad stuff."

"How do you keep loving him, then?"

"Because he's my dad. He has his bad days, but most of the time he's all right. He does his best. And we're family, you know? It isn't perfect, but it's ours. If I did something bad, I think he'd still love me."

Every time there is a flash of lightning, I can see the mural across the kitchen from us. "You painted me, huh?"

Jack taps the card table's leg with his shoe. "I know it isn't good. Cole could've done better."

"It is good, though, because you did it."

"Yeah?"

"Honestly."

Jack presses his shoe against mine. They are both covered in mud. "We should go back. I know you're mad at them, but . . . don't you want to know the truth? You can ask them all your questions."

When I imagine asking my grandparents and my aunts about the fire, I feel sick to my stomach. "I guess . . ."

"And hey, you can always come stay at our place. It's dirty and kind of smells, but we have cookies."

I laugh. "You and Gretchen are both obsessed with cookies."

"Who wouldn't be?" Jack crawls out from under the table and sweeps his blanket majestically around his shoulders. "My queen?" he asks, in a royal-sounding voice.

I take his hand. "Okay. Let's go."

Let's go find the whole truth.

# 41

As we make our way back through the Everwood, the storm knocks branches from trees and whips wet leaves into our faces.

I try not to feel guilty about everyone searching for me. In fact I hope Grandma and Grandpa are worried sick. I hope they are blaming themselves, looking back on their lives trying to figure out where they went wrong.

(I have an idea.)

Ducking under a branch heavy with rain, I hear a scream buried in the wind.

"Did you hear that?" I ask Jack.

"Hear what?"

There it is again—and it sounds familiar.

The world slows down. I feel every drop of rain on my skin.

I know that scream. How many times have I heard her, racing through the house?

It comes from the direction of the First Bridge.

*Ruth.*

I run toward the sound, leaving Jack behind. Mud sucks at my feet; the ground cannot hold any more water.

At the riverbank I look down and nearly fall.

This is not my river. The water is rushing, roaring, cascading. I see rapids, debris carried away in the current.

I see Dex and Ruth.

Dex, on this side of the river, faceup in the water, his shirt snagged on a branch.

Ruth, kneeling on the shore beside him, screaming at the top of her lungs. She pulls on his shirt, but he won't budge.

They must have crossed the Bridge, and then—

"Ruth!" I slide down the muddy riverbank.

At the bottom Ruth throws her arms around me, wet hair in her eyes.

"He fell!" I can barely hear her over the howling wind. "Finley, get him up! Get him up!"

"Stay here. Sit right here and don't move."

I head for the water. With a crack a large branch breaks from its tree and drops into the river. A second later it is swept away.

The branch holding Dex's shirt shifts. The water pulls and pulls at him.

Ruth screams.

Jack slides down beside me. "I'll go."

Jack makes his way down the slippery slope, but I cannot let him go alone. I tell Ruth to stay where she is, and I follow him. The ground flattens, and Jack almost falls, but I catch his hand and hold on tight. He stumbles, almost drags us both down into the water, but I cannot let go. I cannot buckle.

I am a queen. Queens do not fall.

Between the two of us we get Dex out of the water and back to solid ground. He is a pile of wet clothes and cold skin.

Jack suddenly looks lost. "I don't know, I don't know. What do we do, Fin?"

Ruth runs over, wails, shakes me.

We do not have time for this.

I press my hands to Dex's chest. We did this at school last year. We practiced on dummies. Rhonda thought it was stupid, that the dummies smelled like feet and we should not be required to touch them.

I liked it. As we practiced on the dummies, I imagined what it would feel like to save a person.

I thought that if I saved a person, I would no longer feel my sadness. How could you, after such a thing?

But doing this in real life is different.

This is no dummy; this is our Dex.

I press and press until my fingers are sore. Coach Williams said giving mouth-to-mouth is not as helpful as pumping the chest, but I do it anyway, because I am panicking, because I am desperate, because I would give Dex all my air, if I could.

When he starts gasping and choking, spitting up river water, I sit back hard in the mud.

"He's okay?" Ruth clutches his arm. "Is he?"

Dex groans, his eyelids fluttering shut.

"Dex? Dex!"

I hold Ruth still. "Something's wrong."

Jack gently pushes Dex's hair aside—a gash, on his fore-head. A mark red with blood. "Oh no."

Ruth struggles in my arms. "We didn't mean to!"

"Ruth, stop it. Listen to me—"

"We just wanted to find you!"

I catch her hands. "What do you mean?"

"You were missing. Everyone's looking for you, but they were looking all wrong. We knew where you were, but—"

My heart sinks. "So you went to find me."

"We thought if we found you, we could be knights." Ruth's face is a mess of rain and mud. "We wanted to save the queen."

"We shouldn't move him," Jack says. "I'll stay here. You go get help."

But I am frozen to the ground.

This is my fault.

Maybe if I'd never told them about the Everwood—

Maybe if I'd never brought them here—

Jack grabs my hand. "I won't let anything happen to them, okay? Go get your grandpa. Go!"

My fault, my fault, my fault.

"Finley!" Ruth screams.

I take one last look at Dex and climb up the riverbank.

I know I must cross the Bridge. There, through the trees—those flickers of lights. Amber, red, blue. Hart House. Police cars, I assume, looking for me.

(My fault. Dex, Dex, Dex.)

*The Dark Ones stood tall on the queen's back, stomping,*
*kicking, grinding her into the ground.*

*"Sad, sad orphan girl with a sad, sad curse," they cried.*
*"She takes everything happy and makes it worse."*

No. Enough.

"Be quiet." I clench my fists. "Stop it. Stop, right now."

*The Dark Ones shrank back and fell silent.*

(Think, Finley.)

I must cross the Bridge, but it is long, narrow, slick with rain.

I look down. Bad idea.

The river is wild, swift, dark.

I step back, breathing hard, the storm pounding in my ears—along with my heart, along with the rushing water.

I cannot cross the river. My legs won't move that way.

Cupping my muddy hands, I scream toward Hart House, but the storm swallows my voice.

No one can hear me—but I know where I can go for help.

Past the Post Office, up the hill, pulling myself up by the roots—

(I am a queen.)

Across the yard, through the maze of old lawn chairs and half-filled trash cans—

(I am not afraid.)

I fling open the screen door and pound on the door behind it. Please. Please. Please.

The door opens.

"Mr. Bailey," I gasp, "I'm sorry for bothering you. I know you don't like me. But please, can I use your phone? My cousin Dex. He's hurt—the river's flooding—Jack's with him—please—"

I break down, the pieces of me collapsing inward until I am the smallest I have ever been.

Mr. Bailey leads me inside. "Okay, now. It's okay."

He sits me down in a chair. Cole and Bennett run in from the other room.

"What happened?" asks Cole. "Where's Jack?"

Mr. Bailey picks up an old wall phone and dials.

"Mr. Hart?" He rubs his face. "It's Geoffrey Bailey. Listen, your granddaughter's here. Finley. She's okay. But she says her cousin Dex is down by the river and needs help. . . . Yeah, I've been watching the police come and go from over here. . . . Yeah, okay. I'll tell her. Thanks."

I feel like the chair has disappeared from underneath me.

I have done my part. Dex will be okay now. He has to be okay.

Mr. Bailey hangs up and sits down beside me.

"Someone's coming to get you," he says. He seems a bit shaky. I wonder what he is thinking.

A few minutes later the door flies open. Avery and Gretchen burst in, drenched and pale. Behind them Stick calls out my name.

My cousins launch themselves at me. It is the warmest hug I have ever felt.

# 42

THE PARAMEDICS SAID DEX WILL be okay, but it is hard to believe them. When they carried him off on the stretcher, he looked too small and pale to be alive. Like a soaked baby bird.

Aunt Bridget and Ruth went with him.

When I stepped inside Hart House in my wet shoes, the first person I saw was Aunt Bridget, and I thought she would yell at me, but she didn't. She hugged me close and squeezed.

(*You*, pounded her heart.)

(*You*, answered mine.)

Then she swept Ruth up into her arms and they were gone.

We stand around while Grandma and Grandpa talk with the police. They call my parents, tell them it's all right, that I am safe. They put the phone to my ear and through the fog of my shivering and my exhaustion, I hear Dad saying something about the storm making it unsafe to drive. They had to turn around, nearly got run off the road, but they'll get here as soon as it lets up. His voice breaks into jagged crystal pieces, and I realize he was terrified that he had lost me. I want to tell him I'm sorry, but I cannot find the words.

Grandpa calls Dr. Bristow, too, to let her know that I am

safe, and then I feel even worse. I hope she won't get in trouble for leaving her window open.

When the police leave, there are thirteen of us left: my family (minus Dex, Ruth, and Aunt Bridget) and the Baileys.

Thirteen people in a crowded kitchen, and still the room feels too empty.

Aunt Dee is in charge of wrapping the wet people in blankets. When she gets to me, she holds me close, tucked under her chin, and kisses my wet head.

Maybe I should want to pull away from her, but I don't.

Grandma is the first to speak. I can hear every secret that clogs her voice.

"You all had better go home," she says to the Baileys, but she does not look directly at them. "I'm sure you're tired."

Gretchen, red-eyed, shifts from one foot to the other. She stands behind Stick's chair, her arms loose around Stick's shoulders.

Jack scowls at the floor. Cole stands stiff and tall in front of his dad, like a soldier.

The house feels like it is holding its breath. I cannot stand this.

"You could thank Jack," I say.

Grandma turns to me. "Pardon me?"

"I said, you could thank him. He helped me save Dex."

"Yes, and he wouldn't have needed to if you hadn't been so irresponsible as to run away from Dr. Bristow's office."

She's right, of course, but it is worse to hear it said aloud. The words crush me flat.

Grandpa places his hand on Grandma's shoulder. "Candace . . ."

"How could you have been so selfish, Finley?" Grandma's voice shakes, the Hart mask slipping fast. I know she is upset; I get it. I know she was afraid of losing her grandchild.

Still, I cannot believe she is saying these things to me.

(I know the real you, Grandma.)

(I know about your wig. I know you snore.)

(I know the truth.)

"If you hadn't run off," Grandma continues, "the twins wouldn't have tried to find you, and Dex would not have fallen. If anything happens to him, it will be your fault."

"Grandma, please—" Avery interrupts.

"After everything we've done for you, after welcoming you into our home, you do something so blindingly selfish—"

Grandpa frowns. "Candace, that's enough."

"Didn't you stop to think for one second about the consequences of your actions? Didn't you *think*—"

"Selfish?" My brain is stuck on that word. It stings, and it is unfair. "At least I'm not a liar."

Grandma blinks. "I beg your—"

"I know about the fire. Mr. Bailey told me."

The house goes from quiet to quieter. Stick says, "Dad?" and looks at Grandpa like she's a little girl again and Daddy can make everything better.

"What's she talking about, Geoffrey?" Grandpa asks.

Mr. Bailey crosses his arms over his chest, his shoulders hunched. "I'm sorry, Warren. I didn't mean to, honest I didn't."

"You promised us you would never tell a soul." Grandma's voice is wire thin. "Especially not our grandchildren."

"I know, and like I said, I didn't mean to—"

"Whether or not you *meant to* isn't the issue here." Grandma rises, leaning hard on the kitchen table.

Everyone probably thinks she's angry and tired from worrying about me and Dex.

(But me and Avery and Grandpa, we know the truth.)

"We had a bargain, and you broke it," Grandma continues. "I guess I shouldn't be surprised. You've always been irresponsible and good for nothing, ever since you were a boy."

Jack kicks an empty chair. "Stop it. Don't yell at him."

Mr. Bailey grabs his arm. "Jack, it's okay—"

"No it isn't. Why are you letting them treat you like this? They're the ones who started the fire, not you."

Grandma lets out a mean-sounding laugh. "Oh, is that what everyone thinks? Well, allow me to set the record straight."

"Candace," says Grandpa, "let's not do this right now. Everyone's had a long day."

I stand up. "Tell us."

Everyone looks at me. Avery shakes her head slowly. *What are you doing?*

I have no idea. But I am tired of secrets.

"Tell us the truth," I say. "We've been going to the Bone

House all summer. We've been cleaning it, and we found the gravestones. It's ours now. We deserve to know."

Grandma looks like she's ready to either cry or snap in two, but Grandpa says, "Okay, Finley. Okay."

"Dad, *no*," Stick whispers. "Our kids—"

"They deserve to know. She's right." Grandpa looks at Mr. Bailey. "Geoffrey? Is that okay with you?"

"Dad?" Cole asks. "What's he talking about?"

Mr. Bailey nods slowly. "It's all right. Just listen."

"The truth is, I've been wanting to tell this story for a long time," says Grandpa. "We should've told it a long time ago, when it actually counted."

Grandma makes a small noise and goes to the sunroom windows. The world outside is storm-dark.

Then Grandpa folds his hands on the kitchen table and begins.

NCE UPON A TIME, A *wizard lived in the Ever-wood. He had a wife and a small daughter.*

*For generations his family had been poor. He worked in a small shop, where he earned enough wages to feed and clothe his loved ones, and to take care of his crumbling castle.*

*Though it was old and humble, he and his family loved it with all their hearts.*

*They lived a small life, and they were happy.*

*In this same forest there was a river.*

*On one side of the river lived a family of pirates. On the other side of the river lived another family—a king and a queen, and four children.*

*The family of pirates was troubled.*

*The father had long abandoned them, and the mother fell into a deep sorrow. Their son left his schooling to take care of her, and the family's estate fell into disrepair.*

*The family of royals was charmed.*

*The king and queen were wealthy. Their son, the prince, was quiet and studious. Their daughters, princesses three, were golden-haired, beautiful, and clever—but increasingly discontent.*

*There were many rules about how to be proper princesses, and the daughters hated them all. They wanted to* please their parents, but they feared they never would.

One night the three princesses took to the forest in the midnight hours, even though wandering into the woods after dark was forbidden.

Their younger brother, the prince, secretly followed them, for he could tell they were not themselves. They walked unsteadily and spoke too loudly.

The pirate son joined their revel, glad for the chance to escape his troubled home.

The four young people began to drink and dance, filling the forest with laughter.

From the shadows the prince watched, and he began to think his worry needless. They were children, after all, not much older than he. They were only children celebrating the night.

They were wild creatures, and this was their kingdom.

Their revels brought them deeper into the forest, until they were very near the wizard's castle, hidden in shadow and thick trees.

The princesses and the pirate built a fire and danced around it. For a time they forgot everything else. The world was simply them, and their forest, and their fire reaching higher and higher.

But the fire grew quickly, consuming the surrounding trees, and the princesses and the pirate played their games and laughed their hearts free, oblivious to it all.

The young prince ran out from his hiding place, shouting. The wizard's castle was wreathed in flame.

They watched as the wizard fell from a tower window. He did not get up.

Smoke filled the forest, followed by horrible screams. Someone remained in the house. Two someones.

The princesses and the pirate tried to help, but the flames were too great, raging stronger than any known Everwood spell.

They found the man who had fallen and pulled him to safety.

They watched as the castle crumbled, and the screams faded away.

The young prince ran through the forest and across the river to his parents' white castle.

The king and queen summoned help, and they cared for the frightened children as the flames were put out.

They even brought the poor wizard to the best healers they could find, but it was not enough. His hurts were too great.

He woke up long enough to ask them two things: that they bury him and his family beneath the old tree behind their beloved house, and that they tell his family's story and not let their memories turn to dust.

But the king and queen were afraid. They gathered up the truth of that night and locked it away in the darkest parts of their hearts.

The fire had begun through no fault of their own, they

said. It was the poor wizard, who had let his lands become overgrown, who had lit a fire when he should not have. The three princesses saw the flames from afar and tried to help, but they were too late.

The three princesses, then, were heroes, and so it became known throughout the land.

The Everwood disapproved of these lies and decided that the king and queen must be punished. They must give up their crowns and offer up themselves. For all eternity they must guard the Everwood and never reveal its secrets.

The king and queen agreed and became guardians of the forest. They were bound to the trees by deep, old magic, and their hair and flesh turned white and as cold as stone. Through the years they became ever more powerful—though the burden of their many secrets ate away at them.

They told their children to never reveal the truth of what happened that night, for doing so would endanger everything they had built. They commanded the pirate son to do the same, and offered him coin in exchange for his silence.

Some years later the pirate fell in love with a woman who bore him three boys, who all grew up to be pirates as well. But the pirate father was poisoned by drink, and on the days when he raged, he became a monstrous troll, and his family grew to fear him.

The young prince, who hated lies, left the kingdom forever.

*He would not betray the ancient guardians, but he would no longer be theirs to call son.*

*And so the Everwood grew on and on, while the ancient guardians watched over its secrets—until, one day, an orphan girl who did not know she was a queen arrived in the forest, and everything began to change.*

# 43

Now I finally understand.

My aunts—three girls, trying to be happy. Trying to be Harts.

(It's not just about the blood in your veins. It's also about the smile on your face.)

Geoffrey Bailey—Jack's father.

Four kids, around Avery's age.

Four kids, drinks, a bonfire. Out in the forest where they weren't supposed to be. A celebration of forgetting their problems for a while.

(I understand these things.)

An overgrown house, hidden in the trees.

A man who had a family, and then did not.

A melted bicycle, a shoe belonging to Cynthia Travers.

The knife? Maybe it fell from someone's pocket. Maybe it was knocked out of the house when the firefighters arrived.

Dad, watching it all happen. And after, maybe wanting to talk about it. Maybe wanting to tell the truth.

And this is why, isn't it? This is why no one talks about him, why he left, why I am only now meeting my family.

Because he wanted to tell their secrets.

Grandma and Grandpa Hart, hiding it all so no one would see. Paying the right people. Spinning stories and lies and smiles.

That is the truth, the real truth, of the Everwood.

"So that's it," I say into the silence. "That's what happened."

Stick, Aunt Dee, and Kennedy are crying. Mr. Bailey seems like he might be about to. Cole holds Bennett. Avery looks like if she breathes too hard, she will shatter.

Jack watches me. I think he is waiting for me to make the next move.

"How could you do that?" Gretchen blurts out.

(I know how.)

## WHAT IT MEANS TO BE A HART

- You must make the world see you as you want to be seen.

Something inside me detonates. I want to hit something or run somewhere or cry until I can't anymore.

I want to say I hate them. I want to yell and scream and spit and kick.

But I can't do that, because I don't.

I still love them. *I love them.*

This realization has been coming to me in pieces over the summer, but now it rushes at me, fully formed.

(Now? Now, after what I have learned?)

(Yes. Now.)

I love my family.

I love Aunt Bridget, because her heartbeat sounds like mine.

I love Aunt Dee, because she was the first one to say she loves me, too.

I love Stick, because I am her coolest niece, and she belongs to my Gretchen.

I love Grandpa, because he dresses old-fashioned, and he built us a tree patio, and he talked to Dad when no one else would.

I even love Grandma, because she slept beside me, and I see the person she is trying to be.

They are mine, and I am theirs.

We are Harts. It's in the blood.

But it isn't fair, what they have done. It isn't fair that I love them. I shouldn't love people like that.

But . . . people like *what*? They were only kids, my aunts and Mr. Bailey. They were afraid.

And Grandma and Grandpa, they were also afraid—for their children, and for their own sorry, wonderful selves.

I cannot stop imagining Avery doing something like that, and hating herself, and living with the horrible fact of it forever.

I cannot stop imagining what I would have done, if instead of my aunts and Mr. Bailey it had been me and my cousins.

What would *we* have done?

Would we have been the same? Would we have allowed such secrets, to protect one another? The queen and her companions, bound through the power of the Everwood.

What would we have done?

I think about it, a hot bubble building inside me.

Then I decide: We would not have done that. We would not have hidden what we had done.

What will happen to us all?

Maybe the divorce will be a good thing. If the Harts are arrested for keeping so many secrets, Dad will be locked up with the rest of them, and Mom and I can live alone and get stressed and eat cold pizza together.

Grandpa looks old and exhausted without all those words inside him. "So that's the truth," he tells us. "I'm sorry, and . . . I don't know what else to say."

"You hid what happened." I have to say this out loud. Somehow I have to claw through it. "All of you did. You lied about it, for years—"

Grandma turns. "It isn't that simple, Finley—"

"No! *I'm* talking now. *Me.*" My ears turn hot and my skin tingles in waves. "You kept it secret. You paid Mr. Bailey to keep him quiet. You used your money and made sure no one would know. You scared my dad when he wanted to tell the truth. You scared him away, made him angry. That's why you fought. *You're* why I'm only just now visiting. Because you were scared. You were selfish, and you were cowards."

Grandma and Grandpa stare at me like I have told them

the sky is falling, which I suppose it is, to them. Their perfect, cloudless, blue sky for miles.

"Aunt Bridget, Dee, Stick. Mr. Bailey," I continued. "They didn't mean for that fire to go wrong, but it did, and you couldn't tell anyone because you couldn't let anyone know they'd messed up."

Grandma holds her face stiff.

I am shouting now, clutching the chair in front of me. "All you care about is keeping everything beautiful and peaceful and perfect. But not everything is perfect. Not everything is happy and normal and nice. Not every house is Hart House. Do you get that? All of this is because of you. Without you, there wouldn't have been any secrets. I wouldn't have run away. Dex and Ruth wouldn't have come after me. It's your fault this happened. It's *your* fault."

I cannot talk very well anymore. I feel like I could fly out of my skin. My throat hurts so much, I could throw up.

"It was an accident," Grandma whispers. "It was just an accident."

"Hiding it wasn't an accident."

Grandma's eyes meet mine. They look empty, fuzzy, like she has just woken up. She sits in one of the polished chairs and looks too small in it, like a kid in a grown-up's chair.

Everyone is quiet, like they are waiting for whatever this thing is between me and Grandma to snap.

I sway on my feet; Avery helps me find a chair. She sits down and pulls me onto her lap. Her fingers are stained with paint—hot pink and bright orange and forest green. She feels strong, like the kind of person you would want on your side.

She feels safe.

But I cannot relax yet.

What now? What will happen to all of us?

Aunt Dee is still crying; Stick is trying to help her. Mr. Bailey sits with his head in his hands.

Jack. Jack. Where is Jack?

Jack is passing out cookies—fresh ones, which makes me think Grandma was nervously baking until we all got home safely.

(Of course.)

I meet Jack's eyes. *Are we okay?*

He crooks his finger, like a hook.

Pirate.

We are okay, he and I.

The rest of us—that is a less certain thing.


After that, I do not say much.

What is left to say?

I watch everyone mill around the kitchen. Hot chocolate for the kids, coffee for the grown-ups. Kennedy sniffles in Uncle Nelson's lap; he holds her like she is five instead of twelve. Gretchen cleans cups in the kitchen, wearing Grandma's washing gloves and scrubbing like a maniac.

I lean against Avery's shoulder and fall asleep and wake up

again. Someone brings me saltines, strokes my hair, brings a phone to my ear.

It's Mom.

Dad is getting their things together; they will arrive in Billington in the morning.

"Are you okay, sweetie? Finley, my baby Finley."

"Mom, I'm not a baby."

"I know, but you always will be to me."

"Mom. I'm sorry I ran away."

"I know you are. It's okay. We're going to be okay."

Are we going to be okay? I want to say yes, but as I say good-bye to my mother and hang up the phone, I'm not sure.

The world is not a sure place anymore. Maybe it has never been. Maybe it has always been a mess—some kind of twisted, cosmic mess we can't possibly understand.

This room is full of snobs, secret-keepers, liars, and cowards. We hide our mistakes; we drink too much; we get scared and do things we are not proud of.

We feel sad even when it makes no sense to feel sad.

I hear people talking and lift myself up.

"Geoffrey." Grandpa sits beside Mr. Bailey. "I'm sorry about all of this."

"Don't be." Mr. Bailey's voice is rough. "It was about time, wasn't it?"

Grandpa pauses. It looks like something inside him is fighting to get out. "I always wanted to . . . I don't know. Come out and confess. Tell the truth. But I didn't know how. I found my grandkids playing with your boys, a few weeks ago."

Mr. Bailey's eyes flick to me and back to Grandpa. "Jack told me."

"It scared me."

"Yeah. Me too."

Grandpa sighs and tugs his shirt straight. He holds out his hand, and Mr. Bailey grabs on.

"I guess this is the start of something," Grandpa says.

"Warren," says Mr. Bailey, sounding shaky, "I'm scared out of my mind."

"Me too."

Mr. Bailey gives him a sad smile. "I kind of like it. Feels nice."

Grandpa passes him a fresh cup of coffee. "Feels like a beginning."

I feel like telling them that this isn't starting tonight.

It started with us—with me, Gretchen, Kennedy, Dex, Ruth, Avery, Jack, Cole, and Bennett.

It started in the Everwood. We found the truth in those trees.

But I think they know that.


I fall asleep on the sofa in the sunroom. Rain trickles down the windows, pinging on the green glass roof like tiny birds' feet.

When I wake up, it takes me a moment to realize who is sitting at the kitchen table: Mr. Bailey. Aunt Dee and Stick. Grandma.

My chest tightens, but I keep my eyes cracked open. What now? What will Grandma say?

Aunt Dee whispers, "And then what? What will happen to us?"

"It doesn't matter," says Grandma, her voice pure Hart. She sounds ready to clean attics and organize cities. "Finley was right. We've been selfish. All of us."

Stick holds Grandma's hand tight. Everyone is quiet.

Mr. Bailey says, "She's a brave girl, Mrs. Hart."

Grandma says, "You're right, Geoffrey. My Finley is a queen."

Her Finley. *Hers.*

On this couch I am weightless. I want to live inside this moment forever. Through the glass ceiling I see the clouds clearing away to reveal an ocean of stars.

Everyone at the kitchen table keeps talking, quietly, slowly. They are small, scared creatures trying to find their way.

I wonder if I will ever find mine.

# 44

THE NEXT TIME I WAKE up, all the lights are off except one. Grandma is sitting alone at the kitchen table holding a coffee mug.

Sometimes I think whatever is wrong with me is wrong with Mom or Dad, too. Maybe it is a thing I will never be able to shake, because it comes straight from my bad cells.

Sometimes I think I must have done something terrible, or will do something terrible, to deserve such a fate. My sadness might be a punishment.

I wonder if Grandma thinks things like, *How many more cups of coffee will I have in this life? How long will the rest of my life be?*

I wonder if she ever asks herself, *Is this cancer punishment for something I have done?*

(For hiding an accident? For keeping secrets?)

Grandma catches me watching her. "Oh! You're awake."

She comes toward me, pauses, looks around the room, goes to the kitchen, gets another coffee mug, starts making me hot chocolate.

I move to the table, sit, and wait. I feel like I should say something, but I do not know what that would be.

Grandma sits back down. I sip my hot chocolate and watch her face, but she does not meet my eyes.

Every tick of the clock above the sunroom doors is a crash in this silence.

"Not everything is perfect," Grandma says softly. "Not everything is happy."

It takes me a moment to realize that she is repeating what I screamed at her a few hours ago.

"Is that what you've been trying to tell me, Finley? All summer?"

Grandma clasps her hands tightly together and looks at me, waiting.

Everything around me—the whole world, my whole *life*—narrows down to this moment:

Grandma, in her peach-colored blouse, her pearls, her makeup not even smudged, even after everything that happened.

The clock, crashing away.

The soft light of the kitchen, the sky getting brighter outside, the hot chocolate steaming in front of me.

If I am a puzzle, this is the moment in which I find the first corner piece.

There is still a lot of work to do; I still have a thousand pieces of myself to fit into place. But everyone knows you're supposed to find the corners first. They are the beginning.

My family has found theirs, and I have just found mine.

All it took was someone else asking a question, making

me search for an answer I think I already knew.

Maybe we should not be talking about this. After everything I have learned in the past couple of days, don't more important things need discussing?

What will happen to us, if Grandma decides to tell the world the truth?

"Finley?" Grandma folds her soft, warm hand around mine. "Are you all right?"

"Really? Like, honestly?"

"Yes."

Then again, I have heard people say—Mom, when she's stressed about work; Rhonda, when she's trying to sound mature—that it is important to take life one day at a time, one moment at a time, one item on the great big list of life to-dos at a time.

This can be my moment—right now, between me and Grandma. One moment out of a billion ones yet to come.

It is okay for me to have that.

I take a deep breath.

(How many people have I told about this? Ever?)

(No one. Not a single living soul.)

(Only my notebook. The Everwood, of course, already knew. We are connected, me and those trees.)

Everything about this summer comes back to me like I am seeing it for the first time.

"I don't think I'm okay." I stare at the table. "I'm not very happy."

A single knot inside me untangles.

Grandma waits, her hand on mine.

"I'm sad, a lot," I say. "And I get afraid a lot. *Really* afraid. Like, panicky for no reason. And I don't know why."

I tell her it scares me.

I tell her it makes me angry.

I tell her I feel guilty about it. I know I should be happy. I want to carve this thing out of me with a knife.

Grandma smiles—not her magazine smile. More like Mom when she is tired and comes in after a long day to tuck me in.

(Mom says she refuses to give up that parental right, even when I am grown up.)

"I know the feeling, wanting to carve something out of you," says Grandma.

Oh. Of course she does. "I'm sorry—"

"Don't be. I'm going to be okay."

"That's what the doctor says?"

"That's what *I* say."

Even I know that cancer is not so simple. You cannot smile it better. You cannot tell it you are a Hart and watch it obey.

"You should tell them you're sick," I say.

"Who?"

"Everyone."

Grandma's lips thin. "Finley—"

"They would want to know."

"And they will, eventually. For now this house will remain

what it is. For as long as I can keep it that way, I will."

There is no arguing with her. I am used to the expression on her face. I see it on my own, all the time, when I look in the mirror and tell myself, *You will stop feeling sad. You will push it down. You will be okay. You will be happy, now. Right now.*

Maybe Grandma and I are more alike than I have ever thought possible.

Grandma sighs, looks at her hands. "Finley, I did everything wrong, didn't I? All of this: the dresses, Dr. Bristow. Your notebook. I kept thinking I was making you happy, making you better, but I think, deep down, I knew I wasn't. I was doing those things for me, and I'm sorry." She laughs, a puff of soft, sad air. "I was doing all of this for me. For the family. And it was all wrong."

My eyes fill up. I am so tired of that feeling, but I cannot stop it. "Mom and Dad are getting a divorce, and I don't know what will happen now."

Grandma's face goes soft. "Oh, Finley. None of us do, about any of it. But we have to keep going anyway. Giving up is not an option in this house. And if you have to keep going, you might as well smile while you're doing it. Don't you think that's right?"

"Yeah. I guess so."

"You *guess* so?"

My smile is small, but it still counts. "I *know* so."

"Quite right. So, why don't you finish your drink? Then, since you're up, you can help me make breakfast."

"Pancakes?"

Grandma gets up, snaps a dishtowel, and folds it. "Naturally."

This is one of the reasons why you keep going, I think.

Even after everything else has gone wrong, pancakes still smell the same.

### WHAT IT MEANS TO BE A HART

- Giving up is not an option.
- And if you have to keep going, you might as well smile while you're doing it.

That says everything you need to know, really.

# 45

SOMETIMES BEFORE YOU CAN GIVE someone help, the person has to ask you for it, because they have gotten really good at hiding what hurts them.

I know, because I am good at that.

I know, because I am learning that it is okay to ask for help. Otherwise, how will you ever find it?

Jack and I lie on our backs in the Tower.

Across the river, back in the Wasteland, a crew is working to rebuild the Bone House.

Except we do not want to call it the Bone House anymore. It is too macabre.

(Seven-letter word for "representing death.")

I have added this to my list of favorite words. Not to be morbid, but because it will help me remember.

(Also, we have asked the crew to keep Cole's mural of all of us, and they agreed.)

(We will live forever in that house, no matter what happens.)

My cousins and I cracked open our box of dues, because the summer is almost over, and we do not need material items to know we are bound together forever—through blood, of course, but through the Everwood, too.

I close my eyes and let the wind rush over me. I hear birds singing, and Grandma's wind chimes.

Beside me Jack belches.

I want to laugh, but it catches on something in my throat and disappears.

Mom and Dad are here now. Even though they had to take some time off work to do it, they brought their things and are staying for a while, to help with everything. Mom could not resist the chance to recreate the Bone House. She has been in constant conversation with the building crew about the curve of the staircase, the dimensions of the kitchen.

No. Not the Bone House. What will we call it?

We have to figure it out soon. When all this is done, my parents and I will leave. Then one of them will leave again, and I will live . . . where? I will be split between two homes, two parents.

If that pizza boy ever starts delivering pizzas again, he may not know where to find me.

I will be far from my Everwood.

I press my palms flat against the Tower floor.

Sometimes over the past few days so much has been going on that I have forgotten how I really feel.

But when I have a moment to sit back and think, I slip back into that cold, blue water again, and I can hardly move at all.

(Yes. Still. After everything that's happened.)

(Still my sadness remains.)

(It comes and goes in waves, like a never-ending ocean.)

Jack puts his feet up on the painted wall. "I have a plan."

"For what?"

"For keeping you here in Billington."

"Good luck with that."

"No, seriously, hear me out."

I sigh. "Okay. Shoot."

"So, your grandparents' castle probably has a dungeon somewhere—"

"*Jack*. Come on."

"No, this is great. Listen. We find the key, lock your parents inside. We don't let them out until they agree to our terms: (a) They let you stay in Billington; (b) they get over themselves and cancel the divorce."

"There are so many problems with that plan."

"What are you talking about? It's flawless."

"What if there *is* no dungeon? What will we tell my dad's boss and my mom's clients? What if we get arrested for, you know, imprisoning my parents?"

"Okay, so the plan needs some work."

"A little bit, yeah."

Avery's painting music floats down from the garage.

"Hey," Jack says, after a while. "I'm sorry."

"For what?"

"For getting mad that night. When you saw my mom and dad."

"You've said sorry about ten million times."

"Yeah, but I never told you *why* I got mad."

"It's okay."

"Seriously, Finley." Jack turns onto his side to look at me. "I want to tell you."

When I look back at him, I realize too late that I do not know how to handle this situation. Jack is so close that his breath moves tiny strands of my hair.

"Okay," I say. "What?"

"Why'd I get mad?"

"Jack. Yes. Why'd you get mad?"

"Because, well . . . I have this crush on you."

It kind of seems like a joke, with him staring at me, so serious. People who say things like that while looking so serious are bound to be poking fun at you. Right?

Jack and me. Me and Jack. We are in the Tower, and it seems like it's right where we are supposed to be.

"Stop making fun of me," I say.

"I'm one hundred percent serious. It's just . . . I didn't want you to see them. Whenever Mom comes by, she's in such a bad mood, and Dad . . . he's great, but when he gets like that, when he drinks, he's . . ."

"Scary?"

"Yeah."

"He was nice, though, after."

"He is. I love him, you know? I just don't always like him. He's got problems."

I do laugh then. What else can I do? "He's not the only one."

Jack cracks a grin. "Hey, you know what?"

"What?"

"You're blushing."

I sit up and shake my hair over my cheeks. "I am not."

"It's okay." Jack grins. "You can have a crush on me, too."

This is getting out of hand. "How can you just *say* things like that?"

He shrugs. "That's the way I am."

"Well, you want to know the way *I* am?"

Jack sits up. "Definitely."

I have only said these words out loud twice—to Grandma, to Mom and Dad.

And now to Jack.

"I have these things I call blue days," I say. "When I get sad for no reason."

Jack nods and waits. He hasn't run away screaming *yet*.

"And I don't mean normal sad. At all. I mean sad for *no reason*. Heavy sad. I wake up feeling happy and then anything can happen, or *nothing* can happen, and all of a sudden I'm sad, and I can't stop being sad, even though I want to. Sometimes I freak out so bad I can't breathe. Sometimes I pretend to be sick to stay home from school because it feels impossible to get out of bed. That's how I came up with the

Everwood. I started writing about it to make myself feel better."

I stop, feeling dizzy. Each time I talk about this, each time I let out the words, I feel . . . lighter. Clear like the Everwood sky.

"So?" I say. "Do you still have a crush on me?"

"Yep," says Jack.

"Why? How can you?"

"Too long to explain. But I do have a question."

I sigh. He is exasperating. He needs to comb his hair. "What?"

"Were you happy in the Everwood? With all of us?"

"Yes." I answer that without thinking.

"But you were still sad, too?"

This I answer more slowly, because it makes me angry to admit it. "Yes."

"Well, okay. So that has to mean something. Right?"

"Like what?"

"Like maybe you have to really try and fix it now. The stuff that's been bothering you. The blue days. Because if you're sad even when you're happy, even when you're doing stuff you like doing, maybe you can't just ignore it forever."

His words remind me of what Mom said, the other night, snuggled up in my bed here at Hart House: "You can't hide in the Everwood anymore, sweetie."

Dad sat beside the bed, in a chair.

(Before, he would have been in there with us.)

(But that was before.)

"We can help you, Fin," Dad said. "There are lots of ways to help you with this. But we've all got to try, together. Okay?"

And now I am sitting beside Jack, and he shrugs. "Maybe you've got to ask someone to help you figure it out. I don't know."

"I guess so," I say.

Jack smiles. "No big deal."

"No big deal."

"I'll help, if you want. You can write me letters and tell me everything."

"What about the dungeon plan?"

Jack holds my hand. "Is this okay?"

(If this day had a color, it would be as gold as the sun.)

"Yeah. It's okay."

(It is so okay that it surpasses all possible definitions of the word.)

"So, the dungeon plan."

"In progress." Jack sticks his other arm out into the sun and closes his eyes. "But don't worry. We'll figure it out."

He is right.

This is a work in progress.

I will figure it out.

For reasons beyond my understanding, Dr. Bristow is not mad about the open window incident.

She gives me an enormous hug the moment I step into her office, in fact.

That doesn't seem entirely professional to me, but I like it anyway.

I have a substantial amount of good huggers in my life. This might not be something everyone enjoys.

We settle on the couch. Mom, me, Dad. Dr. Bristow in her chair.

"So, Finley," she says, "what's on your mind today?"

I breathe in and breathe out.

"I've been thinking," I say. "I talked a lot with Mom and Dad."

"That's good. What about?"

"About me. We've done some research."

I breathe in. I breathe out.

(It's okay, Finley.)

(Let her see.)

Dad squeezes my hand.

"I think I have depression." I hesitate. "And anxiety, too."

When I say it, the words float away from me and leave nothing behind.

They are only words. They are only part of me, and I am still here.

I do not need to be afraid of them.

"Sometimes I have panic attacks," I say. "Sometimes I can't sleep. Sometimes I sleep too much, and sometimes I hurt and can't breathe."

Dr. Bristow says, "What happens, when you start to feel like this? What do you do next?"

I think for a second and then glance at Mom. She smiles at me and pulls my notebook out of her purse.

I settle it on my lap and open to the first story I ever wrote about the Everwood—about how the Everwood came to be, when the world was very young and full of magic.

I told this story to Mr. Bailey that night, sitting under the stars with him and Jack.

This is the story of my heart.

"I think I should read some of these stories to you," I tell her. "They explain everything."

Dr. Bristow smiles. "That sounds perfect."

So I scoot back until I am wedged tight between Mom and Dad. I find the beginning, and I start to read.

# 46

WHY MY LIFE IS BEAUTIFUL

- I know a lot of good huggers.
- Jack and I will continue to write letters.
- We do not yet have a new name for the Bone House, but we will think of one.
  - (We still have so many fun things left to do. We are only just beginning.)
- There is now a memorial near the finished Bone House, in honor of the Travers family.
- Grandma and Grandpa want to tell people the whole truth.
  - That in itself is scary, but I have learned it is important to tell the truth, even if it is frightening.
  - And no matter what, we will all have one another, now and forever.
    - ♦ We are all linked, we Harts.
    - ♦ (We share blood and bones. We are a battleship, and we will not sink.)
- Mom and Dad will always love me, even though Dad now lives in another apartment.
  - His apartment overlooks a giant wooded park.

- He says that is why he chose it—for me, so I could see trees, even when I am not in my Everwood.
- I am in the process of introducing Rhonda to the Beatles. She is not yet convinced, but I am persistent.
- Avery will leave for the Rigby Institute next year.
  - We are already planning my first visit.
  - She texts me picture updates of her newest paintings every week.
- It is okay to be sad.
  - It does not mean I am broken or strange or a non-Hart.
- Dex is alive.
- I am alive.
- Grandma is alive. Right now.
- Right now is all that matters, because right now is what we know.
- The future is wide open, and the world is full of people who get scared and lie and are sad and happy.
  - That is how it is supposed to be.

**T**HE QUEEN'S MOTHER AND FATHER *had returned to her at last, and though they were changed, they were still themselves in the ways that mattered.*

*They told her she would no longer have to hide herself, or face the darkness alone.*

*Most importantly, they told her they still loved her and always would—yes, even though she carried her sadness inside her.*

*Her sadness, they said, was not a thing they must look past to love her. It was a part of her, and therefore it was a part of them.*

*The queen brought them to the Everwood and introduced them to the trees, the river, the wind. She wore her crown. The fog had gone from the forest, leaving everything fresh and golden and new.*

*"This is where it happened," she explained to her mother and father. "This is where I have been, all this time. This is where I came to know my friends."*

*The artist. The lady knight. The champion and the two young squires, who were soon to be knighted for their bravery. The three pirates, and the wizard's ghost.*

*The queen thought of them, and she knew that her sadness was now not the only thing she carried inside her heart, nor the most powerful.*

*Now everything would be different—for her, for her*

*friends, for everyone in the Everwood—in ways she could not yet imagine.*

*Things would change, as they do.*

*But the Everwood would remain, and so would the bond among those who lived there.*

*She would make sure of that.*

*"Is it time?" asked the queen's mother.*

*"Are you ready?" asked her father.*

*"I am," said the queen, and she stepped with them out of the trees and into the sun.*

# A Reading Group Guide to
# *Some Kind of Happiness*
### By Claire Legrand

## About the Book

Eleven-year-old Finley Hart knows this summer will be the most terrible one of her life. And why wouldn't it be? Her parents are shipping her off to live with grandparents she has never met, and surrounded by cousins she doesn't know, while her parents will be home deciding if they will stay a family or get a divorce. At the same time, her blue days are getting worse—the times where she feels she is so heavy that she can't get out of bed—where her sadness sticks in her like a sword. Her only escape is the Everwood, the forest kingdom that exists in the pages of her notebook. When she realizes that her grandparents' house borders a lush and mysterious forest, her reality and fantasy begin to collide. Setting out to uncover a family secret, Finley enlists the help of her cousins and a trio of forbidden brothers to uncover the dark past of the forest. What is revealed will force Finley to not only confront her family, but her greatest fear.

## Discussion Questions

**1.** Consider the book's title: *Some Kind of Happiness*. Does happiness have kinds? Discuss what happiness means to you? Are there different ways to be happy? As you read the text, think about the concept of happiness as it pertains to Finley and the other members of the Hart family. After reading the story, discuss why the author may have given her book this title.

**2.** Why does Finley feel the need to "hide" herself upon meeting her grandparents? In this context, what does the verb hide denote? Why does she not tell her parents about the physical and emotional feelings that trouble her? Discuss what Finley means when she thinks, "How can the world look so perfect when I feel so broken?"

**3.** Discuss Finley's first encounter with the larger Hart family. How does the author's use of figurative language help to visualize Finley's complex emotions: "The Harts are a storm, and I am its bewildered eye. I feel like I'm being dragged through a fun-house mirror maze that reflects distorted versions of myself." At this point in the story how does Finley perceive her extended family? Why does she compare herself to a smudge on her grandmother's crystal glass?

**4.** Throughout the text it is clear that Finley feels separate from the larger Hart family. In addition to her physical separation to this point in her life, why does Finley feel so different from her extended family? Discuss Finley's feelings of *wrongness*: "The wrongness of the tight, jumbled knot that is my insides. And how heavy it feels. And how it is pulling and pushing and molding me like clay." How much of Finley's feelings are caused by the outside forces of her family members versus the internal forces that she is coping with?

**5.** Discuss Finley's early encounter with Gretchen. Why do you think that Finley decided to share the Everwood with Gretchen? How is it a personal risk for Finley to tell Gretchen about the Everwood? How does Gretchen's acceptance of Finley forge their early bond? Do you agree/disagree with Finley's statement: "You can't simply become part of something that doesn't belong to you, something you've only just learned about." How does the statement relate to her feelings about the Harts?

**6.** Over the course of the story, Finley dismisses her own emotional pain (fear, sadness, shame, guilt) by talking herself out of whatever negative feeling or thought she has. How do these internal dialogues both help and hurt Finley? Why do you think she does not feel entitled to her sadness? Why does she assume that Grandma and the other Harts wouldn't understand if she told them about her 'blue days" and feelings of "losing herself"? Discuss the meaning of empathy. How does Finley (and the orphan girl in the Everwood tale) display empathy?

7. Grandma is a complex character in the story, and one that Finley has decided is her nemesis from the moment they meet. How does Grandma make Finely feel like an outsider? Do you think this is Grandma's intention? Explain. Discuss Grandma Hart as her character evolves over the course of the story. Early in the story Grandma says, "We do not talk about upsetting topics at the dinner table." How is this statement a metaphor for the Hart Family? When Finley discovers that Grandma is ill and has been keeping the news from the family, how does their personal dynamic shift?

8. Keeping secrets is one of the major themes of this story. Discuss how all of the major characters keep secrets. As much as she despises the truth/s that are being kept from her, Finley is excellent at keeping her own secrets. Discuss this duality in the main character. How are secrets and lies connected? How are they different? What does Finley mean by a "Grandma mask"? Fox says that the orphan girl is "afraid of herself." How can one be afraid of him/herself? What does Fox mean when it says, "We all carry secrets. The more we ignore them, the heavier they become." How does this statement pertain to Finley?

**9.** During Finley's first drive with Grandpa, she plucks up the courage to him about her father's estrangement from the family. Finley asks Grandpa why they cannot simply apologize, to which he replies, "Sometimes things are too big for sorry." Do you agree or disagree? Discuss a time in your life when you either apologized or received an apology that made a situation better or solved a problem.

**10.** Discuss Finley's relationship with Jack Bailey. Why do you think they relate to one another so well? How does discovering the Travers family graves strengthen their bond? How are Jack and Finley similar? After Jack shares his fears with Finley, she cannot bring herself to utter the word divorce. Why do you think that Finley is unable to say the word even though she knows that it is going to happen? How is Jack's friendship a kind of lifeline for Finley? When Finley finally tells Jack about the divorce, why does she think, "though it is awful, it is the easiest thing to say"? Why is it Jack who helps Finley realize that she has to get "the whole truth" about the fire?

**11.** After the kids find the Travers graves, Finley's intense feelings of sadness and anxiety threaten to overcome her. At first she tell herself that she is undeserving of such feelings in the face of what she perceives are greater sadnesses, but then attempts to block them entirely: "I focus on pushing these feelings down to a place where they cannot touch me anymore. I will push on them, and push on them, until they have nowhere else to go but out of my head entirely." Why do you think that Finley refuses to reveal these painful feelings? Do you think this is a good way to deal with pain and confusion? If you could advise Finley, what would you say to her? How does writing about the Everwood help Finley cope, but also keep her stuck in place?

**12.** Discuss Finley's thoughts about "sitting alone in a quiet room" where she feels she can be her true self and not pretend to be happy. Why does Finley feel compelled to fake happiness? What is pretense? Discuss how the Harts pretend at being happy. Discuss the following passage: "Most of the time I think I could be perfectly content without saying a single word, but no one else seems to function that way. There is so much talking in the world, and so much expectation to talk, even if you don't feel like talking." How does this passage relate to your own life and the experiences of growing up?

**13.** Finley is keenly observant. She notices details about people that belie her young age, such as this observation of Grandma: "Because most of the time I cannot see past her smile—but when I do, I see someone who is angry and sad and tired." Discuss other instances in the story that highlight Finley's powers of observation. Why do the other members of the family seem to be unaware of the signs of Grandma's illness?

**14.** Reread Chapters 22 and 23, which describe the emotional and physical symptoms that Finley experiences when she "loses herself." Discuss the meanings of depression and anxiety. Finley refers to the feelings as "it." How does her concealment of these feelings help to deepen and continue them?

**15.** When Avery hugs Finley in the bathroom, what is revealed about the older cousin that Finley has been so intimidated by? In the car Avery confides to Finley that she is jealous of her because she "got away" from the expectations that come with being a Hart. How does this knowledge begin to change Finley's perceptions about her family? How can being held to high expectations be exhausting?

**16.** When Grandma takes Finley to her first appointment with Dr. Bristow, she tells Finley that, "This will get everything back to normal, you see? A normal summer," and "Everything is fine, now." Why does Grandma have such a deep need to make things *normal* and *fine*? How is Finley's internal dialogue to make herself happy similar to what Grandma is saying in the waiting room?

**17.** Discuss Dr. Bristow's statement to Finley about honesty: "I like honesty, and I think sometimes adults decide not to be honest with children because they think doing so will protect them, but I don't agree with that philosophy."

Do you agree or disagree with Dr. Bristow? Is there ever a circumstance where it is right for parents to be dishonest with a child? Is Finley's concealment of her mental illness a form of dishonesty?

**18.** As Finley's blue days become more frequent, the Dark Ones not only enter the Everwood story but also appear in Finley's actual life: "Lots of other things are on my mind. Particularly the Dark Ones on my back. Sometimes when I look in the mirror I think I can see them, even though I am fully aware that they are figments of my imagination." How are the Dark Ones symbols of the actual pain that Finley experiences? The Dark Ones yell to the Queen, "Free she's not!" How is mental illness, if left untreated, a kind of prison? How does Finley's reality fuel her imagination, and vice versa?

**19.** Discuss the list that Finley makes titled: What Has Changed This Summer. How have her cousins become more than strangers who happen to resemble her? Compare this list to the one that opens Chapter 1. After Grandma takes away Finley's notebook, a subtle realization occurs to Finley ("Finley girl, Finley girl, what do you see? I see a Hart, and she looks like me"). How is this chapter a turning point in the story?

**20.** Why doesn't Finley confront Grandpa after learning the truth about the fire and cover-up? How is her avoidance of learning the whole story of the fire similar to her denial of her parent's divorce and her own internal pain?

**21.** Discuss Finley's need for control and how it parallels with her grandmother's need to maintain appearances. How is writing about the Everwood a way for Finley to control what is happening to her emotionally? Does Finley or Grandma truly have control over what is happening to them? Explain. In Chapter 40 Finley decides that she will "go into the deepest parts of the Everwood that no one has yet explored—where no one lies, and everything is truth." How is this thought an illusion? Why do Finley/orphan girl feel so alone?

**22.** When Finley realizes that it is up to her to save Dex, how is she able to quiet the Dark Ones? When her cousins "launch themselves" at Finley in Mr. Bailey's house, she describes the embrace as "the warmest hug I ever felt." Why does she describe the embrace this way? Describe how the characters react when Grandpa decides to tell the truth about the Travers fire. What does he mean by: "We should've told it a long time ago, when it actually counted"?

**23**. When Finley realizes that she loves her family, even with the knowledge of their role in the Travers fire, she thinks: "This realization has been coming to me in pieces over the summer, but now it rushes at me, fully formed." Discuss the pieces of her realization. Why is it important to tell the truth, even if it's frightening?

**24**. Go back and reread the first Everwood entry. How is this introduction a metaphor for the entire story?

**Extension Activities**

**1.** An allegory is story in which the characters and events are symbols that stand for ideas about human life or for a political or historical situation (source: merriam-webster. com). The story that Finley creates about the Everwood is an allegory for her own life: her emotional pain, her fears, and her secrets. The many characters in the Everwood represent the actual people in her life. Reread the Everwood portions of the text in order. As you do so, record how the allegory of the Everwood parallels the characters and events of the story-proper.

**2.** Finley is a list-maker. One of the lists that appear in the story is titled: What It Means to Be a Hart. Create a list, substituting the Hart name with your own surname. Generate as many items as possible. When the list is complete, choose one item and expand it into a poem, short story, or personal essay.

**3.** References to music appear throughout *Some Kind of Happiness*. The Blues (Ray Charles; Jimmy Reed), Beethoven, The Beatles, and The Clash are some of the styles/artists that Finley and her relatives listen to. Assign groups to one of the musical styles/artists from the story to research. Have each group present their findings in an audio/visual slideshow.

**4.** The author's use of simile and metaphor to describe character's thoughts and feelings, as well as the physical settings of the story, such as the Bone House or the Ever-wood, are highly visual. Go back through the text and locate a description that you connect with. For example: "I must keep myself held tightly together, straight up and down, like someone has stuffed me into a too-small bag and zipped me up." Make an illustration inspired by the text. Integrate the text into the image, or use it as a caption.

**5.** Write a fantasy short story inspired by the Everwood. Work with a partner to draft an introduction and a first chapter. Create illustrations that depict characters, setting, and details.

**6.** Secrets, truth, fear, control, family, trust, friendship are the major themes in *Some Kind of Happiness*. Assign small groups sections of the book to reread. As you read, record examples of the themes in a list. Next, using magazine clip-pings, meaningful words, phrases and descriptions from the text, and original artwork, work together to create a theme collage. Choose a strong central image for the piece, and add layers of images and text around the center.

*Guide written by Colleen Carroll, literacy specialist, education consultant, and author of the twelve-volume series, How Artists See (Abbeville Press).*

*This guide has been provided by Simon & Schuster for classroom, library, and reading group use. It may be reproduced in its entirety or excerpted for these purposes.*

# Did you LOVE reading this book?

Visit the Whyville...

## Where you can:

- Discover great books!
- Meet new friends!
- Read exclusive sneak peeks and more!

Log on to visit now!
bookhive.whyville.net

Olivia Stellatella may not be having the best year, but she is about to make some new friends.

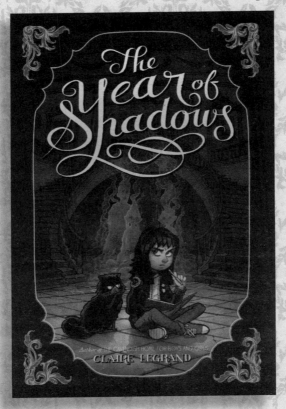

From **CLAIRE LEGRAND,**
author of *The Cavendish Home for Boys and Girls*

PRINT AND EBOOK EDITIONS AVAILABLE
From Simon and Schuster Books for Young Readers
KIDS.SimonandSchuster.com

# YOU CAN GO IN,
# BUT YOU MAY NEVER
# COME OUT. . . .

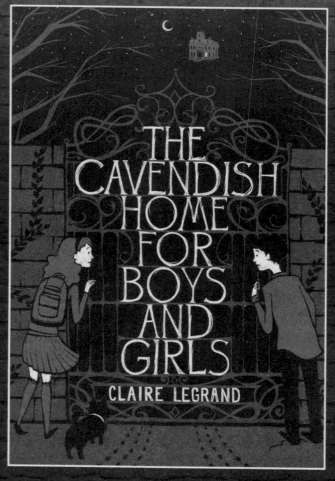

THE CAVENDISH HOME FOR BOYS AND GIRLS

CLAIRE LEGRAND

**PRINT AND EBOOK EDITIONS AVAILABLE**
From Simon & Schuster Books for Young Readers
KIDS.SimonandSchuster.com